The Silent Maid

ANNETTE SPRATTE

Copyright © Annette Spratte 2021
Im Kappesgarten 6, 57636 Mammelzen, Germany

All rights reserved. No part of this publication may be reproduced, stored in a retrieval system, or transmitted in any form or by any means, electronic, mechanical, photocopying, recording, or otherwise, without the prior permission of the copyright owner.

All the characters in this book are fictitious, and any resemblance to actual persons living or dead is purely coincidental.

This publication follows the rules of British English.

Cover Design: Vercodesign, Unna, Germany
Illustrations: Annette Spratte © 2021

Contents

Prologue 1

1 Arrival 6

2 Friendship 21

3 Riddles 27

4 Closeness 36

5 Invention 47

6 Escape 56

7 Fighting Spirit 67

8 Fright 74

9 Grief 87

10 Revelations 96

11 Opportunity 108

12 Rescue 116

13 Confession 127

Arabella 135

14 Uncertainty 138

15 Overseer 147

16 Move 158

17 Thunderstorm 168

18 Return 178

19 Disillusionment 188

20 Tenants	197
21 Changes	214
22 Suitors	227
23 Riding	238
24 Relapse	246
25 Bones	258
26 Forgiveness	267
27 Life	276
28 Selflessness	286
29 Contract	296
30 Accident	307
31 Awakening	314
Epilogue	321

Prologue

SHE WOKE FROM a chilling drop hitting her cheek. Her eyes flew open and she tensed immediately. She might as well have left them closed; it didn't make any difference. Another drop hit her face, just below her eye. She could hear soft dripping all around her, and the oddly muffled sound of the trees above her sighing in the wind. A sob escaped her throat. She curled up and hugged the damp blanket around her, shivering. Something slimy touched her neck and she screamed, scrambling frantically to get away from whatever it was.

Her shoulder hit the soggy wall and moist lumps of earth crumbled from it. Her sobs turned into pitiful crying. This time she would die. This time the roof would cave in, the tree's roots would no longer hold the earth and she would be buried under masses of mud.

The thought was almost welcome.

Prologue

Brigham Hall, October 24, 1710

Dearest Mother,

Please forgive your son for his tardiness in writing to you, but the most extraordinary circumstances have prevented me from keeping up my regular correspondence. If you have written to me in the meantime, I am afraid those letters have not reached me, since I have resigned from Baronet Goodricke's services and moved to an altogether new position. Please allow me to start my narration at the beginning so you may learn all that has occurred in the right order.

I told you in my last letter that Baronet Goodricke had given me the sole responsibility for taking his ageing broodmare to market in York and to find a suitable replacement. It was not an easy task since his mare was not of the finest breed — although he seemed to think so — and wouldn't fetch nearly as much money as he had hoped.

Nevertheless, I was excited at the prospect of spending two days at the most prestigious horse market in the area and couldn't wait for the day of my departure. I was stunned when I finally arrived. Never in my wildest dreams had I imagined the sheer size of the market with hundreds upon hundreds of people and horses milling about the place. A great melee, indeed. I left the horses with the lad who had accompanied me and started my search. Most of the horses seemed unacceptable to me; in fact, I often wondered how the owners could expect any decent man to spend even a farthing on what they had to offer. But there were a few very fine animals, which of course cost a fortune. One mare in particular caught my eye as being in line with the fine local breed of the Brighams, located near Bridlington. Where exactly that was, I didn't know at that point, but I had already come across a number of those excellent horses. This one wasn't marked with the stylish brand, though. It's a B adorned with wings, which I think represents the horses perfectly. They are sturdy and strong, but fleet footed, nonetheless. I haggled with the seller but stood no chance.

I returned to my horse and spent the rest of the day trying to find a buyer for the mare. Having seen what else was for sale, I gained confidence because our mare was in good health with a fine coat, clear bones, and a pleasant disposition. By the end of the day, I had sold her for a good price.

The lad and I rewarded ourselves with dinner and a jug of ale. In the noisy crowd that filled the tavern to bursting, I overheard a gangling man with a peculiarly high voice complaining about the fact that he could not find a decent mare to buy at the entire infernal market. Before I knew what I was doing, I had told him about the mare I had tried to buy earlier, even mentioning the Brigham resemblance I had detected. The man's eyes bore into mine with a frightening intensity. He did not respond; instead, he drained his jug in one large gulp.

"Show me the horse, now," he said and grabbed my arm, pushing me out of the door. I led him to the enclosure in which several horses were kept and pointed the mare out to him. Thank God she was still there. He threw another long look at me and then examined the horse. As I was about to depart, thinking my role in the proceedings done, he called me back and told me to wait.

I did not have to wait long. Within ten minutes he had concluded the deal and returned to me with the first smile I had seen on his face.

"Allow me to introduce myself," he said and held out his hand. "I am Baronet Brigham and you have just aided me tremendously by helping me secure a valuable addition to my brood stock."

Dear Mother, you can imagine my surprise! The Baronet himself! He asked me all sorts of questions about my origins and experience. You have taught me to always be truthful and so I did not try to make myself grander than I am, especially since I was in doubt as to why he wanted to know all these things about me. Of course, I suspected he might have a position to fill in his stables and silently prayed

Prologue

for God's guidance. But when he offered me a position with the grand title "Master of Horse" (despite my young years), I was too surprised to respond at first.

How could I not accept? Even though I chided myself for a fool, a mere under-groom of three and twenty aspiring to take charge of a Baronet's renowned breed, my heart sang with joy at the thought of being around these fine animals day in, day out, caring for them, shaping them, training them. No, I had to accept.

My master was not happy to learn of my decision. He had relied on me to stay another year. Now he would have to go out to the Michaelmas mop market and find a new groom. In fact, he was so angry that he refused to pay the rest of my wages and threw me out without another word.

So here I am now, at the beautiful Brigham estate, which is situated a few miles from the coast above Bridlington. Several tenants farm the estate. The stables are spacious; large pastures surround them and there are paddocks and even a riding arena. I have never seen such grandeur before. Brigham Hall is a beautiful structure, though not as large and old as Ribston Hall, where I have served before. On one side, it borders a forest, while the back looks out over a lovely valley with a small stream. On the western corner, the building sports a little tower with large windows, which is likely to offer a splendid view across the pastures.

The old Master of Horse, by all referred to as Ole Pete, is still in residence, but he is feeble and prone to rambling incoherently. But sometimes his mind clears and when it does, I find in him a deep well of wisdom and horse-related knowledge that I soak up and try to preserve by writing into a notebook I keep handy whenever I go to visit him.

Mother, the heavens have smiled upon me and granted me my deepest heart's desires. I am overjoyed, even though my position isn't permanent yet. That troubles me, as I'm unsure what is expected of me and whether I will be able to meet those expectations. I will have to prove my worth and shall set all my energy thereon.

Your grateful son,
Daniel Huntington

1
Arrival

DANIEL STEPPED OUT of the stable and observed the courtyard. Dense fog shrouded the buildings and rendered the riding arena on the left, as well as the other stable across the yard, nearly invisible.

"Bastian? Willie?" he called but received no answer. Where were those lads? A lonely broom leaned against the hitching post by the majestic chestnut tree overshadowing the yard. Everything else was hauntingly empty. He walked along the wall to the wide entry gate which was large enough to admit a carriage. An eerie feeling gripped him. Across from him he could just make out the gate posts of the servants' entrance, but the large residence was invisible, as were the pastures which stretched out to the left into a gentle valley below Brigham Hall.

Perhaps he had dreamed it all? Perhaps he was dreaming now and would soon wake up in his old chamber at Ribston Hall…

"Nonsense," he said to himself and walked purposefully over to the main house. With each step, another detail rose out of the mist: the small gate, the herb garden, and finally the walls of the house with the low door leading to the servants' quarters.

Daniel needed to stoop through the door despite his average height. On the right, stairs led up to the sleeping quarters of the house servants. He slipped out of his boots and took a pair of felt slippers from under the stairs. The pile of boots already lying there gave him a clue as to where his stable lads had disappeared to. He turned left toward the kitchen.

There was hardly any talk around the large table, but the room was far from quiet. The clanging of spoons in bowls and the noisy chewing told of the quality of the cook's stew. All eyes turned to Daniel upon his entry. The three stable lads pulled their heads between their shoulders and hastily continued to shovel stew into their mouths.

"Oh, here you are," Daniel stated drily and glared at them. He wasn't really angry, but he knew he needed to establish authority in his new position. The two younger boys looked guilty but the older lad, Bastian, made a big show of being completely unimpressed.

"Lunchtime," he informed Daniel with a negligent shrug.

Being watched with amusement by the staff, Daniel approached the table and put both of his fists slowly down next to Bastian's bowl, leaning in closely.

"As we have not talked about this before, it is well for now. But tomorrow, boys -" He let his gaze linger on each of the lads and continued as softly as before, "lunchtime starts when your tasks are done and I give you leave." With a satisfied nod he watched Bastian swallow hard. The lad had obviously noticed the steel in Daniel's voice.

Having resolved this situation to his satisfaction, Daniel straightened up and looked around. Most of the names and faces were still strange to him. Before he could feel

Arrival

lost, one of the maids jumped up and waved at him. She was an ample young woman with dark hair, who now gave him her brightest smile.

"Sit over here, dear Master of Horse, there is enough room. I'm sure you're starving after missing breakfast this morning."

"Breakfast?" Daniel asked in surprise and was rewarded with equally surprised glances from around the table.

"Of course, there is breakfast," the cook exclaimed indignantly, as if it were a personal affront to assume there was none. "Three meals a day is the rule in this house. Those who work hard need to eat well, is what the master says."

This was music in Daniel's ears. With his former master, he had only had one meal a day and often been hungry.

"I don't mind that," he said and sat down at the table. The maid, Fanny by name, waved her hand at a girl sitting on a stool by the hearth. She jumped up immediately, grabbed another bowl from the shelf and ladled stew into it, offering it to Daniel with downcast eyes.

He accepted it with a word of thanks and followed her with his gaze as she returned to her stool. She looked haggard and dirty; her clothes far more worn than those of the other maids. Daniel wondered why she was excluded but didn't dare ask.

Thanks to Fanny, he got to know the other servants a little better during the meal. She chattered away and introduced each person around the table with a little anecdote.

"You already know the three urchins who always smell of dung," she said with a perky grin, pointing at the stable lads. Bastian raised his head in protest.

"I'm no urchin!" he called and couldn't understand why everyone started to laugh.

"The fat one is Mo," Fanny continued and put her hand on the shoulder of a chubby twelve-year-old boy. "I'm sure he's got a real name, but I forgot it. With anything edible he'll ask if he can have a bit mo'. Never leave your food unattended or it will disappear." The boy grinned from ear to ear, obviously unworried about his reputation.

"I want to be a cook," he stated with his mouth full and received a stern glance from the cook.

"You'll need to learn a lot for that to happen," she said pointedly.

"Always be nice to Ellie," Fanny advised with a nod at the cook. "She is the secret mistress of this estate…"

"Oh, that's ridiculous!" Ellie called out but Fanny remained unperturbed.

"…and the heart and soul of this place. We owe it to her that we are so well-fed." With this, Ellie was pacified. Fanny's gaze wandered to a non-descript girl intensely studying the contents of her bowl.

"That's Lizzie. She's supposed to be a parlourmaid, but she can't do anything. Don't ever hand her something fragile or she's bound to break it. I don't have a clue why the master hired her but perhaps she has some qualities I'm not aware of." The face of the light blond girl flushed crimson up to the roots of her hair.

"Fanny!" Ellie called in a stern voice. She approved of neither the disrespectful words nor the feisty tone in which they had been delivered. Daniel didn't comment on any of this but raised his eyebrows questioningly. Only one man shook with laughter.

Arrival

"That's Russell, the footman. He deems himself incredibly important, despite the fact that he doesn't do anything all day but stand around and keep everyone else from their work," said Fanny, continuing her introductions. The man's laughter turned into an outraged snort.

"What do you know, silly kitchen maid? Cutting greens and plucking chickens is all you know how to do," he shot back at her.

"That's more than you have to show for yourself! You only open doors," she replied with a sneer. Daniel couldn't suppress a short laugh and more than one amused giggle sounded around the table.

"I'm Harry, the gardener," a small, steely man with deeply tanned skin said, giving Daniel a friendly nod and cutting Fanny short. "And if the master doesn't ride, I'm also the driver."

With that, everyone around the table was introduced. Daniel's gaze wandered to the girl in the corner. "What about her?" he asked. The girl didn't look at him but kept her glance lowered to the floor. She was short, hardly more than five foot, with light reddish-brown ringlets that had escaped her cap in several places. Her face was pale and dotted with freckles. Uncomfortable silence spread through the room.

"Just pretend she's not there," Fanny finally said in a chipped manner and rose to clear the table. As if on cue, everyone else got up as well and returned to work with a few mumbled words. Confused, Daniel followed suit. Something tugged at his heart upon seeing the girl's hunched shoulders.

You're too soft-hearted, his father's voice echoed in his memory and he nodded involuntarily, pushing all thoughts of the girl aside. She was none of his business. He had enough to worry about, such as having his authority questioned by a teenage lad.

"HAVE YOU STILL not finished doling out the hay?" Daniel yelled at Willie, who jumped as if stabbed with a hot poker. He grabbed the handles of the wheelbarrow and hurried across the cobblestoned yard in such haste that it tipped over and spilled its load all over the ground. The boy froze in place, staring over his shoulder at Daniel with eyes the size of saucers. With a grunt, Daniel put down the water buckets he had been carrying. He crossed his arms and towered with an angry glare but did not move towards the frightened boy.

"Well, pick it up again, you fool," he called and watched with silent amusement as the lad raked the hay off the moist ground with his fingers and put it back in the wheelbarrow. He made his way to the opposite stable without another accident.

Daniel turned with a shake of his head. Willie was only ten and had arrived merely a week before Daniel himself. He was frightened, bewildered and homesick, a feeling Daniel knew only too well. He had been nine when he had started his first job and the first months had been hell. He had cried himself to sleep every night in his lonely sleeping spot in the hay loft, miserably missing his mother.

But there had been no choice, Daniel was the youngest of eight children and there wasn't enough bread for them all. His father had tried to find work for him close to home, to no avail. His mother's whispers in his hair when she had hugged him goodbye would stay with him forever. *God bless you, my sweetest, my heart, my love…*

If he had tipped over the wheelbarrow like the lad did just now, his master would have beaten him. Daniel wouldn't do that, though. No need to frighten the boy any more than he already was. If he ever got cheeky, that would be another matter.

Daniel picked up the buckets and put them inside the stalls. The horses were restless, stomping their feet impatiently. Unlike the brood mares, the geldings were kept ready to hand, but the master had not been out over the past days, so the horses needed exercise. He talked softly to them and they pricked up their ears and blew into his face. Tomorrow, he would let them out to pasture and hoped they wouldn't jump around so much for joy that they broke their legs. He would need Bastian to help. The small boys would be dangling on the lead ropes like flags on a ship's mast. No need to have them trampled. Bastian was a big lad; he would be able to handle the restless souls.

"Everything settled for the day?"

Daniel whirled around to find Baronet Brigham looking down at him. The man had an unnerving habit of sneaking up on people. He was unnaturally tall and long-limbed, and his eerie high voice didn't fit his size at all. In combination with his glare, the receding hair, and dark clothing, his entire presence was intimidating.

"Yes, sir, everything is settled." Out of the corner of his eye Daniel saw Willie make his way back with the now empty wheelbarrow, faltering upon sight of his master. Daniel couldn't blame him. To a lad of ten this man was a walking nightmare.

"Good. When you've cleaned yourself up, come and see me in my office. I want to go over the books with you."

"Very well, sir," Daniel replied. Baronet Brigham was not afraid to get dirty when working with the horses, but in the house he was meticulous. Once, Daniel had stepped into his office with mud on his boots, and he certainly wouldn't do so again. After his master had exploded and yelled at him at the top of his voice, Daniel had known why the servants were so mistrustingly respectful. In that moment, he had seriously wondered if it had been such a wise decision to work for the baronet. But as quickly as it had come, the anger had evaporated, and Baronet Brigham had treated him as usual. It calmed Daniel and confirmed his decision. Never before had he owned two sets of clothes, but now he was Master of Horse at the Brigham estate and proud to own a frock, trousers, and a shirt tailored to his needs in addition to his work clothes. No more hand-me-downs.

It was with a fair amount of apprehension that Daniel entered the baronet's office, looking snug and clean in his new clothes. He was painfully aware of his shortcomings, never having attended school. While he had taught himself to read and write with the aid of his mother's Bible, his understanding of numbers and sums was limited. The baronet knew this, having asked Daniel about his education prior to employing him, but seemed inclined to teach him all he needed to know. Why he would go to such lengths was beyond Daniel.

"Come," the man ordered and turned back to the large book he had been studying. He stood at his high desk by the window, a sharpened quill and ink ready to hand. In addition to the high desk, there was another desk, two armchairs in front of the fireplace, and shelves covering the walls from floor to ceiling. Three large windows gave light during the day, but now it was dark outside, the curtains were drawn, and several candles burned.

Daniel stood beside his master, running his gaze along the columns of words and numbers.

Lord, don't let me make a complete fool of myself, he prayed silently. To his immense surprise, the baronet didn't ask him to do anything except watch him closely. He then proceeded to write the day's dealings into the ledger: what the cook had spent at the market, which tenants had paid their dues, how much they got for the sale of a pig. Then he balanced the accounts and closed the ledger with a heavy thud, placing it on a shelf where many others like it already stood.

"I consider you a clever man, Mr Huntington," Brigham said as he turned back to Daniel. "You will watch and learn, every night. If you have questions, ask."

Daniel gave a slow nod. With a flick of his wrist, the baronet dismissed him.

DANIEL OCCUPIED A small, but comfortable room above the stables on the left, while the lads shared a chamber in the other wing, next to the hayloft. He was glad of this arrangement. Having to deal with the boys all day long and getting them to do their tasks was often tiring and he felt a deep sense of relief every time he closed his door behind him. Tonight, he didn't drop off to sleep as soon as he had crawled under his blanket, though. Too many things were twirling through his mind, all the new impressions and expectations finally catching up with him. He desperately wished for the master to approve of him and make his position permanent. He wasn't worried about his work with the horses, knowing that he was a natural with the animals. But everything else? The breeding, the organization of the stable, handling his employees? Heretofore, others had taken care of these things and he wasn't at all sure if it wasn't too much for him. The baronet hadn't specified how long his trial period would be and Daniel had been too intimidated to ask. All he could do was give his best, anyway.

After tossing and turning for a while he sat up with a grunt. It was no use; he needed to get something to eat. Putting his trousers and boots back on, he took his lamp and trudged down the narrow stairs into the stable, crossed the yard and followed the path to the servants' entrance and the kitchen. In the hallway, he bumped into Harry, the gardener.

"Up late, are you, Master of Horse?" the older man asked in a friendly manner.

"My stomach won't let me be," Daniel explained and smiled crookedly.

"Right, the young lads." Harry grinned back and winked. "I go out to the village once in a while. You're welcome to join me if you like."

"The village?"

"Yes, to Flamborough. It's quite a walk, but well worth it. If you want to know what's happening in the world, there's no better place than the *Seabirds*. And the gin is decent, too."

"If you say so," Daniel said evasively. At his former place, the lads had liked their gin as well and not a few

Arrival

fights had derived from it. Daniel also preferred to avoid the drinking establishments because his mother had warned him time and again to stay away from alcohol for the love of God. Harry immediately noticed his hesitance.

"Don't worry, I don't fill up like some do. I drink a glass and listen to what folks have to tell. There are always sailors coming in, talking about their voyages, about the war with Spain and whatever else is going on. Like I said, you're welcome to join me, if you want." With that, he nodded and climbed the steep stairs, while Daniel wished him good-night and went into the kitchen.

It was a good thing he had brought the lamp, because the fire had been banked and the room was dark. He held the lamp high in search of something edible and then nearly dropped it because a shape suddenly rose up from the bench behind the table. Light was momentarily reflected in a pair of frightened eyes before they squeezed shut to avoid being blinded. Tousled curls bobbed and Daniel wiped his brow with relief. It was the maid. He let out a sigh mingled with embarrassed laughter. That girl had almost made him turn on his heel and run!

"Goodness, what are you doing here in the middle of the night? You gave me a good scare." He walked up to the table and placed the lamp on it. The girl was hugging a blanket around herself, alternately blinking up at Daniel and glancing over her shoulder. She bit her lip but said nothing.

"Is there some food left? I'm very hungry," Daniel went on and looked around once more. The girl flicked her gaze over to a large cupboard in the corner but made no move otherwise. When Daniel opened the cupboard, he found a good number of supplies stored inside. He helped himself to some bread and cheese as well as a few slices of ham. Returning to the table, he noticed that the girl was in her shift under the blanket, her clothes piled on the floor beside the bench. It gave him a start.

"Are you sleeping here on the bench?" he asked incredulously.

"Up late, Mr Huntington?" the baronet's voice cut in sharply. The man stepped out of the shadows by the opposite door. Daniel jumped, then coughed and frantically swallowed the bite of bread he had taken.

"I was just hungry," he croaked and coughed some more. The girl hunkered down on the bench as if she wanted to dissolve on the spot.

"I see you've resolved that problem," Brigham said in a tone of dismissal.

Daniel hastily grabbed his lamp as well as the food and nodded to his master. "Sir," he mumbled and took his leave, although he very much wanted to know why his master slunk through the house in the middle of the night. Had he also been hungry? For some reason, Daniel doubted it. It rather appeared as if the baronet had watched over the maid. That was ridiculous. Why didn't she have a cot to sleep in? Surely there was enough room in the house! Was she being punished for something? Daniel made his way back to his room and stared thoughtfully at the wall while chewing his late-night meal. He couldn't make sense of it. The girl had kept looking towards the door, as if she had expected someone to come in. Why didn't she speak? She obviously had understood everything he had said to her, so she wasn't deaf. Why was she so afraid of the baronet? Daniel gave an unwilling grunt. He really didn't want to pursue that line of thought. He was well aware that any master, no matter what his social standing, thought he could do with his maids whatever he wanted. Even the footmen and butlers were known for chasing every skirt. Curiously enough, there was no butler here. Perhaps Russell fulfilled some of the tasks. Or the baronet wouldn't suffer a butler's presence. Stuffing the rest of the bread and cheese into his mouth, Daniel extinguished the lamp and lay down again. *What is her name?* he wondered as he finally drifted off to sleep.

IT TOOK DANIEL several weeks to get up the nerve to ask the baronet a question about the accounts. He had watched closely and understood the general concept of bookkeeping. There was stock; things that went out had to be deducted from the stock; things that came in were added. The baronet's quick calculations remained a mystery to him, though. With burning cheeks, he admitted his helplessness, which was met by an amused smirk.

"Good thing you finally swallowed your pride, Mr Huntington," Brigham said with a chuckle. "I was afraid you might choke on it." He pulled a slate out of a drawer and proceeded to explain the general concept of numbers and sums. Then he pulled one of the older ledgers off the shelf and pressed it into Daniel's arms. "Use this for practise," he advised and sent him back to his quarters.

Henceforth, Daniel spent every night doing sums in his room above the stables. At first, he thought he would never make sense of it, but remembered thinking the same thing when figuring out letters. He had stoically kept at it and then, like a flash, it had suddenly come together in his brain and he could read. He expected the same to happen with the numbers. Besides learning to calculate, he also learned a lot about how the estate was run and applied this knowledge to his daily chores.

Good hay was essential to the health of the horses and hayfields were a valuable asset. Daniel's former master had paid little heed to the quality of his hay, and the horses had forever been coughing, especially in winter, when they had all been stabled. Daniel had never before encountered anyone who kept horses outside in the winter, but Brigham swore by it. He said horses had to move in fresh air and didn't need to be holed up inside when it got cold. Ole Pete said the same thing and Daniel could see that the horses were all healthy and strong, without the slightest trace of a cough.

At first, Daniel had wondered at the many hay sheds he saw on his training rounds with the horses, which were often in better repair than some of the tenants' cottages. He learned that the baronet produced a lot more hay than he needed, selling the surplus off during the winter. His own animals always received the best first cut.

When Daniel saw the income generated by hay sales in the books, he suddenly understood – and developed a strong respect for his gangly master. That money certainly helped to keep everyone on the estate fed and clothed.

Arrival

Brigham Hall, November 12, 1710

Dear Mother,

I was overwhelmed by a bundle of letters today; all of them written by your loving hand. They seem to have been collected and then sent on to my new residence, by whom I will never know. I have not had the chance to read them yet, but I will do so — one at a time — and respond accordingly. This is just a quick note to let you know I am well and to advise you of the address to use now.

Your loving son,
Daniel

2
Friendship

"YOU CERTAINLY HAVE a healthy appetite, Mr Huntington," Ellie teased. He stopped chewing only for a moment to give her a wide grin. After a few weeks he had come to know the staff and was on good terms with most of them. He had his stable lads under control now and Fanny seemed to be fairly smitten with him, taking excellent care he was well fed, even in between regular meals. He wasn't sorry about it; his new job kept him on his toes from sunrise to well after dark and the hard work made his stomach feel like a bottomless hole. He could eat anything, anytime. So, he was glad to have Fanny come over to him at the paddocks or stable with a kerchief filled with goodies, although he did wonder if he was the only one receiving such treatment. When he had asked Russell, the footman, about it, he had merely laughed and winked at him.

Surprisingly, it was Ole Pete who shed light on the matter. After another such encounter, he hobbled over to where Daniel was repairing a fence and clapped him on the shoulder in a friendly manner.

"Should reward that girlie with a kiss, you should," he said and cackled. Daniel's eyes widened with astonishment. "Surely you should, no need to goggle, don't you know

Friendship

you're a sought-after bachelor? Tall and handsome with a good prospect…"

Pete let it hang between them in favour of looking at the horses that grazed peacefully under the overcast sky. Daniel swallowed. He had been a dirty, penniless stable lad for so long; he found it hard to believe anyone could be interested in him. His height was medium, his brown hair cropped short because he lost every ribbon and hated to have his hair fall into his face. His eyes were brown, too. He supposed he wasn't ugly, but so far in his life, girls had avoided him and now he wasn't sure what to do with the attention he received. Kiss Fanny? No, that couldn't be right if he didn't have serious intentions. Russell would do such a thing, but not he. Daniel dismissed the topic from his mind. Pete seemed to be having one of his better days, so maybe he could get some valuable horse information out of him.

While they were leaning on the fence talking, one of the maids stealthily approached the paddock, constantly glancing back over her shoulder. Ole Pete fell silent, watching her. Daniel recognized the girl as the silent one. The one who never sat with the others. The one nobody talked to except to give her a task. He still hadn't heard her utter one word. She was always working whenever he encountered her – even when the others were taking a break. And during meals, she always sat apart in the corner, never at the table.

Now she sidled up to the fence and whistled softly. Immediately, a small white mare lifted her head. Before anything else happened, Ole Pete erupted in a violent coughing fit and Daniel had to hold on to the old man to keep

The Silent Maid

him on his feet. When he looked around again, the girl had disappeared, and the baronet was walking towards them.

"You shouldn't hang around here and keep my Master of Horse from his work, old man," he said and tipped his head in the direction of Ole Pete's cottage that stood a little way behind the stable. "Get back to bed." Pete coughed some more, hawked, and spat, barely missing the baronet's boots. Then he turned and hobbled away. Daniel dared not look up at his master. Surely, he would rant and rave again. It was something Daniel found hard to bear. Amazingly enough, Brigham made no comment on the old man's rude behaviour.

"We are having some gentlemen visit tomorrow, looking to buy horses. See to it that these are polished to a shine, saddled and bridled in the riding arena, ten o'clock sharp." He handed Daniel a list. "The boys need to wash, too, and sweep the stables. You will present the horses under the saddle. Make sure to work them well beforehand, but I don't want them showing a sweat. We want to make a good impression." Without another word, he turned and walked back to the house. Daniel let out a long sigh and went back to his repairs. While he was thrilled by the prospect of impressing potential buyers with his charges, his thoughts revolved more around the silent maid. He studied the white mare, which had reacted to the girl's whistle. He hadn't worked with her yet, thinking he was too heavy for the delicate creature. Should he do so? He'd have to ask the master.

Friendship

IT WAS A FEW days later that Daniel observed the girl again. As before, she sneaked up to the fence, constantly glancing back over her shoulder as if it was forbidden, then whistled to the horse. This time, there was no interruption, and the horse came up to the girl, greeting her like an old friend. It nuzzled her neck and hair while she repeatedly kissed its nose. Then their foreheads touched, and they stayed like that for several minutes, as if drawing strength from each other. Daniel kept himself hidden behind the stable door and watched in fascination. The intimacy between the girl and the horse touched him deeply and kindled a familiar longing in him. So far, he had not managed to create such a close bond with a horse. After a moment, the girl sighed and turned back to the house, a peaceful look on her face for once. The mare whinnied after her and stomped its hoof. The girl turned to look at it and shook her head before breaking into a run.

Daniel left his place by the stable door and walked up to the horse, which was still staring after the girl. He reached out to pet its neck, but it immediately flattened its ears against its head and snapped at him. Daniel took a surprised step backwards. "Whoa there, I'm not hurting you," he said, but the mare had already turned away.

The Silent Maid

Brigham Hall, November 25, 1710

Dearest Mother,

I am overjoyed to hear that you and father are well and that you are managing to save up a little for bad times. With all the comforts I am enjoying in my new life here, I am also able to put a bit aside, a situation entirely new to me. I might even begin to consider marriage sometime next year, although I must admit that despite the amount of attention I am receiving from a young girl here, she is not the one I would want to spend my life with.

There is a great puzzle here, though, of which I must tell you. I am very curious to hear your thoughts on the matter. Working in the kitchen and the wash house is a maid. Well, there are several maids working there, to be precise, but this one is special. She does not speak to anyone and I have so far never heard more from her than a gasp or a sneeze. The other servants treat her harshly, which tears at my heart, I'm afraid. You know me, Mother, injustice goes against my grain. They give her all the heavy or unpleasant tasks they want to avoid themselves, and the girl has no way of refusing or complaining. I have seen Fanny (the maid paying me so much attention) threatening to hit her if she is reluctant to do what she demands, although I've never witnessed the actual deed. Usually, the girl complies. Mother, you would also feel pity for her if you saw her fragile frame and frightened eyes. It is beyond me how she manages her heavy workload.

When Russell, the footman, noticed my watching her, he pulled me aside and whispered in my ear to stay well clear of that girl. He said she was cursed, which was why she couldn't speak. I'm prepared to laugh that off as superstitious nonsense, but what really troubles me is that nobody knows the girl's name. Isn't that awful? She sleeps in the kitchen like a dog, but even dogs have names you call them by. This poor maid seems to have none. Her only friend is a horse, a

Friendship

small white mare with a feisty temper. I've tried to catch it, but it wouldn't let me come near it. Yet the girl can touch it and it will even come to her at a whistle. What say you to this riddle?

Your puzzled son,

Daniel

3
Riddles

THERE SHE WAS again. Daniel held his breath and tried to melt into the background. She hadn't noticed him, and he ducked down a little behind the large brown mare with the small gash on its shoulder he had been meaning to look at when the silent maid had appeared in the mist. She whistled and the white mare immediately left the hay. The two of them were so intent upon each other that Daniel risked straightening up and slowly moving closer. He stayed well out of reach of the mare and only when he had almost arrived at the fence, did the maid notice him. Her eyes grew round with surprise, but before she could turn and run, he put his hands up soothingly.

"It's all right, please, don't go away."

She stayed where she was but cast a quick look around. There was no one else in sight except a few crows looking for something edible among the horses' feet. Daniel climbed through the fence and approached the girl, smiling kindly at her. "It's fine," he repeated, as if she herself was a nervous horse. The mare eyed him suspiciously, so he stopped. "She really likes you," Daniel observed.

The maid blinked in reply and slowly took up stroking the mare's neck again, her fingers red with cold. She buried them deep in the horse's thick winter coat, yet her eyes never left his face.

Daniel felt absurdly proud that the girl didn't run from him and grinned widely. A wondrous expression crept into the maid's eyes. For a moment, they stood like that, merely looking at each other, and Daniel could feel a subtle shift in her demeanour. Something changed between them, but he couldn't tell what it was. She blinked at him again and then turned to slowly walk away, despite the drizzle. He followed her with his gaze until she was out of sight.

Daniel went into the stable to find Bastian, who was grooming the master's favourite stallion.

"Tell me, Bastian, when you're cleaning the mares' hooves, do you ever check that small white one?"

Bastian hesitated a moment in his brush strokes. "No," he answered and frowned.

"She won't let you near her?"

Bastian shook his head. All the other horses were easy to handle and didn't even need to be tied when picking up their feet.

Daniel looked the stallion over. "This is good enough. Put him back in his stall and then go and try to halter up that mare. We don't want her to pick up a stone in her hoof and go lame," he ordered and turned away to check on the lads. They were supposed to be scrubbing the mangers, but he couldn't see them anywhere. While he was still searching for them, he suddenly heard the baronet's shrill voice.

"What do you think you're doing?" Brigham yelled.

Daniel immediately went out to the paddocks, just in time to see the baronet stride up to Bastian and slap him hard across the face.

The boy staggered back, a look both of surprise and resentment in his eyes. "Master of Horse said to pick her hooves," he said defensively.

The baronet grabbed the boy's shirt and pulled him close until their noses almost touched. "I have told you more than once that you're not to lay one finger on that mare," he hissed. "I take care of her myself." He gave the lad a violent shove, sending him flying. "One more time, Mr Higgins, and you will find yourself another job."

"Is there a problem, sir?" Daniel asked, warily approaching the scene.

"Yes, there is, Mr Huntington," the baronet replied hotly, wiping his hands on his trousers. "Nobody touches that mare; do you understand me? If that pig-headed idiot tries one more time, dismiss him. No, lash him first and then dismiss him."

Daniel was taken aback by the vehemence in his master's tone. "I thought we should check her feet, sir," he replied carefully, wondering why the baronet was so particular about this horse.

"There is no need!" Brigham snapped and glared at Daniel. He even took a step towards him and Daniel feared he'd be the next one landing in the dirt. But Brigham controlled himself just in time. "Leave that mare alone and take care that everyone else does, too. Especially that girl," he added with a cruel snarl. He didn't elaborate on which girl he was referring to but pushed past Daniel in a rush of fury. When he was out of sight, Bastian picked himself up out of the muddy paddock. He didn't meet Daniel's gaze.

"You knew that," Daniel stated.

Bastian shrugged; his gaze glued to the ground. Nevertheless, Daniel saw the amount of anger burning inside him. "Why didn't you tell me, if you knew?"

The boy didn't answer, slinking away into the stable, rubbing his cheek.

Daniel let out a long sigh. That lad was looking for trouble.

WHEN RUSSELL AND Daniel entered the kitchen shortly after dinner time, the girl hurried past them with a tray of food.

"Maybe you'll get lucky and she'll poison Ole Pete one of these days," Russell said and stretched his back before dropping down on the bench. The servants had already left, apart from Ellie and Fanny.

"Hey, Ellie, I'm starving, get me some grub," Russell called.

"If you don't learn to say pretty please, I'll be happy to let you starve," Ellie replied and slapped the back of his head on passing. He laughed and patted her ample rump, getting his fingers smacked in return, which only made him laugh harder.

Daniel didn't join in the banter.

"Here sweetheart, you know how to behave, I'll give you food and gladly," Ellie said to him and handed him a plate filled to the brim.

"I took extra care the others left enough for you," Fanny chimed in and gave him a pretty smile.

"Thank you kindly," Daniel replied and sat down across from Russell, who started complaining immediately.

"He didn't even ask for food! You two are not being fair."

They ignored him.

Russell rolled his eyes. "Dearest Ellie, would you please give me my dinner?" he asked as sweetly as he could.

"Well, there you go. That wasn't so hard, was it?" With a laugh and a wink Ellie put his plate before him.

They ate in silence for a while, but Daniel's thoughts churned on Russell's earlier comment.

"What did you mean I would be lucky if that girl poisoned Ole Pete?" He tried not to let Russell see how disturbing the thought was to him. So far, he got along well with the footman, but that could change in an instant if Russell got wind of Daniel's soft side. And admitting to a fondness for the old man would certainly be considered soft.

"Don't you know? The cottage rightfully belongs to the Master of Horse. I've no idea why the master lets the old bugger stay in there."

"So …" Daniel couldn't bring himself to say it. Russell had no such qualms.

"If the old man dies, the cottage is yours. Maybe you should whack him over the head with a shovel when he's crawling around outside. Then he won't make a mess in your future bed!" Russell roared with laughter, but Ellie stood next to him with her fists propped to her sides.

"Russell, you're a mean beast. That old man has served the Brighams for longer than you've been alive and it's due to him the breed has such a brilliant reputation. Show some respect, you impertinent fool!"

Riddles

"As if you know," Russell replied, his voice turning haughty, "you haven't worked here longer than I. It could all be a myth."

"How long have you been here?" Daniel asked.

"Four years, same as Ellie. Nobody has worked here longer than four years, except Pete. The baronet had us all start on the same day. A few came later, such as Fanny and Bastian and the little lads, right, Fanny? Everyone else started four years ago."

"Why?" Daniel had never heard of such a thing before. "What happened to the other servants?"

"Nobody knows," Fanny replied, eyes wide. "There were rumours about the haunted chapel, where the former master was burned to death. Maybe the other servants were afraid and fled."

"Yeah", Russell added and opened his eyes so wide it looked like any second they'd pop right out of his head. Then he lowered his voice to a confidential tone and said, "The last bloke who was supposed to be Master of Horse saw a ghost. A white shape skulking around the pastures at midnight. After that, he didn't want to stay another day."

Daniel shuddered. He had seen the charred remains of the chapel, situated in a lovely grove about half a mile from Brigham Hall. The roof had caved in and two walls had crumbled, leaving an ugly ruin everyone avoided like a sore tooth. Daniel had never ventured near it, even if he didn't believe the ghost stories. The place was spooky, nevertheless.

"What about the girl?" he asked.

"What girl?"

"The silent girl? Was she here when you started?"

The Silent Maid

Russell said nothing. Ellie clamped her lips shut as well, but Fanny replied with vigour. "She was already here, wasn't she, Ellie? The little witch. Don't trust her. She's evil. I wish the master would find her another place to sleep. It's so awkward with her sleeping in the kitchen."

"Witch? I can't imagine that," Daniel put in, but didn't get any further.

"Oh, don't be fooled by her!" said Fanny. "There are reasons why the master always keeps an eye on her. I wouldn't mind if he locked her up in the cellar, so she'd be out of the way."

"Don't you think that's a bit hard? She's only a girl…"

"Only a girl, he says!" Russell scoffed. "You'd better listen to Fanny and keep out of trouble, my friend."

Daniel swallowed his protests and didn't pursue the subject. They didn't seem to want to budge from their harsh opinion.

When he got up to leave, Russell unexpectedly stopped him in the doorway. "Stay away from that girl," he whispered in Daniel's ear. "I know she's a pretty little thing, but the master will tear you apart with his bare hands if you touch her. He's mad. He treats her worse than a dog, but if you try anything funny with her, he's all over you. Mark my words." When he saw Daniel's questioning look, he continued. "One of the lads wanted to have some fun with her, dragged her off into the hayloft. Thought she couldn't scream, right? Before he could get started, the master caught on, went up there and threw him out of the loft. Broke his leg and a few ribs. Master had him whipped, anyway. Never saw the lad again after that. Believe me; you want to stay away from that girl."

Riddles

Brigham Hall, December 27, 1710

Dear Mother,

You need not worry about me, bless your gentle heart! I really do not believe the girl is cursed, although everyone wants to convince me otherwise. If God has blessed me with only a touch of common sense, I know for sure this girl has a good heart. And yet I must heed their warnings for quite different reasons. It seems that the baronet is very particular about the girl and will not suffer anyone to mistreat her, even though his own treatment of her is more than cruel. He does not beat her, as far as I know, but she is obviously frightened of him. What puzzles me most is her connection to this horse, which the master seeks to interrupt at every opportunity. He will not suffer her to come near the horse and has instructed me repeatedly to drive her away. Yet she keeps coming back, despite her fear of being discovered. I have to admit, I cannot send her away, even though I disobey my master's direct order. I simply don't understand it! Why does he mind if she touches that horse? Or if anyone else touches it, for that matter? I simply cannot come up with a sensible reason. She knows I allow it. I tried talking to her and although she didn't reply, I felt some communication pass between us. If it had lasted any longer, I believe she might have smiled.

I can picture you scolding me for making a foolish choice again and I promise I will not put myself in danger. I know now that the master will react violently if crossed, so I won't cross him. His faith in me seems strong, and my abilities with numbers and calculations have much increased since he has given me a few lessons. I can now follow his bookkeeping and have even made some suggestions on how to improve the running of the stables, which he approved of. He's not a man to praise easily, but I feel that he is satisfied with my work and does not regret hiring me. A steady stream of gentlemen visits the stables in search of a good horse, and we have managed to sell quite a few since I've come here.

In the beginning, the master watched me closely while I trained the horses, but now he only stops by sporadically, which is enough praise for me. I have earned his trust and am proud of it. I will soon have to look for a new groom, though. Bastian is giving me more and more trouble and sooner or later he will have to go, as he doesn't follow orders and is often rough with the horses. As harsh as the master is with his servants, he wants his horses treated gently. This man is a walking riddle.

He didn't want to have anything to do with Christmas, as if the holiday didn't exist. Ellie prepared a bit of a feast for us and we rested a little. Nobody went to church. It is quite far away, and the weather was awful – sleet and a cruel, cold wind.

But inside it was nice and warm, and Ellie decorated the kitchen with pine and mistletoe and rosemary. I was glad to be busy in the stables or I would have missed you too much. I wonder if we will ever spend Christmas together again. I would like that very much.

Love,

Daniel Huntington
Master of Horse, Brigham Estate (hopefully for a long time)

4
Closeness

IN THE NEW YEAR, Daniel was way too busy to worry about the maid. Foaling season had started early after the harsh winter, and he was with the mares almost all day and night. Baronet Brigham helped him a lot, taking the stable lads and the exercise of the horses off his hands, which surprised Daniel.

The disadvantage was that Bastian's mood turned ever sourer. During one of his rounds, Daniel caught Bastian hitting one of the horses repeatedly because it hadn't stepped aside quickly enough.

"Hey!" Daniel called from the stable door. "That's not how we treat horses here!"

He reached Bastian in a few strides; the lad putting his fists on his hips and giving Daniel a contemptuous glare. "I treat the horses the way I want," he hissed and spat in front of Daniel's feet. Everything in Bastian's eyes challenged Daniel to rebuke him.

Daniel felt heat rise in his cheeks, but he breathed deep and fought his anger down. Slowly he let out his breath and consciously relaxed his arms and shoulders. Bastian was almost his height and a little heavier. He wasn't at all sure he could keep on top in a fight. He decided not to do what Bastian expected. "You get enough beatings," he said so quietly, Bastian had to strain to hear him. "Used to be the same for me. It's never good to be beaten. It makes you angry and helpless at the same time." Daniel was sure Bastian was listening closely, now. He broke eye contact and looked at the horse. He didn't add anything else but passed by Bastian to check on Thunderboy, the estate's breeding stallion, on the back pasture. If his words would make a difference, he couldn't tell, but at least he had deescalated the situation.

Shortly after that, he heard noises from the stable, clattering and thumps, as if buckets were being thrown about and posts kicked. He was about to go back when he saw the baronet's ferocious figure appear in the doorway. He approached Daniel with long strides.

"What's happened?" Daniel wanted to know, but the baronet only made a dismissive gesture.

"So, how is our bonny lad?" he asked and doted on the stallion with a satisfied smile.

"Perfect," Daniel said. He felt a little queasy because he didn't know what Bastian was doing inside the stable. If the baronet had beat him again it was well possible the boy had lost his temper. That could affect the horses or Willie or Tom. He bit his lip, unsure whether he should address this or not.

The baronet's thoughts moved along other tracks, though. "I'm going to take two horses for my rounds to the tenants, so you won't have to exercise them," he said and was already turning to go.

"That is a great help, thank you, sir," Daniel replied. "To be honest, I wouldn't know how to handle everything otherwise."

Closeness

The baronet stopped. "These horses are the heart and soul of the Brigham estate. They are the best for miles around and every gentleman wants to ride one. Most of the ladies, too. It is your responsibility to make sure not a single one of this year's foal crop is lost, Mr Huntington. I might ask a lot of you, but I do not intend to work you to death. I know we are understaffed because Bastian isn't doing his job. As soon as this is over, we will hire another stable hand and a groom. I have already put word out."

"I'm glad to hear that, sir," Daniel replied.

"Don't let Bastian work the young horses. That boy has as much horse sense as the next fence post. I'd rather have them started late than ruined by that idiot. You start them. You know what you're doing."

Daniel almost stopped breathing with so much praise. "In that case you should send him away as soon as possible. Every time I turn my back, he's doing things he's not supposed to do. He thinks very highly of himself, does young Mr Higgins." Daniel did not mention the scene in the stable. It wasn't necessary.

The baronet emitted a low growl. "I know," he said through clenched teeth. "He won't stay longer than absolutely essential." He left. Daniel busied himself with his tasks and made his way across the pastures to get to the mares.

Before long, Ole Pete tottered up to the fence. He stood watching Daniel for a long time as he went from mare to mare. When Daniel had finally finished his round, he took a moment to talk to the old man.

"Any foals tonight?" Pete asked, his face alight with interest.

The Silent Maid

"There might be two, maybe three," Daniel informed him.

"Keep an eye on that black one. She fooled me more than once. And that brown one's looking ready to burst?"

"Yes, she will most likely foal tonight," Daniel responded.

"No. Next week, earliest." The old man cackled loudly when he saw Daniel's unbelieving face. "I've sat next to her night after night, for a fortnight at least. Nothing. And then, when I was so tired, I fell over, right there in the straw, what do I find when I wake up? The foal. Just leave her alone. She'll be fine. The more you check on her, the longer she'll keep it. The bay one over there, she needs help. Almost lost her on the first foal and she's been nervous ever since. Makes damn fine fillies, though." He grinned his toothless grin and Daniel couldn't help wondering what he would do without his wisdom. Ole Pete knew every single horse on the estate, and a lot of them from the day they were born. Daniel sent a quick prayer to Heaven, asking God to grant Pete a few more years on earth. He hooked his arm under the old man's and helped him make his arduous way back to his cottage.

When they arrived there, the silent maid had already laid out his dinner for him and was busy cleaning his chamber pot. Daniel pulled the chair out and seated Ole Pete at the table. Pete slumped down as soon as he sat, mumbling and shaking his head.

"What is it?" Daniel asked.

"Shouldn't do that, no," Pete grumbled, his forehead deeply wrinkled in a frown.

"Do what?" But Pete didn't respond. He sagged heavily to the side and Daniel grabbed him to keep him from toppling off the chair. "I think you had better lie down," he said gently. Pete kept shaking his head and mumbling incoherently but did not resist when Daniel pulled him to his feet again and led him over to his bed. He tugged his boots off and settled him under the covers. When he turned, the maid was back, the bowl of broth ready to feed the old man.

"Do you want me to prop that extra blanket behind his back so he can sit up a little?" Daniel asked the girl. She nodded slightly, her gaze lingering on Daniel's eyes. Although her face was serious, he felt that she was grateful to him for his kindness. She seemed to care deeply about the old man. Upon leaving, he heard him grumbling again. "Shouldn't do that, can do it myself, poor sweet girl, shouldn't do it…" Daniel glanced over his shoulder as the girl leaned close to Ole Pete, holding the bowl for him while he ate. The scene was immensely peaceful.

IT WAS MID-APRIL when the wind turned from West to North, driving a frightful storm across the land. That night, Daniel found no rest. The gusts of wind were so strong Daniel felt the roof must surely be lifted off the building. He sat on his bed with the lamp lit, feeling his insides begin to churn. He had reacted to thunderstorms like this even as a child and knew he would have to go to the privy soon. No prayer helped. He went, although he loathed it. Hurrying back and wishing he had brought something to ward off the rain, a scream stopped him in his tracks. Lightning ripped the darkness apart and for a split second he could see a white shape bumping into the gate post by the servants' entrance. The following thunder could not drown out another panicked shriek. Daniel froze. His entire body consisted of goose bumps and he was no longer sure at all that those ghost stories were pure imagination. Everything in him wanted to flee but he stood rooted in the rain. Suddenly, he heard groaning cries and then something barrelled into him. The next flash of lightning revealed the nameless maid, eyes wide with fear. By reflex, he caught her in his arms, greatly relieved she was no ghost. She started to scream again, fighting to get free.

"Stop it, it's me, Daniel," he called, but she didn't seem to hear. He grasped her around the middle and unceremoniously carried her off into the stables.

As if passing a magic barrier, she suddenly stopped struggling. Daniel set her on her feet again. In the feeble light of the lantern he had left by the door, he saw that she was in her shift, feet bare and muddy. She stared mutely at him for a moment before breaking down into pitiful sobs. He pulled her drenched, shivering form to him, mumbling soothing nonsense, while his brain worked overtime.

What on earth had possessed her to run out into the rain like that? He shook his head and guided her to a box to sit down on, but her shivering and crying increased to such an extent that she simply collapsed. He caught her up once more and placed her on his lap, pulling a horse blanket around them both for warmth. She buried her head against his shoulder and cried and cried.

Daniel didn't know what else he could do except hold her and wait. Part of him wished he had gone into one of the horse stalls instead of the privy to relieve himself. Then he wouldn't have run into her and would have been spared this emotional upheaval. At the same time, another part of him took enormous pleasure from the soft, female form pressed against him, leaving him in a state of thorough confusion.

After what seemed like an eternity, her crying finally abated. The girl didn't move, though, remaining wrapped in his arms, her head resting against his furiously beating heart. He wanted to stroke her wet, tangled hair. Before he could do so, she slowly raised her eyes to meet his.

He swallowed hard. Never in his life had he seen such an expression of utter, pain-filled sadness. She blinked and a spark of gratitude lit up in her gaze, followed by a hand tentatively laid against his cheek. Her cold fingers had barely touched his skin before she slipped off his lap and disappeared back into the stormy darkness outside. He rose and followed her but stopped in the gateway of the yard when he saw the baronet pull her back into the kitchen during the next flash of lightning. He must have been looking for her. How would he have reacted if he had found her on Daniel's lap? Following Russell's tales, he'd rather not know.

Returning to the stable, he wondered for the hundredth time what this girl's story was. She seemed older to him now, not a young girl of fifteen but rather close to twenty. That was a surprise. Her slight figure made her appear girlish but the expression in her eyes spoke of a lot more life experience. He had to find out more about her. Perhaps old Pete could tell him something after all. None of the other servants knew anything about her and stayed well away. He really should do the same, but his cursed, compassionate heart wouldn't let him. Same as his curiosity.

He went to retrieve his lantern, closed the door, and folded the blanket. Suddenly realization hit him like one of the flashes outside. She had screamed. Did she have a voice after all? If she did, then why didn't she speak? He shook his head, puzzled.

Her eyes were green with golden specks in them. He was sure they sparkled when she smiled. Would he ever see her smile?

Closeness

Brigham Hall, May 9, 1711

Dear Mother,

Thank you for your long letter and all the news about my brothers and sisters. I'm pleased to hear that Mary has recovered. Please send her greetings and my sincerest best wishes. Fortunately, I am in good health and no accidents have happened.

Miraculously, all of the foals were born without complications and it is a tremendous joy to see them frolicking in the pasture. It will ease your mind to hear that I get sufficient amounts of sleep again. My workload has lightened considerably, since the baronet stayed true to his word and dismissed Bastian from his services, which is a great relief for me. The young lads, Willie and Tom, are so much easier to handle now that he is gone and there is a new groom, slightly older than I am, but with a mild temper. We get along well, although it still costs me an effort to give him orders. The master continues to look for a replacement for Bastian. The new groom, Oliver by name, gets much more work done than Bastian ever did and seems quite content to keep the stables clean. Perhaps the master told him that I'm responsible for training the horses. Oliver keeps one lad with him, while I have the other to lend me a hand, which makes for a great working arrangement.

There is no news regarding the riddle of the silent maid, except that I suspect her capable of speech after all. One dreadful stormy night, I heard her scream, when the lightning and thunder must have frightened her. She still comes to visit the white mare as often as she can, but whenever the baronet is in the vicinity, she doesn't dare approach. I have made it a habit to keep some dry bread or an apple in my pocket to give to her to feed to the horse. She seems disproportionately happy about this and I have even detected the trace of a smile on her usually serious face. I know I am defying my master by doing this, but his actions appear so irrational and cruel to me that I cannot help myself. But I do take great care not to have any witnesses.

While the baronet is normally a determined and intelligent man with clear goals, his behaviour occasionally causes me to question his sanity. Last night, for example, I wanted to enter his office for our usual meeting, when I heard him raving loudly inside. "How did he do it!" he yelled. "His methods were ineffective, he was wasting time and blowing money to the wind, and yet his proceeds were higher! It's impossible." Then I heard a loud thud. I contemplated leaving, but before I could do so, the door was thrown open. "There you are," Brigham said to me and all but pulled me inside. He strode forcefully over to his desk and slapped his hand hard on the ledger lying on it. "I want you to look at this," he informed me and thrust the book into my arms. "Look at it and tell me what I'm missing." I was quite speechless, and he must have observed my confusion. "It's one of the former baronet's ledgers. His running of the estate was much different from mine. I am convinced that I have made many improvements, like crop rotation for instance. I have started growing clover and turnips which improves the soil and we even have winter fodder for the livestock. Yet the numbers don't show it. I should be making much more money than he ever was, but I'm not. Look at it," he repeated. "Tell me what I'm missing."

I promised him to do my best, though I'm not convinced I will be able to help him. So far, I haven't had time to really study the ledger, but I am curious, I must admit. The Brigham estate is well-to-do, the tenants have produced good crops and the horse sales are generating a handsome income. And since the baronet isn't married, there is no woman spending fortunes on dresses and entertaining guests. The baronet himself doesn't seem interested in socializing and only entertains guests for business reasons. There's one minor debt which will be paid off in the course of next year, most likely, so why would the baronet fly into such a rage over the former master's handling of affairs? Does he feel there is a competition? And if so, why?

I can see you shaking your head and hear your reprimands. I know it is none of my business, but he has involved me, so how can I not wonder? I long to see you again, dear Mother, to discuss all of these strange goings-on with you.

With all my love,

Your son Daniel

5
Invention

ON A BEAUTIFUL day in May, Daniel heard a carriage rumble into the yard. Before Willie could disappear out of the stable full of curiosity, Daniel grabbed him by the collar and turned him around to face him. "First you finish rubbing down and watering the horse. The hooves need to be checked as well. Then you tie it properly, not like last time when it walked around the stable half the night, working mischief. And then – and only then – can you go and see who arrived, understand?"

Willie dropped his gaze to the ground and chewed his lip. Daniel gave him an encouraging slap on the back and then stepped out into the yard. A long waggon had stopped beneath the wide branches of the chestnut tree. Russell had greeted the visitor and was about to go and summon the baronet, but he was already approaching with long strides. "Do you have a delivery for me?" he called from afar, an unusually expectant light gleaming in his eyes.

"Yes, if you have ordered a seed drill from Mr Tull, sir," the man replied while folding down the waggon's back board. He then proceeded to set two planks against the waggon bed.

Invention

Brigham rubbed his hands. "That I have, indeed," he said and watched the man climb up onto the waggon. "Be careful with the precious thing, I've paid a fortune for it," he warned.

Curiously, Daniel stepped closer. The man shoved a strange looking contraption to the end of the waggon and tried to manoeuvre its wheels onto the planks.

"Come on Russell, give a hand," Daniel said to the footman and together they rolled the machine safely to the ground.

"Nice, very nice," Brigham mumbled and smiling, walked round the device. It had two handles to push it by. At the front, it had two wheels and a smaller drum at the back. In the middle, there was a large container under which several plough-like spikes were attached.

"Whatever could that thing be good for?" Russell asked, completely flummoxed.

"It makes sowing much more effective," Brigham answered. "The machine creates a furrow in the soil. Through this tube…" Brigham stooped low to point at a tube underneath the container, his arm so long his finger rested right on the object of interest. "…the seeds fall into the furrow. These spikes here cover them with earth and the drum presses it down. Not a single seed wasted because it was thrown too far or left on top of the soil. It's superb!"

Daniel had never seen Brigham so excited. He acted like a small boy with a new toy.

"Russell, show this man into the kitchen so he can refresh himself. Mr Huntington, take care of the horses."

"Shall I unhitch them, sir?" Daniel asked the delivery man.

The Silent Maid

"No, a bit of water and a handful of oats will suffice. I need to leave again right away," the man replied and followed Russell into the kitchen.

Daniel fetched a bucket of water and nosebags for the grateful horses and then returned to Brigham's side.

"It's too late to test it now, isn't it?" he observed.

Brigham frowned. "Unfortunately, yes. I ordered it last autumn, right after I learnt of this invention. It's been available since 1701, so I know it's well tested, and the reports are overwhelming. It is said that the plants grow a lot better." His hands moved across the handles and then he closely examined every little detail of the machine. "Look at this!" He pointed at a bar at the side which also sported a thorn. "This marks where to start the next row. You will have perfectly uniform spaces, no more removal of plants growing too closely together. It is a brilliantly clever design." Brigham looked at Daniel. "What do you say?"

Daniel laughed in surprise. Did he really want to hear his opinion? "To be honest, I can hardly imagine how it would work. One would have to test it for oneself." He shrugged.

"You are right," Brigham said enthusiastically. "And we will, despite everything. Ride over to Miller. He was sick last autumn and is sure to have a field lying fallow. Tell him he receives the outstanding honour of having this invention tested on it. No, wait. Saddle two horses. We will ride together. And tell the boys to keep their fingers off the machine, under all circumstances!" Brigham hastened over to the house.

"Don't touch! You heard the master," Daniel warned Willie who stood in the stable doorway, wide-eyed and watching everything. "Go and saddle Thunderboy. I think the master will want to leave as soon as possible."

Daniel fetched one of the younger horses, a gelding with way too much energy. A long, swift ride would do the horse good and hopefully clear some cobwebs out of his head.

Once on the road, the youngster nearly bolted but Thunderboy knew his role as a favourite of the master of Brigham Hall and kicked the young gelding squarely in the chest when he tried to overtake him. Brigham laughed out loud and petted his horse's neck while galloping on. Daniel did not laugh because the gelding bucked for a few paces before settling into place behind the older horse. After little more than half the distance, he ran out of breath, and Daniel had to ask the baronet to slow down.

"Why did you have to take the greenhorn?" Brigham asked impatiently but when Daniel explained his reasons, he nodded approvingly. "Not dumb, Huntington, not dumb at all." With an amused grin he watched the gelding's submissive face. "It seems to me he learned his lesson."

Even Daniel couldn't suppress a smirk now. "Sometimes you simply need another horse to teach them manners. I knew I could rely on Thunderboy."

The tenant Miller seemed unenthusiastic about the baronet's unannounced visit. He bowed slightly and then eyed his master suspiciously.

"Am I right in assuming you have fields lying fallow?" Brigham asked without delay while swinging down from his horse. He threw the reins to a boy standing by and stared down at the farmer, arms crossed.

"Two thirds I have tilled," the farmer replied defiantly. "The rest needs a break anyway."

His wife stepped up and put her arm around him. "He really did work very hard, sir, you have to believe that!" she pleaded. "The children and I have all chipped in, but they are so little…"

The baronet cut her off with a swipe of his hand. "I have good news for you, Miller. Show me the fallow field. I have bought a new machine with which the work is made a lot easier. We will test it on your fields. I'm going to supervise the test myself. If it is successful, which I expect it shall be, come autumn, you will be the first one to sow his fields with the new machine."

"A machine for sowing? Never heard of such a thing." The farmer harrumphed but the baronet was already mounting his horse again.

Miller sent his son to show his master the fallow field. The boy ran in front of the horses and led them to two larger lots surrounded by a low stone wall.

"Are there many stones in the ground here?" Daniel asked.

The boy nodded. "Father always says, they grow better than any grain."

"Could that impair the machine?" Daniel asked the baronet.

He frowned for a moment and then shook his head. "I do not know. As you said before, we will have to test it."

The way back took a lot longer because they didn't want to push the young horse beyond its limit. Surprisingly for Daniel, this led to a rather personal talk with his master.

"Perhaps you have wondered why I have hired you, Huntington," the baronet said pointedly. "A poor sod with nothing more to show for himself than his brains."

Invention

Daniel swallowed hard. After receiving much praise from the baronet of late, this description was rather sobering.

Brigham hooted with laughter. "Don't blame me for naming things as they are. I know exactly how you feel, believe me." A mysterious smile crossed his features and Daniel wondered what the man was hiding. "You are smart, Huntington, and you possess an outstanding power of observation. This gives you more horse sense than some who call themselves experts. In a way, I'm quite glad you have never been to school, so nobody robbed you of your natural curiosity."

Daniel had no idea what to reply to that.

"There are not many people with whom I enjoy a conversation, you know," the baronet went on. "Most people are so terribly simple. No fantasy. Ignorant. Ugh." He spat on the grass. "You, on the other hand, have retained a certain openness, even if I'm sure they tried to beat it out of you. Am I not right?" He cast an inquisitive glance at Daniel.

"I'm not sure what they tried to beat out of me. But there were lots of beatings," Daniel admitted. First by his father, later by his master. And the other stable lads.

"Relax, Huntington. You won't receive any beatings from me. I respect you. And I would talk to you a lot more if you weren't so terribly submissive. It makes me angry. Stop that, understood?"

"Yes, sir," Daniel replied.

"Yes, sir?" echoed Brigham.

Only then did Daniel realise how contradictory his statement was. He blushed. The situation was so unusual that he had didn't know how to handle it. At the same time, he had to laugh. Brigham joined in with his eerie, high voice, and suddenly Daniel knew with perfect clarity that Baronet Brigham was a very lonely man, and had been for a long time.

Invention

Brigham Hall, May 28, 1711

Dear Mother,

You will never believe me when I tell you how things have developed around here. The baronet is trusting me more and more. At the beginning, I was very sceptical and constantly wondered what he was planning. He has such a furtive, calculating manner which unsettles me time and again. And yet his interest in me seems to be genuine. He leans on me for help and support and as of late, has started to discuss many things with me during our nightly meetings. For example, how to convince the farmers to use the new seed drill he bought. He forced one tenant to sow two fields with it, despite it being the wrong time of year. In the end, the baronet had to use the machine himself, which of course was tattled around all the farmsteads. During my training rounds with the horses, I heard a lot of ridicule and was quite shaken by the way the tenants talked about their master. They despise him while fearing him. His explosive temper is known to all.

So far, I haven't mentioned any of this to him, but I think he is aware of it. It's probably his reason for seeking closer contact with me. He needs someone to talk to. He fosters me and explains a lot so that I begin to understand the complex running of the estate with its servants, the horse breeding and the tenants. It's almost like an organism, all conjoined into one larger entity.

He has asked me about the ledger of his predecessor which I haven't had the chance to look at yet. I shouldn't put it off much longer because I sense his impatience. He wants my opinion on it and hates waiting.

I haven't dared ask him after the silent maid. On several occasions, I have seen him watch over her as if she was a precious treasure, only to reduce her into a bundle of fear with a few harsh words a moment later. I'm sure there are incidents in the past giving her reason to fear, even if there are only threats right now. I wish I could help her. But how?

Love,

Daniel

6
Escape

DANIEL WAS ABOUT to drift off to sleep when the sound of hooves on stone reached his ears. Not the sharp clanging of iron shoes, but the soft clopping of unshod feet. One of the mares. Daniel sat up and strained to hear. Yes, only one horse. He climbed out of bed and stood by his window, from which he could see the inner courtyard between the stable buildings and a stretch of road that was paved up to the paddock entrance and then turned into a grassy path. Without moonlight, the night was dark, but he could make out two white shapes moving onto the road.

With a frightened jolt he stepped back. That's what Russell had told him about! White shapes slinking around the pastures at night! For a while, he stood in the middle of the room, his heart pounding. He didn't want to end up like his predecessor, so he stepped up to the window again. Peering so hard into the darkness that he felt his eyeballs would soon touch the windowpane, he identified a person and a white horse. A small person wearing a dress. Was that the girl? She was doing something to the horse's head. Daniel watched her motions and suddenly knew she was tying the loose end of the lead rope into the halter to create reins. Daniel rolled his eyes. Nobody in his right mind rode a horse without a bit. The horse suddenly knelt down, enabling her to climb onto its back. As soon as she was astride, the horse scrambled up again and walked off, breaking into a canter upon reaching the grassy path. They disappeared into the night.

For a moment, Daniel wondered if he had just imagined the two of them. He lit his lamp and went down into the stables. First, he checked the tack room, but all saddles and bridles were in their accustomed spots. She was obviously riding bareback, extremely unusual for a girl. If it was a girl. Slightly hesitant, he went out to the pasture. With his lamp in hand, it wasn't completely dark, but he still felt a bit queasy. "Never heard of a ghost stealing horses…" he said under his breath. The sound of his own voice made the bright shape seem a lot less ghostly right away. There was only one white horse in this group, and that was the small white mare nobody was allowed to touch. He couldn't detect it anywhere. Constantly glancing over his shoulder, he slowly retraced his steps, lingering by the stable door. Should he go into the kitchen? If the silent maid wasn't sleeping there, on the kitchen bench, he knew who had taken the mare for a midnight ride.

He went. He needed to know to satisfy his own curiosity. One of his charges was gone and it was his responsibility to identify the culprit.

Daniel entered the kitchen quietly and held his lamp aloft. He moved around the table but found both benches empty. The girl was gone and none of her clothes were lying on the ground, either. A sigh of relief escaped him. He was about to turn and go back outside, when the baronet entered the kitchen from the other side.

It took him only a split second to grasp the situation.

"Where is she?" the baronet hissed, glaring at Daniel.

Escape

"She took the horse," Daniel answered.

"Why didn't you stop her?" Brigham demanded and rushed past him.

Daniel swallowed hard. "I thought I'd seen a ghost," he replied tonelessly.

Brigham huffed and ducked through the low servants' door. Daniel followed. When he caught up with the baronet by the pasture gate, the man was walking up and down in front of it, muttering furiously to himself.

"At least you came to investigate," he said bitterly as Daniel reached him. "The last fool hid under his bed."

Daniel made no reply but was extremely glad to have overcome his fright.

They didn't have to wait very long before they heard the approaching thud of hooves. It slowed from a gallop to a walk and stopped just outside the ring of light of Daniel's lamp. In three long strides the baronet reached the horse, grabbed the halter and forcefully pulled the girl off. She hit the ground with a cry of pain. The mare reared in panic, but the baronet's iron grip forced it to come down again. He led the prancing horse up to Daniel and thrust the lead rope into his hands.

"Take her into the pasture," he ordered and turned back to the girl. Daniel was hard pushed to keep the agitated beast from pulling free. It snorted and stomped, alternately crowding him and jumping away. With a fair amount of luck, he managed to open the pasture gate, manoeuvre the mare inside and get the halter off without getting bitten or trampled. He jumped back just in time when the mare shot its hind legs in his direction before running off to the safety of the other horses.

The Silent Maid

A slapping sound followed by a yelp brought his attention back to the baronet and the girl. The man was towering over her. He had dealt her a slap that was hard enough to draw blood. Daniel expected her to cry and be frightened, but instead she scrambled to her feet, her face a mask of purest fury. She rushed at the baronet and started pummelling her fists into his belly. One blow must have landed in a sensitive spot, for Daniel heard him grunt. He cursed and swung her off her feet, threw her slender form over his shoulder and carried her back to the house.

Daniel followed him. He couldn't let the baronet mistreat the girl any further. Right in front of the low kitchen door, the baronet set her down and pushed her through before him, while he ducked in after her.

"You'll feel the consequences!" Daniel heard him rant, then a door slammed. Cautiously, he peered into the kitchen. The baronet was nowhere to be seen. In the dim light, he made out the maid sat at the table with her face buried in her hands.

Suddenly, the door to the hallway opened again. The maid started, but it wasn't the baronet. It was Lizzie who quietly entered, candle in hand.

"Oh, you poor thing," she whispered when she saw the maid's face. She fetched a bowl of water and a cloth and started to wipe off the blood.

With trembling hands, Daniel closed the door. It was much better for the other maid to take care of the girl. If the baronet got wind of Daniel helping the silent maid, their good relationship would probably meet its end. Slowly, he walked back to the stable, only to find Oliver hovering inside the door.

"What was that all about?" the groom asked.

Escape

"The silent girl took that white horse and went for a ride," Daniel answered wearily. He felt helpless and didn't really have an explanation for any of it.

"Master beat her?" Oliver guessed.

Daniel's gut clenched at the question. He nodded. The baronet was easily capable of crippling the girl if he so wished. Daniel sent a silent prayer upwards for protection. He was immensely relieved that the baronet had left her behind in the kitchen and Lizzie was looking after her. He had never observed anything of the kind before.

"I hope he doesn't damage her. She's a pretty little thing. Do you believe she's cursed? Russell said so." Oliver seemed unsure what to make of that statement.

"I don't think so," Daniel replied and made his way back to his room, too bewildered to discuss events with Oliver. Questions flooded his mind. Who was this girl? Why could she ride a horse without a saddle, a horse that nobody else could even touch? What was the baronet's role in this? Why his vehemence with regard to both girl and horse? And why didn't she speak, but could scream and cry? He still didn't believe in a curse and was sure there was another explanation for her silence.

Given the circumstances, what she had done tonight was sheer madness, her desperate bout of fury included. One thing was certain: he had to get to the bottom of this or it would drive him mad.

Lying back down in his cot he decided to ask Ole Pete about the girl. Hopefully, the old man would be able to tell him something. Ole Pete hadn't been in very good shape lately, staying mostly in his cottage, and Daniel hadn't had the leisure to visit him. Tomorrow, he would make the time.

The Silent Maid

IT WAS EVENING of the next day before Daniel knocked on the cottage door. Although he heard no reply, he let himself in.

"No," Ole Pete protested.

His curiosity aroused, Daniel stepped into the single room and found the maid sitting by Pete's bed with a bowl of food, but the old man was waving his hands about. "No, no, you mustn't do that!" he exclaimed repeatedly.

The girl tried again to feed him, but Pete was getting more and more agitated and finally knocked the bowl out of her hands, sending broth flying all over the floor.

"Now look at that, look at that," Pete scolded. "Don't you dare wipe it up, I made the mess; I'll clean it up. Go. Go!" He flung his blankets back and struggled to gain his feet. Twice he plopped back down before he stood swaying like a reed in a storm. Daniel hastened across the room to lend him a hand.

"Tell her she mustn't do that! She won't listen to me!" he implored Daniel.

Daniel looked at the girl and inwardly winced. The whole right side of her face was puffy and bruised with a deep cut showing on her swollen lip. Apart from that, she seemed to be fine.

"She only wants to help." He tried to soothe the old man, but he would have none of it.

"She mustn't do this; it's not right," he insisted and then turned to the girl again. "Leave it!" he yelled so angrily that the girl finally dropped the rag with which she had meant to wipe up the broth. When she rose to leave, Daniel could see her eyes were brimming with tears, but there was also a determination in them he hadn't seen before.

Escape

As soon as she left the cottage, all fight went out of Pete and he dropped back down on his bed, his hands and knees shaking. Daniel helped him lie down and stuffed the blanket around Pete's bony frame. The man sighed and closed his eyes.

Daniel cleaned the floor as best as possible. "Why won't you accept that girl's help?" Daniel asked softly.

"It's not right, not right," the old man mumbled.

Daniel straightened up and sat beside him. "Why not?"

"Hm?" Pete asked and opened one eye just a slit.

"Why isn't it right?" Daniel repeated.

"She's the master's daughter. She mustn't serve me. It's not right."

Daniel gaped at him, trying to grasp what he had just said.

"This girl is the master's daughter?" he asked in disbelief and shook his head. No, this was impossible. No man would treat his own daughter like that. Last night's violent scenes flashed through his mind. No, it couldn't be. Besides, there was no resemblance whatsoever between the baronet and the girl. Ole Pete must be more confused than he had thought. In spite of that, he decided to give it another try and ask him about the mare. "Pete?" Daniel probed. "What can you tell me about the white mare?"

Now Pete opened both eyes. "The small one?"

Daniel nodded.

"Don't try to ride her, she'll buck you off. Nobody can ride that mare, except Bella. She's Bella's horse," Pete mumbled, the last words slurring while his eyes closed once more.

"Is that the girl's name?" Daniel asked quickly, but he didn't get any more answers. Pete was softly snoring.

"So, it's Bella," Daniel murmured.

When Daniel left the cottage, he found the girl sitting hunched on a rock by the path. Although she was usually extremely watchful, she didn't even turn her head in his direction. All energy seemed to have drained out of her. Daniel stopped beside her, thoughts churning. "Bella?" he whispered, his heart thumping in his chest.

The girl slowly turned her head in his direction and equally slowly rose to her feet. When her gaze met his, it was filled with an expression of complete horror.

Daniel swallowed hard. "Is that your name? Bella?" he asked and saw her eyes widen even more. She quickly closed the distance between them and covered his mouth with both her hands, vehemently shaking her head. She caught Daniel by surprise. He curled his fingers around her wrists and eased her hands away from his lips, taking them in his own. She blinked rapidly a couple of times, begging him with her eyes not to say anymore.

"Why? Why doesn't anyone know your name? I don't understand," Daniel went on regardless, gently caressing the back of her hand with his thumb.

A tear rolled down her unbruised cheek and he let go of one hand in favour of wiping it away. She gazed into his eyes and placed the forefinger of her free hand on his lips again, her expression becoming deadly serious. She pulled her other hand from his grasp and mimicked holding a knife and slicing her throat with it. In the next instant, she was out of his reach, running up the path back to Brigham Hall.

Even though she had not spoken a word, her message was perfectly clear to him. He had read it in her eyes and

Escape

felt it in her trembling fingers. Her name must remain secret, or her life would be forfeited.

The Silent Maid

Brigham Hall, June 3, 1711

Dear Mother,

The riddle around the silent maid is growing more mysterious by the minute. Despite her obvious fear of the baronet, right in the middle of the night she stole, or rather borrowed, the white mare to go for a ride. Can you believe it? The baronet was beside himself when he found out and punished the girl by beating her. I was unable to intervene and am relieved she seemed fine today, apart from some bruises.

I don't understand any of this. Why would she do such a thing? She must have known what would happen if she got caught. Ole Pete said the horse was hers, but if that were the case, why wouldn't the baronet want her to go near it? And since the baronet treats her so unjustly, why did she return at all? Questions and more questions.

At last, I believe I have learned her name, but she gave me to understand it must remain secret. Pete told me. He also said the girl is the baronet's daughter, but I cannot believe that, Mother, I just can't!

The baronet summoned me into his office this morning, ordering me once more to intervene should the girl go near the horse again. He also tried to arouse my superstitious fear by telling me that the girl was an evil witch, and that I should take great care – the same rumour going around among the servants. It's so different from his usually sober manner. How did he put it? "Those sweet freckles and gold-specked eyes will have you bewitched sooner than you know."

I was quite chagrined when he pointed out to me that he had observed my gentle heart, but he did not hold it against me. "It's what makes you such an excellent horseman, Mr Huntington," he said, which pleased me a lot, as you may imagine. He assured me that he had solid reasons for acting the way he had and that I shouldn't judge him prematurely for what must seem unjust and cruel to me.

Escape

I am confused, Mother. Never in my interactions with the girl have I noticed an evil streak in her. Could I be so very wrong?

How I wish I could talk to you about all of this! You have always known how to straighten out my muddled thoughts.

With much love,
Your son Daniel

7

Fighting Spirit

DANIEL DIDN'T TAKE his eyes off the young stallion as it circled him in a wide arc. Working with the horses in the riding arena gave Daniel a whole new set of possibilities, which he discovered bit by bit. Originally, he had started to train the young horses individually in the arena to teach them various commands. While doing so, he noticed a pleasant side effect: he was able to build a relationship with the horses that influenced their entire handling.

The youngster he was dealing with at the moment was not easy to direct. Daniel had named him Copper, because his coat gleamed unusually dark red, making it shine like copper in the sun. A beautiful horse which the baronet intended to use for breeding. With a click of his tongue, Daniel set the horse to a gallop. It always obeyed this command, without exception. With a wild snort and two bucking jumps it raced around Daniel as fast as the size of the arena would allow. Daniel waited until it slowed down of its own accord and then stepped into its path with raised arms to make it change direction. This time the stallion shook its head and kicked at Daniel before racing off the other way around. Daniel clamped his jaw. The stallion was recalcitrant and had its attention everywhere, except on

Daniel. He simply couldn't get the youngster to concentrate on his commands. With quite an effort and several changes of direction he finally made the stallion go back to a walk, but it was a far cry from real obedience.

"Enough for today," he grumbled and attached the lead rope to the animal's halter. He led it to the gate where the baronet stood. Obviously, he had been watching for a while.

"He's making good progress, our capital fellow," he said, full of pride, and petted the stallion's sweaty neck. "You've got a good grip on him; I have to admit." He gave Daniel an approving smile, but Daniel didn't return it.

"Hm," was all he replied.

"You're dissatisfied?" The baronet seemed surprised. "He did everything you wanted. What more do you expect?"

Daniel tied Copper to a stall and started to rub him down with wisps of straw, a procedure the stallion enjoyed immensely. He stretched his head into the air and pushed out his upper lip. Willie, who was busy mucking out the stalls, couldn't help chuckling, but one glare from the baronet quickly silenced him.

"He obeys, but only reluctantly. He's not with me." Daniel threw the straw on the ground and unhitched the lead rope to take the stallion back to the pasture. Baronet Brigham fell in beside him.

"I'm sure all he needs is a little more time. All young stallions are unruly. It's part of the game." It seemed as if he wanted to add more but refrained from doing so. Over the horse's neck, Daniel caught a look on the baronet's face that included confidence and pride as well as a contradictory pain he couldn't place at all. He had no idea how to react. His opinion differed widely from his master's, but could he dare to tell him?

They had reached the pasture gate and Daniel led the stallion inside, turned him around and took his halter off. Instantly, the horse jumped around and kicked. Lumps of dirt flew through the air, flung up by the galloping hooves. Daniel had expected it and ducked. Now he closed the gate and cast a questioning glance at the baronet.

"Speak, Huntington."

"By your leave, sir, but I think we should castrate him."

"What?" Brigham yelled shrilly and turned red as a beet root. "Are you crazy? Just take a look at that fellow, he's going to make us a fortune! His build is perfect and the colour! Everyone will want his foals!"

In reflex, Daniel stepped back. The baronet's outburst was just as sudden and fierce as that of the stallion. What should he do? Drop his gaze and agree? Or stand up to him? Daniel took a deep breath and looked the outraged man in the eyes. The baronet had made him Master of Horse because he trusted his judgement. And he had repeatedly asked him to show more confidence.

"You're right, he's truly beautiful," Daniel said and nodded. The words seemed to soothe the baronet. "But what use is the best exterior if we can't control him? I tell you, by next spring he will be so keen on mating that nobody will be able to restrain him. He's not like the others. He doesn't want to please. I don't think we'll get that out of him. And the will to please is one of the most outstanding traits of the Brighams."

"Tut tut! Every horse can be trained. Perhaps this one needs a firmer hand than you have applied so far," the baronet objected.

Daniel knew instantly that this was not the case. It was the reason why he had stopped just now. This stallion would never give in. He would fight to his last breath.

"May I make a suggestion, sir?" Daniel said. "You work him. And then you decide."

Brigham started. "Don't you feel up to it?" he asked suspiciously.

A smile crossed Daniel's face before he could stop it. "I certainly feel up to it, but I don't see any sense in it, because I'm sure he'll turn aggressive. He will not be subdued."

Brigham snorted. "All right, I'll take him on tomorrow. Let's see if you're right."

The next day, Daniel was about to go to the pasture to fetch Copper, when the tenant Miller showed up, the man whose field the baronet had sown with the new machine. He approached Daniel and pulled his cap from his head. "Good morning, sir," he said in polite greeting.

Daniel nodded at him. "Good morning, Mr Miller," he replied and wondered what the man wanted. It also irritated him that Miller addressed him in such a respectful manner. He must have made some progress in life if he had risen from 'hey you!' to 'sir'. The tenant shifted his cap from hand to hand.

"Is there anything I can do for you?" Daniel asked.

"Well, yes, I'm here about the field, you know, the one we laid to seed? It's growing really well. Who would have thought. And all in pretty rows, too. Great for going in and weeding. I only wanted to give word; in case the master would like to look at it. I don't expect we'll be able to harvest anything, though. It won't ripen in time."

"He's in the house, you can tell him yourself," Daniel said and put his hand on the pasture gate.

Miller looked at the ground. "Well, I thought, perhaps you could just give him the message. Don't have to bother him right now," he mumbled evasively and then briskly turned about. "Have a good day!" he called over his shoulder.

Daniel looked at his receding figure. That sort of thing happened more often of late. With Harry, the gardener, and mostly with Oliver. He could understand it with Oliver since he was his superior, but the gardener had absolutely no reason to turn to Daniel when needing to tell the baronet something. And now the tenant, as well. Strange.

THE INSTANT THE baronet cracked the whip, Daniel knew there would be trouble. He observed the proceedings from the entrance. Copper had been uptight ever since Daniel moved out of the arena, leaving him alone with the baronet. The man's dominant attitude unsettled the horse and the animal watched him with his ears laid back in distrust while circling him – a lot slower than Daniel was used to. Brigham must have also noticed the lack of sprightliness and increased the pressure accordingly, achieving contrary results. Daniel was just about to issue a warning when the baronet used the whip. Instead of fleeing, the stallion attacked. With bared teeth he ran at Brigham. The man flung his arms in the air and whipped the horse across the head. That made an impact. The horse about turned, but not without kicking. His hoof hit Brigham's shoulder and made him stumble backwards.

Furious, he switched the whip to his other hand and went after the stallion with shrill screams. Copper bucked through the arena, suddenly stopping in a corner and going for Brigham again who managed to get out of the way just in time. The stallion kicked at him once more, but this time Brigham dealt him a sharp blow. For several minutes, the horse raced along the arena wall in blind panic. Daniel feared he would slip and fall, but then Brigham stepped into his path to slow him down. Copper stemmed his legs into the ground, then reared. His flying front hooves barely missed the baronet who backed off with a yell. He tripped and landed in the sand, going down with dreadful jolt.

Daniel crashed opened the arena door, thereby diverting the stallion's attention. With flailing arms, he shooed the horse into a corner. There it stood, blowing and snorting, eyes wide and rolling.

"Everything all right, sir?" Daniel asked without taking his gaze off Copper. Out of the corner of his eye he saw the baronet gain his feet and brush the sand off his clothes.

"Cut off the damned beast's balls," he said hoarsely and left the arena.

The Silent Maid

Brigham Hall, June 11, 1711

Dearest Mother,

How much my view of the world has changed over the months I've been here. Not even half a year has passed, and I feel like a new person. I have fought so hard for approval, with Father, with my masters; and it was always denied me. And now, when I had no longer hoped or searched for it, now I receive it and sometimes it frightens me to think on it. Those who don't amount to much in the world have no responsibility. They fulfil their tasks and don't have to think, because thinking is the job of those who give instructions. But now I give the instructions. No, even more, I make decisions about the stables, my subordinates, and the breed. I'm even able to hold up my opinion against my master, that's how much he respects me!

My responsibility weighs heavily on me, and yet it gives me strength and courage and a confidence I've never known before. I can and may prove my worth.

What surprises me most is that there are an increasing number of people on the estate who prefer to come to me with their concerns, not to the baronet, even if it doesn't have anything to do with the horses. I don't know how to take this development. I also don't know if the baronet is aware of it or what he would think about it. So far, he seems to be happy not to have to deal with the people himself. Oh, I still owe him an answer, that's why I have to go now. Such a strange man. On the one hand, he is so good to me, and on the other hand, I fear him and his cruel streak. I don't think you would like him but perhaps I'm wrong. You have such a generous heart…

Love

Daniel

8
Fright

IT WAS WAY past midnight and Daniel was still poring over the ledger the baronet had given him. He wasn't sure what Brigham expected him to find, so he took note of anything and everything that differed from what he was used to seeing. Studying the former baronet's flourishing script, there was only one profound difference: the man had been deeply religious. He had employed a priest who had lived in his own quarters adjoining the chapel. All servants and tenants had been expected to join the service on a Sunday, which was a work free day for everyone. Only the most basic tasks such as feeding animals, tending to fires, and cooking had been required.

There was never any interest charged if one of the tenants was given a loan and a lot of money was simply given away to the needy.

Brigham was right, the former baronet had spent much more money, but his income had been higher. Brigham spent nothing on charity or a priest; he had fewer servants and nearly the same number of tenants, fields, and livestock. In addition, he required his staff to work more, only granting a free day every fortnight. Interest was charged if tenants required a loan, and yet the income did not exceed that of the former baronet. Daniel was just as puzzled as Brigham.

He kept reading until he came across an entry that read "Sabbath Year". With growing fascination, Daniel saw that for one year all fields had been let lie fallow, while the entire estate had lived off the surplus from the previous harvest. Grain that grew of its own accord had been gathered, but nothing had been ploughed or sown. "Impossible," he murmured, while going over the numbers and comments. He knew that every field was left fallow once in a while to recover its strength. Brigham was following a new concept by adding crops like clover and turnips to the rotation system. According to him, these crops helped improve the ground much more than merely leaving the fields lie fallow. It also provided additional winter fodder for the livestock, making the usual autumn slaughter unnecessary. They were now able to feed the livestock throughout the winter and only had to slaughter what they needed. Personally, Daniel found Ellie's turnip stew delicious and a most welcome change from cabbage which they had far too often for his taste.

The ledger only covered two and a half years, so Daniel was extremely curious to know if the former baronet had done this on a regular basis. According to the book, the estate had not only survived, but been able to sow and plant in the following year. Yes, after planting stocks had been depleted, but there was still money left to buy necessities, because the sale of horses and cattle brought in a substantial income. It was the craziest thing Daniel had ever heard of, but it rang a bell.

He had read about this before. He took his treasured Bible off the small shelf by his cot and opened it to the books of Moses. He had to read up to Leviticus 25 before he found the rules about the Sabbath Year, the year in which the land was given a rest in the same way that man should hold his Sabbath and rest from his work on the seventh day. Never before had Daniel heard of anyone enforcing these biblical laws. He sat still, pensively staring into the flickering flame of his lamp. Then he rose, put the Bible back on the shelf and closed the baronet's ledger. He wasn't sure if Brigham wanted to hear the explanation he had.

The following evening, when Daniel entered the baronet's office cradling the ledger in his arms, Brigham instantly snapped to full alert. He had obviously been waiting for Daniel's response.

"Have you found anything?" he asked eagerly, taking the heavy volume back from Daniel.

"Yes and no," Daniel replied and sighed deeply.

"Out with it," the baronet demanded.

Daniel looked him in the eye. "I am as puzzled as you are, sir. The man spent a lot more money than you do, so it would only be logical for you to have more income. But you don't, I have come to that conclusion as well."

Brigham thumped his fist on his thigh and dropped into the armchair positioned at a comfortable distance from the fireplace. "Damn!" he exclaimed and ground his teeth. "Do you have an explanation?"

"Not a logical one," Daniel said.

Brigham gave a mirthless laugh. "What is that supposed to mean?" He motioned Daniel to take a seat on the second chair.

Daniel hesitantly followed the invitation but did not lean back. He remained perched on the edge of the chair. To sit in the presence of his master like an equal went against his grain yet a less modest part of him revelled in the honour. "Well, obviously the former baronet was a God-fearing man. The only reason I can see why he would be better off than you is that God had blessed him."

Brigham's face froze in a mask of outrage. He huffed several times before finding his speech again. "That is complete nonsense, Mr Huntington," he hissed through clenched teeth, jumped up from his chair and paced the room. "There is no such thing as a god preferring one person over another! We are all in this game of life with the odds thrown in our faces and we have to make the best of it!"

Daniel kept his silence but rose, too. He had suspected that the baronet did not hold with religion. Many people had lost their faith in these times, but Daniel felt that there was a higher being and found great solace in the reading of the Bible.

"You have found nothing else?" the baronet demanded.

"No, sir."

Brigham returned the ledger to the shelf. For a moment he rested his hand on it before he turned back to Daniel. "Are *you* a God-fearing man, Mr Huntington?" he asked.

"I am," Daniel admitted with a lump in his throat. Would it cost him his position? The baronet approached him with a fierce look in his eyes.

"Well, Mr Huntington, there is one thing you need to know and always remember: on Brigham estate, *I* am God." He underlined his statement by smacking his open

Fright

palm against his chest. Stepping even closer and leaning down, he pushed his face up to Daniel's so that they were merely inches apart. Despite the coldness in his gaze his eyes seemed to burn with an inner fire. "That will be all for tonight," he whispered with so much venom in his voice that Daniel shuddered. He turned on his heel and fled from the room.

His trembling legs carried him into the stable courtyard, where he sank down on the stone rim of the horse trough and splashed some water onto his face. The sun hadn't set yet and a flock of sparrows frolicked in the branches of the chestnut tree above him, chirping cheerfully. He looked up into the widespread leaves, bathed brilliantly orange by the rays of the setting sun. The devilish cold that had grabbed his heart at Brigham's words slowly dispersed. The man was insane. No person in his right mind would call himself God. Daniel wiped his brow with his hand. What had he got himself into? The idyllic peace of the evening suddenly seemed like a mirage. He thought of the many discussions he had already had with Brigham. Most of them had been really good. Only once in a while was Brigham overcome by a mood, a craze as it seemed to Daniel, which transformed him into a monster. What caused it? Was he mad and managed to appear normal most of the time, or was he normal and repeatedly overwhelmed by something? A riddle, as confusing as that surrounding the silent maid.

With a heavy sigh, he made a last round of the pastures. Whatever was wrong with his master, Daniel would have to live with it. He would pray for him but had no intention of giving up his position just because his master behaved strangely at times.

The Silent Maid

"THERE NOW, UP YOU go," Daniel said and held out his hand to help Willie into the saddle.

"Do I really have to?" the boy asked anxiously, eyeing the horse with suspicion. He was confident leading and grooming the horses, Daniel had observed but thought it was high time Willie lost his fear of riding.

"You only learn to ride by riding," Daniel answered and heaved the boy up. He sat on the horse like a frightened rabbit, bent almost double with his knees drawn up.

"There's really nothing to be afraid of, Willie. Old Larry here is the gentlest fellow you could wish for. He won't lose you. Didn't you ever ride before?"

Willie shook his head, his lower lip quivering.

Daniel stepped closer and reached up to put a soothing hand on the lad's shoulder. "Want to know what I started riding on when I was five?" he whispered confidentially.

Willie nodded.

"A pig."

That actually made Willie smile. Daniel laughed too and went over to his own mount. He swung into the saddle with the easy grace of long practice. "It's true," he said and picked up his reins as well as the rope to lead the boy's horse. "There were no ponies around I could snag, so I jumped onto the neighbour's pig. That's how badly I wanted to ride. It's fun, you'll see."

Willie relaxed a little. "But we're not going to canter, are we?" he asked, grasping the saddle's rim with all his might.

"No, we won't. Now sit up straight. We'll just take a nice easy walk. Next week I expect you'll be begging me to canter," Daniel replied and clicked his tongue. The horses moved off at a leisurely pace and Daniel chuckled to himself as the boy started to prattle about the animals in his family's neighbourhood. He was adjusting nicely to his new situation; he only needed a little encouragement to overcome his fears. Daniel listened with half an ear to what the boy was saying, keeping an eye on their surroundings as they rode. He knew most of the tracks fairly well by now and kept to open spaces between fields to avoid deer or pheasants spooking the horses. It wouldn't help at all if the boy fell off on his first ride.

The grain had grown nicely and started to turn yellow. Some of the hay fields had been mown recently and the sweet smell of cut grass lingered in the air. Where fields and grass were still high, the wind touched it in gentle waves, giving the blades a silvery shimmer. Daniel loved this view.

Willie talked almost nonstop the whole time, and Daniel was looking forward to getting back to the stable. As they were passing Ole Pete's cottage, Willie suddenly paused.

"What's that on the ground?" he asked, pointing.

Daniel reined the horses in and peered over. In the next instant he was off his horse, throwing the reins into Willie's hands. He dashed over to the lifeless form lying on the ground in front of the cottage door. It was Pete.

The old man obviously lay exactly where he had fallen, his arm bent under his body at a painfully wrong angle.

"Pete!" Daniel exclaimed and knelt down, putting a hand under the old man's head. His skin had an unhealthy grey pallor, but his eyes fluttered open with the touch. He focussed on Daniel with agonizing slowness.

"Pete," Daniel repeated. The gaze became clearer and a spark of recognition lit the old man's face. He tried to speak, though nothing but a croak escaped his throat.

"Quiet, Pete, keep calm. I'll help you." Daniel lifted the emaciated old man as carefully as he could. Nevertheless, Pete groaned in pain. "I'm sorry," Daniel murmured. Most likely, Pete's arm was broken.

"Is he dead?" Willie's question seemed to be coming from a different world. The boy stood in front of him with both horses, his eyes wide with fear.

"No," Daniel replied and bit his lip. He had almost added 'not yet'. "Run up to the house and let the baronet know that Pete has had a fall. Hurry!"

The boy turned around and hastened away, dragging both horses after him. Daniel carried Pete into the hut and gently laid him on the bed, trying not to hurt the injured arm.

"Don't worry, Pete, help is on its way." His heart tightened as he brushed hair from the old man's clammy forehead. If at all possible, he seemed even greyer than before. Restlessness overcame him now and he tried to sit up.

"Quiet, Pete, lay down and rest. Everything will be all right," Daniel tried to calm him, but Pete shook his head.

"Beware… of… Riley," he whispered hoarsely. He lifted a bony hand to Daniel's wrist, his grasp icy cold. "Beware of… Riley. He killed… the… master…" A long wheezing breath escaped his throat and it seemed to take forever before he breathed in again. "…master… in the chapel… burned it… down… beware…" His eyes clouded over. He never took another breath. His head lolled back, and his hand slipped off Daniel's wrist, dropping back to the bed with a soft thud.

Fright

"No, Pete!" Daniel called and grasped the old man's shoulder. "Pete!"

No reaction. Daniel sat there as if frozen. "Pete," he whispered and felt his throat clog with sadness. The feeling of loss was so overwhelming that he couldn't even think about Pete's words. He just sat there, unable to move.

He wasn't sure how much time had elapsed, but after a while he became aware that Baronet Brigham was beside him. He slowly looked up at his master. There was a genuine expression of sadness on the baronet's face, which somehow surprised Daniel. He hadn't thought the man was capable of caring.

"What happened?" Brigham asked softly.

"Found him on the ground outside the door," Daniel answered curtly, his voice rough from crying.

"Ask Russell and Oliver to dig a grave down by the chapel. I will get a coffin. We'll bury him tomorrow," Brigham said. He stood silent for a moment longer, then turned and left.

Daniel sighed, took off his cap and said a prayer for Pete's soul. For some reason he was glad the baronet hadn't asked him whether Pete had been dead when he found him.

While he slowly made his way back to the stables, the strangeness of it all struck him. Beware of Riley? Daniel didn't know any Riley. Maybe Ole Pete had been talking about something from the distant past, something he had witnessed years back and which had come up now in the hour of his death. These things happened, didn't they? He met Oliver and Russell huddled together by the coach house with a pick and a shovel each, yet they seemed extremely reluctant to get to work. The baronet must have already given them instructions.

Daniel drew himself up. "Well?" he asked. "What are you waiting for?"

The men stepped from one foot to the other in obvious discomfort.

Finally, Russell asked, "Did the master really say by the chapel?"

"So he did," Daniel replied. At last, his sluggish brain made the connection. They believed the chapel to be haunted and didn't want to go near it. Daniel looked up at the sky, shielding his eyes with his hand. Then he looked at the men again. "Only around three in the afternoon. If you get to it, you'll be done before sunset." When they still didn't move, Daniel lost his patience. "Get going you fools! Or do you want me to come along and hold your hands?"

With a start, they grabbed their tools tighter and finally trudged away.

When they were out of sight, Daniel searched for the girl. He felt he should tell her that Pete was dead. Without prior warning, she would be shocked if she came in with his dinner later and found him dead on his bed.

She was laundering sheets in the washhouse. When Daniel approached, she straightened up, drying her arms and hands on her apron. A worried look crept into her face. Daniel had never before sought her out. There was a lump in his throat so big he didn't know how to get the words around it. She caught his sadness even before he managed to whisper, "Pete". Her lips formed a silent 'no' before she simply dropped to the ground and buried her face in her hands. Daniel squatted down beside her and put a comforting hand on her quivering back, his own eyes spilling tears as well.

After a while, she gained control of herself again and fumbled a kerchief out of the folds of her dress, wiping her eyes and nose with it. She gazed up at Daniel, then in a questioning manner, looked over his shoulder in the vague direction of Pete's cottage and back into his eyes.

"He's in his bed. The master said he will get a coffin and we will bury him tomorrow. Russell and Oliver are digging the grave by the chapel." For some reason, this information seemed to give her peace of mind. She nodded and rose, turning back to the laundry.

Daniel wiped his eyes and reluctantly returned to the stables. He still had two horses to exercise. He would take them down to the chapel to check that the men were doing their job. The boys would have to do the mucking out by themselves today.

The Silent Maid

Brigham Hall, June 21, 1711

Dear Mother,

Surely this was the saddest day of my life so far. I have suddenly realized how blessed we have been! There has been no death in our immediate family as long as I remember, which is quite a miracle.

Ole Pete has passed. Even though I have only known him for a few months, he has found a place in my heart that is now painfully vacant. He taught me so much and his great love for the horses in his care was exceptional. Even the baronet, who is usually very taciturn and rarely shows what he feels, shed a few tears by the old man's grave. It made me wonder what their relationship was. He said some warm words of praise for the old man's life and named his accomplishments, which I found very moving. A life of honest dedication he lived. Hearing the baronet speak, I suddenly understood why he had granted the old man to live in that cottage up until his death. It was a show of respect and reverence.

When he had finished, he surprised me even more by asking me to say a prayer. I know he's not a religious man, he told me as much, but he said that Ole Pete had been a believer and therefore he wanted me to do right by him. I recited the twenty-third Psalm, finding much solace in the age-old words. Some of the servants were present, but by far not all, and most of them hurried away as soon as I had said my amen. I watched them casting fearful glances at the broken chapel. Most of them have probably never been near it before for fear of ghosts.

The girl stayed, though. She was silently weeping throughout, holding a small bouquet of wildflowers pressed to her heart. When all was said, the baronet gave her leave to drop her flowers into the grave, which she did with the most heart-breaking expression. She truly looked as if her closest friend had left her, and now she was all alone

85

in the world. It nearly tore me apart and I was hard put to keep my composure.

The baronet asked me to close the grave and then left without taking the girl with him. This was highly unusual, as he normally watches over her like a hawk. Either his own sadness occupied him, or he showed a rare moment of grace to allow the girl to grieve the old man. She did not stay, and I thought she had hidden away somewhere. But when I had finished my dreary work and intended to walk back to Brigham Hall, I found her around the corner of the chapel, crying her eyes out.

Mother, you know me. I act upon my heart before my thoughts can catch up. I did not think about evil or witches. All I saw was a soul needing comfort and I went to give it. She clung to me and buried her face in the folds of my shirt, while I gently stroked her wayward curls. It was a moment of shared sorrow, quite innocent despite the physical closeness. It gave us both comfort and we parted strengthened, walking back to the house in companionable silence.

Your grieving son,
Daniel

9
Grief

OVER THE NEXT FEW days, Daniel felt as if he were moving through water. Everything seemed to require more strength than he had and needed to be done quicker than he was capable of.

While most of the other servants went about their business as usual, more than once Daniel noticed the silent maid sitting in a quiet spot under a tree and felt an almost supernatural pull to join her. Every time he was tempted to give in to his longing, the baronet would appear and shoo the girl back to work. His master's bout of sympathy was obviously spent.

Daniel himself felt it in the baronet's attitude when he came to check on the horses. With a shrewd perception of Daniel's sluggish movements, he ordered him to take the stallion out for some exercise. The order was delivered in a tone that suffered no contradiction. Daniel swallowed hard. He almost refused but knew instinctively that to do so would mar his good standing with the master. He couldn't afford that. Thus, he agreed with a sigh and went to fetch the stallion.

Of course, the baronet was right, the lively beast desperately needed to be exercised. Daniel had neglected it

Grief

because he hadn't felt up to the challenge. While the horse wasn't mean in any way, Daniel still needed his wits about him to ride it. He couldn't let his mind wander, or the horse would wander, too. And this horse wandered swiftly and wasn't afraid of jumping ditches or walls, either.

He needed Oliver's help to mount, for the stallion was so full of energy, it wouldn't stand still. As soon as his backside touched the saddle, they were prancing down the lane and Daniel was hard put to get his feet in the stirrups. When they reached grass, he gave the horse its head and it sprang away in long strides. Leaning over the stallion's neck, the wind rushed into Daniel's face and he felt the powerful pumping of legs under him. A smile spread across his face, pushing tears out of the corners of his eyes. He laughed and cried at the same time, letting the force of freedom rip the sluggish sadness off his soul.

On and on they raced, much further than Daniel had ever been before, until finally the horse slowed down of its own accord and snorted in a deeply satisfied manner. Its neck and flanks were streaked with sweat and Daniel felt its heart pumping heavily against his leg. A bit breathless himself, he patted its shoulder and let it walk on a loose rein. Then he looked around to get his bearings. They had pretty much gone in a straight line from the estate, so he didn't worry about finding his way back. What fascinated him were the ruins of a castle looming up ahead of him. He decided to continue. Ten minutes later he had reached the outer walls of the ruin, which were no more than breast high in most places, while having disappeared altogether in others. The horse easily picked its way through one of the gaps in the wall and Daniel found himself in the shade of a lonely tower nestled in the corner of two intact walls.

Stones and other remnants of the castle lay strewn everywhere, overgrown by grass and weeds. Afraid the stallion might stumble on some loose stones, Daniel dismounted and led it to a single old tree growing in the middle of what must have been the courtyard.

Leaving the stallion tied, he went exploring, having discovered some solid stairs leading up to the castle wall. The view when he reached the top took his breath away. The wild, sun-dappled sea spread out before him, medium-sized waves rolling against the cliff on which the ruin stood. The sheer drop from the wall to the bottom of the cliff made him dizzy. He had known the sea wasn't far off, theoretically. He had known what the sea was, theoretically. But he had never seen it before. For a long time, he stood mesmerized, admiring the wild beauty, feeling the salty wind tearing at his hair and listening to the woeful cries of gulls.

At length, he turned away, his spirit restored.

"Thank you," he whispered into the stallion's ear when he untied it from the tree. He mounted and rode back, much more in control than before.

The baronet awaited him, his long arms crossed tight across his chest and a frown on his brow.

"That was an unseemly long ride, Mr Huntington," he said in a dangerously low voice. Daniel dismounted next to him and acknowledged the criticism with a nod.

"Yes, sir. I'm sorry, sir. He was so full of go I couldn't get him to stop. He took me right down to the sea."

Brigham snorted derisively. "I don't believe you. I'm sure you could have stopped him if you'd wanted to. Never mind. As long as you're fit to work again, and this beast stops kicking the walls."

Grief

Daniel made no reply. He deemed it wiser, and the baronet didn't seem to expect a response. He had already turned away.

"Don't do that again," he admonished over his shoulder.

"No, sir," Daniel murmured. He handed the now docile stallion to Willie to rub down and feed.

THE RIDE HAD lifted the invisible weight resting on Daniel since after the funeral and he felt renewed. He still missed the old man, but the odd sluggishness was gone, and he could work normally again. As yet, the baronet had not mentioned the cottage, which was Daniel's by rights, and he was reluctant to ask for it. He felt comfortable in his room above the stables. He had so much work to do that he only saw the inside of it at night, so there really wasn't any point in moving into the larger cottage.

He wasn't the only one wondering about the cottage, though, as he found out during one of his lunch breaks. It seemed that every single servant wanted to know what would happen to it now that Pete was dead, and questioned Daniel excessively during the meal. Especially Fanny, the kitchen maid, kept pointing out the advantages of the small domicile, until eventually it was raining double-meanings and Daniel realized the girl was hoping to move in there with him. He was a bit flustered when the truth hit him, which of course, led to more banter.

Fanny sailed through it all with a cheeky smile and her sparkling eyes locked on his blushing face. She unashamedly kept winking at him. He suddenly felt that he had no say in the matter, already receiving a congratulatory thump on the back from Russell. He looked around helplessly at the smirking faces, until his gaze landed on the maid watching silently from a corner. Pain and sadness were etched onto her features. He didn't know if it had to do with the discussion at the table or if it was her grief for Pete, but her expression grounded him instantly, blowing his helpless consternation away. Feeling resolute and in control again, he rose and said, "My solitary room suits me very well, thank you all kindly for your concern." With an apologetic smile at Fanny, he left.

All afternoon his thoughts revolved around the scene. Yes, Fanny was a nice girl and she had made him aware of her affection on several occasions. He had thought his own actions rather discouraging, but today's encounter made it more than obvious that this wasn't the case. Everyone seemed to believe the two of them were a couple – or soon would be.

But what about the silent girl? *Bella*, he thought, but immediately stopped himself. He mustn't call her that, not even in his thoughts. The danger of letting her name slip was too great, and then what? Under no circumstances did he want his imprudence to cause her trouble. If he was honest, he couldn't deny feeling much closer to her than to Fanny. Or being a lot more intrigued by her. Or thinking much more about her.

He caught himself leaning on the hay fork and staring off into space while he recalled every single freckle on the girl's nose and every single gold speck in her green eyes. Her silence bothered him a lot less than Fanny's constant babble and as for her reserve, he found that much more attractive than Fanny's winking and the 'coincidental' touches she made happen whenever possible.

He coughed and shook his head, reprimanding himself. One thing was clear, he would not move into the cottage with Fanny, no matter what everyone else thought. He would have to tell her in no uncertain terms.

Having made up his mind, all he had to do was catch her alone to talk to her. This wasn't as easy as it sounded, because the cook kept her on her toes all day long. Maybe he would have a chance after dinner was cleared away and everyone settled for the night.

That evening, Daniel lingered in the kitchen, bemusedly watching the chubby twelve-year-old, Mo, stuffing left-overs into his bulging shirt. The moment Mo clapped eyes on him, Daniel raised his eyebrows, chuckling at the boy's startled expression, which quickly changed to a wide-eyed pleading gaze before he shot off with his booty.

"What's so funny?" Ellie asked as she passed him, but Daniel only shook his head. Instead, he watched Fanny and Lizzie doing the dishes. Both seemed to have their focus more on him than the plates and pots. But while Fanny used every opportunity to smile or wink at him, Lizzie appeared to be getting more nervous by the second. She was blushing again, too. Every time Daniel looked at her or talked to her, she blushed. Perhaps he had better leave before she dropped something. As soon as he had thought it, a plate burst into a thousand pieces on the floor.

"What are you doing, you silly cow? Can't you watch out?" Fanny scolded.

"I'm sorry," Lizzie whined and ran off to get a dustpan and brush. She had to crawl around half the kitchen to collect all the shards and Daniel could see that even the crown of her head was glowing crimson beneath her white-blond hair.

Seeing Daniel's reluctance to leave, the cook quickly put two and two together and sent Fanny outside into the herb garden, giving Daniel a meaningful nod. She probably also wanted to make Fanny stop yelling at Lizzie. The poor girl was already close to tears.

Daniel followed Fanny outside. He had barely turned the corner of the secluded patch of green when Fanny's beaming face was before him and her arms locked around his neck.

"There you are! Finally, we are alone," she breathed and pressed herself against him, ensuring that Daniel felt the warmth of her womanly curves against his body. For a moment, he forgot why he had wanted to talk to her. Her lips were deliciously close and all he had to do was bend down a little to kiss them. What would she taste like? He was extremely tempted to find out. A gasp reached his ears, but it did not come from Fanny.

Before he could even look around, the girl in his arms uttered a harsh warning. "Go away, you little witch!" she hissed, "don't even dream of coming near him. Go and work your evil spells on someone else."

The silent maid stood at a distance, completely ignoring Fanny, her gaze riveted on Daniel's face.

"Go away!" Fanny shrieked and let go of Daniel in favour of chasing the maid away. Daniel shook himself and rubbed a hand over his face. When he looked up again, the maid was gone and Fanny was ambling towards him once more, her hips swinging seductively. This time, he didn't

Grief

fall for it. He drew himself up and squared his shoulders, the gesture stopping Fanny in her advance.

"What's the matter?" she asked with a hint of annoyance.

"I believe there is a misunderstanding," Daniel said and cleared his throat. "You are a nice girl, Fanny, really, but …"

She glowered at him. "Huh! That little witch has already enchanted you. I see. You don't need to say anymore." Her voice was cold as she turned and stomped away.

Daniel let out a long sigh. That was not exactly how he had wanted it to go, but at least she understood his meaning. He only hoped she wouldn't take it out on the maid.

The Silent Maid

Brigham Hall, June 29, 1711

Dear Mother,

What am I going to do? The kitchen maid made an advance towards me and I turned her down. No, please, don't roll your eyes. She is mischievous and manipulating, talking about me behind my back. Russell shared all that he's heard.

First, she told everyone we were a couple, which was a lie. The other servants seriously believed I was about to propose to her, such was her storytelling! Now that I have refused her, she spreads venom everywhere, saying I have taken advantage of her. Another lie. Russell thought it was funny, but I don't see it that way, especially when she has it in her mind that the silent maid is to blame for it all. She's making her life even harder than it already is. I witnessed the cook reprimanding her for it twice, and once, I almost intervened as well. In the end, I kept my silence because I reckoned I would only make things worse if I spoke up for the girl. She bears it all stoically, though. I haven't seen her around the stables in a long time and ever since the funeral I haven't had a moment alone with her. She's always working, always on the periphery of things and always excluded. I'm glad that Ellie, the cook, and Lizzie, another maid, seem to be nice to her.

Apart from all of that, I am well. The baronet has asked me into his office tomorrow morning, which is very unusual. I wonder if he wants to talk to me about my contract. Perhaps my trial period is over, and this is the reason for his summons. Pray for me, Mother! By the time you receive this letter, I might be officially confirmed as Master of Horse at the Brigham estate – or looking for employment.

Your nervous son,

Daniel Huntington

10
Revelations

THE SUN WAS smiling down on Daniel when he rode proudly down the main street of Flamborough. It all felt slightly unreal. The small place appeared absolutely picturesque to him with its shops and workshops lining the main street, the marketplace filled with people walking outdoors to enjoy the lovely weather and standing together in groups. He felt as if in a dream. The baronet had informed Daniel at their meeting the previous morning that he intended to make his position as Master of Horse permanent.

"You've learned fast and work hard," Brigham had said, "and you have a fine hand with the horses. You will stay." He had then given Daniel a raise on his wages and told him to take the next day off.

Daniel was still stunned. Most of his life he had worked for his keep. His previous position had been the first to earn him meagre wages, which he had saved up meticulously. His wages now were lordly by comparison. His eyes were wide with the sheer magnitude of possibilities suddenly open to him. He might actually marry if he wanted to. The baronet had offered him the cottage, but Daniel had declined for now because he found his chamber sufficient. Hesitantly, he had added that he would take up the offer later in case he wanted to start a family. There had been a queer expression on the baronet's face when he had wanted to know if Daniel had any concrete plans in that regard. Daniel wondered if the rumours about Fanny had reached even the ears of the master of the estate.

An old horse caught his eye across the street. Its brand seemed to be Brigham and Daniel was inclined to take a closer look. The gentleman atop the horse was in the process of dismounting in front of a tavern, when all of a sudden, a boy came running around the corner, triumphantly waving a girl's ribboned bonnet; its owner following closely on his heels emitting loud protesting wails. The horse spooked and knocked its elderly rider to the ground, where he landed hard on his rump. It backed up until it careened into Daniel's horse. Daniel reacted quickly, leaned over and grabbed the reins, talking softly to the frightened animal. It calmed down right way, probably because Daniel's horse wasn't troubled at all. Daniel dismounted and led both horses up to the gentleman, helped him to his feet and bestowed a friendly smile.

"Thank you kindly, sir," the gentleman said and proceeded to dust off his clothes.

"Are you all right, sir?" Daniel enquired.

"Oh yes, yes, fine. I'll have a bruise on my backside, I'm sure, but otherwise I'm fine." He looked around for the little rascals who had caused the incident, but the children were nowhere to be seen.

"This is a fine horse you have there, sir," Daniel said and handed the reins back to the owner, who smiled a little wistfully.

"Oh yes," he said and petted the horse's neck affectionately, "he's been serving me for over twenty years, haven't you, old boy?" Upon seeing Daniel's surprised face, he laughed. "Yes, he's carried me over stick and stone for twenty-one years now. Never had a better. But I'm afraid he's ready for retirement. His eyes aren't what they used to be, and as you saw, he spooks more easily. Five years ago, he wouldn't have turned an ear in a situation like this."

Daniel was duly impressed. "Brigham?" he asked.

"So he is," confirmed the gentleman. "Know a bit about it, do you?"

"Well, as a matter of fact, I am the current Master of Horse on the estate," Daniel said, gaining immense enjoyment from the sound of his now permanent title. A cautious look came into the older man's eyes.

"Is that so?" he asked guardedly, and Daniel wondered at the sudden change in his demeanour. Then it struck him. Twenty years ago, the former baronet must have still been alive.

"Did you know the former Baronet Brigham?" Daniel asked outright. He couldn't help it. Maybe this man could finally give him some answers to the mystery surrounding the silent girl.

"Yes," the man replied and took a step away from Daniel, half turning.

"Please, sir," Daniel implored. "I have some questions. Doubts."

The gentleman stopped and seemed to ponder his next move. Then his shoulders sagged, and he gave a reluctant nod. "I was about to have some lunch at the tavern here. Join me if you must."

They led their horses to the attached stable and handed them over to the ostler, who loosened their saddle girths and offered them water and feed. Daniel followed the other man inside the tavern, where they sat at a table in a corner and ordered a meal and a jug of ale.

"My name is Daniel Huntington. I started work at Brigham Hall a few months ago," Daniel said by way of introduction and held out his hand.

The gentleman shook it. "William Montgomery Ainsworth, solicitor, at your service."

Daniel took a deep breath. Where to start? "I have learned that none of the servants working on the estate have been there longer than four years and none of them knew the former master," he said. "It strikes me as odd. There was one exception though. Do you know Ole Pete?"

"Ole Pete?" A look of genuine surprise crossed Mr Ainsworth's face, replacing his obvious reluctance to talk about the past. "You mean he's still alive? He must be pushing on ninety if he is."

"Unfortunately, he passed away a month ago," Daniel said sadly. He still missed the old fellow. "Most of the time he was rambling incoherent things, but once in a while his mind would clear, and he told me a few things. Disturbing things." Daniel paused and noticed Mr Ainsworth's jaws clenched tight as he avoided Daniel's gaze. At that moment, the innkeeper approached with their food, which he put on the table with so much momentum that quite a bit was spilled. The ale followed soon after and Daniel preferred to take the mug out of his hand so as not to waste a single precious drop.

For a while, both men ate in silence.

"How well did you know the former baronet?" Daniel finally enquired.

"I was his solicitor. He was also a close friend of mine," Ainsworth replied and finally looked up at Daniel again, who could read the pain in his expression. "His death remains a mystery, as much as the disappearance of his daughter on the same day. We searched high and low for her. There was no trace. Riley said they must both have burned in the chapel."

Daniel started. "Riley?" he asked. "Who is that?"

A sneer drew down the corners of Mr Ainsworth's mouth. He looked around the room which had filled up a bit, making sure the other guests were not listening in on their conversation. Despite the background noise, he lowered his voice. "Riley was the overseer at Brigham Hall. The baronet, Nathaniel Alexander Brigham, had taken the ten-year-old lad in after his own father had given him up to die. His brute of a dog had attacked the boy and had chewed off his privates."

Daniel swallowed hard. "How on earth did he survive that?"

Ainsworth gave a bitter laugh. "Hard to believe, I know, but these parts are not vital. Nat's wife nurtured him back to health and since his father wouldn't have anything to do with his castrated son, Nat took him in, bless his generous soul. He was still childless at the time and probably thought he'd make the boy his heir if it shouldn't change. Riley was bright, quick to learn and made a good overseer. He wasn't very well liked, though, not like Nat. Everyone knew what had happened to him and there was always something odd about him. That, in combination with his looks…" Mr Ainsworth left the words hanging between them.

Daniel's head swam, Ole Pete's last words echoing in his mind. The cloying smell of pipe smoke drifting over from another corner in the room suddenly made breathing difficult.

"Are you all right?" Mr Ainsworth asked. Daniel coughed. As yet, he hadn't told a soul what Pete had uttered with his dying breath.

"Would Riley be capable of murder, do you think?" Daniel asked in a hushed voice.

"What makes you ask that?"

"Ole Pete died in my arms and with his last breath he warned me of Riley. He said Riley had killed the former master. Where is Riley now, do you know?"

A stony gaze met Daniel's eyes. "You are working for him."

"What?" Daniel exclaimed, suddenly breaking out in a cold sweat. He looked around the room nervously, but none of the other guests had taken note of his exclamation. "How could that be?" he whispered. He had never wasted a thought on the fact that he didn't know the baronet's first name.

"Riley produced the baronet's last will, naming himself heir to the estate with all rights and titles. The signature was undisputable. He inherited the Brigham estate and became the new baronet."

"Good Lord have mercy," Daniel whispered, thoughts churning. If Riley was castrated, he couldn't have had a daughter. But Pete said, the girl was the master's daughter. This left only one conclusion …

"The girl is the missing daughter," Daniel murmured.

"What girl are you talking about?" Mr Ainsworth asked.

Daniel took a sip of his ale and tried to sort his thoughts. "There is a maid at Brigham Hall, a silent maid. I've never heard her utter a word. And what is even more peculiar: nobody knows her name. All the servants swear she was there before them and they never learned her name. They think she is cursed and treat her accordingly. She gets to do all the uncomfortable chores nobody else wants to do. She has nothing, no room, not even a cot to sleep in. The baronet makes her sleep on the kitchen bench. He watches her all the time and treats her cruelly, much harsher than the other servants."

Mr Ainsworth seemed to hold his breath while he followed this tale, his mug forgotten in his hand.

"It was her task to take care of Ole Pete. She would clean his cottage and see to it that he was fed and warm. A few times I caught him rambling that it wasn't right, she shouldn't do this. I asked him why. And he said she was the master's daughter."

Mr Ainsworth gasped and slapped his hand on the table. "What does she look like?" he exclaimed, moving to the front of his seat with eagerness.

"She is a very delicate person and has curly reddish-brown hair. And freckles. Her eyes are green with little golden specks in them." Daniel felt himself blushing as he said this.

"Arabella," Ainsworth whispered and shook his head in disbelief.

"Arabella? Called Bella for short? That's a name Pete mentioned. But if she isn't the master's daughter, I mean Riley's …"

"She is Nathaniel Brigham's daughter, Arabella Alexandra Brigham."

"But you said the baronet was childless," Daniel put in, desperate to bring light into the chaos.

The Silent Maid

"At the time he took Riley in, he was. Arabella was born eight years later. It was tragic. Her mother didn't survive the difficult birth. She was only thirty-three. Nathaniel was devastated, but he doted on Arabella and, I must admit, raised her rather unconventionally. As of a certain age, he took her everywhere with him, constantly explaining things to her. He always said she needed to be strong and smart to keep her place in a man's world. There was no more question of Riley inheriting the estate. Nat worked on his will with me for days on end to make sure the girl could not be cheated out of her inheritance." For a while, the older man gazed out of the window, lost in memory.

"How old was she when he died?"

"Twelve. But she disappeared. On the day the chapel burned and Nathaniel died, she disappeared. Riley insisted she had gone to the chapel with her father, but he still joined the search. Only when it was called off did he produce the new will. I had never seen it before, but it was written in Nathaniel's hand." Both men fell silent trying to figure out what all of this implied.

"It can't be her," Ainsworth finally said with a heart-broken shrug.

"What about the horse?" Daniel asked.

"Good God." The words escaped the solicitor's throat in a weak whisper.

"I saw her ride that horse one moonless night, without a saddle or bridle, just with the lead rope knotted into the halter. The baronet was furious and told me to keep that girl away from the horse. It's the one command I have disobeyed," Daniel informed the older man.

"A small white mare?" Ainsworth asked unbelievingly. Daniel nodded.

"Nathaniel's daughter raised that mare herself. The mother had died in birth, just like her own. Day and night she spent in the stables, feeding that filly. They formed a very special bond and the horse never suffered anyone on its back but Bella. She could ride like the devil, that girl could. Taught the horse tricks, too." Tears welled in Mr Ainsworth's eyes. "If you saw this girl ride the white mare, then we have proof. Arabella Brigham is alive, and she is the rightful owner of Brigham Hall. I have the papers to prove it. Nathaniel had lost his faith in Riley. He told me he wasn't sure anymore what went on in Riley's head. That's why he insisted on leaving his will and all relevant documents in my care. The original will, not the modified thing Riley presented."

"Why didn't you intervene when Riley made his case?" Daniel asked.

"What for? If Arabella had been there, I would have. But without her? There was no other living relative to inherit the estate. Let him have it." Ainsworth shrugged.

"Why would the overseer kill the master, though, after all he had done for him?" Daniel questioned.

The other man sighed deeply. "That remains a mystery. Besides, we don't know if he did. Nobody knows what happened."

"Except Arabella."

"We have to get her out of there! How can we get her out of there?" A burst of excitement brought Ainsworth to his feet, only to slump down on his seat again a second later. "I can't just ride up there and demand to see her. Riley knows me. As soon as he sees me, he's warned. As long as we don't know for sure what he is capable of, we should not confront him. He can be unpredictable."

"In my opinion, he is volatile. I cannot sort him out. And I can't take Arabella away. I wouldn't have a reason to and he watches her very closely. He watches everyone closely. If he would leave the estate, there might be a chance. But as long as I have been there, this has never occurred. Would you give me your place of residence, so that I may send you notice if I've thought of something?"

Ainsworth called to the proprietor to bring him some writing materials. "Don't ever let Riley find this," he said, once he had noted down his name and address and folded the paper twice.

Daniel carefully placed it in his pocket. "I will memorize it and burn it," he promised, then rose to take his leave.

Mr Ainsworth grasped both his hands and shook them vigorously. "Thank you so much, Mr Huntington. Please make sure nothing happens to her! The precious girl."

Daniel could see he was still in a state of emotional upheaval with these new revelations.

"I'll do my best," he promised.

Revelations

Brigham Hall, July 7, 1711

Dearest Mother,

You won't believe what happened here. First of all, congratulate me! My position was confirmed. But this extraordinary occurrence has paled in the light of the revelations I have received at the hands of one Mr Ainsworth, the solicitor and close friend of the previous baronet Brigham. It was a chance encounter in town, brought on by his horse, which I recognized as one of our breed.

If we have come to the right conclusions, and we have talked about it at length, the silent maid is none other than the daughter of the former baronet! The current baronet must have hidden her away somewhere for years after her father's death (we are still uncertain if he caused that death or not), then dismissed all the servants and even all the tenants except Ole Pete, who he probably couldn't do without. In one stroke, every person connected to the former baronet was gone. Only then did he produce the girl again to work for him, and hire new servants, who were unaware of the girl's identity.

This is all so confusing. What is going on in his head? Why would anyone do such a thing? When I see him at work, I cannot believe it to be true. We must be wrong. He runs the estate with such enthusiasm and an alert, fresh spirit. But then I see him with the girl and I deem anything possible. He appears to be obsessed with her and watches her jealously, keeping everyone away from her. What does he hold over her to make her obey? I'm quite certain that she could speak if she wanted to, since I have heard her scream. And yet she stays mute day in, day out. Even Ole Pete didn't offer any explanation, or nobody listened to him because they thought he was senile. I was probably the only one who noticed he wasn't confused all the time.

How can I help her, Mother? The baronet nearly sits on her and rarely leaves the estate. I dare not address the topic with him. Who knows what he would do? He might be a murderer, if Ole Pete's last words can be trusted.

No, I have to be very careful, indeed. But this injustice must end! I will do anything in my power to return this girl to her rightful position as baronetess of Brigham Hall.

Warmest greetings,

Daniel Huntington
The proud Master of Horse

11
Opportunity

DANIEL FELT AWKWARD. Knowing what he did made him restless, especially the dire need to keep this knowledge to himself. There was absolutely no one on the estate he could talk to about the matter, not even the girl herself. It had upset her enough that Daniel had called her by name, and with the vigilant watch the baronet kept on the girl ever since her moonlight ride, he would surely notice if she behaved differently in any way whatsoever. No, Daniel had to share her silence to protect her.

As luck would have it, the baronet had made an official announcement to the staff about Daniel's position, so everyone accepted his nervousness as a fresh boost of energy due to his new social status. And then there was Fanny, of course. By now, even the last servant had found out he was not going to marry her, and gossip ran like a river. Daniel was glad he had no time to idly sit around, like Russell. More often than not, his work with the horses kept him from joining everyone else for meals, although his stable hands managed to keep the eating schedule without a problem. He didn't mind. Horses, especially the young ones, could not be rushed. If one rushed them, one usually regretted it later.

The Silent Maid

It was on such a day, when a young horse had taken a lot longer than Daniel had anticipated, that he entered the kitchen well after dinner time. Fanny was still busy cleaning up. As soon as she saw him, her joyful humming accompanying her work stopped. She frowned, turning her mouth into a thin line. Daniel knew Ellie always kept some food back for him. Usually, he simply took it, but Fanny had positioned herself right in front of the larder.

"Did Ellie put some food back for me?" he asked as politely as possible.

Fanny crossed her arms. "No," she countered. Her eyes turned to slits and she pushed out her chin in defiance. Her entire posture was challenging.

Daniel was sure she was lying to get back at him. It didn't make him angry because he knew why she was reacting like this. In a way, he felt guilty, even if it wasn't his fault that he did not feel about her as she had hoped. Which was nonsense, of course. Angry with himself, he shook his head and also crossed his arms. He was really hungry and had no clue how to get past the perky maid.

In that moment, Ellie entered the kitchen. "Daniel!" she called delightedly. "There you are. I have your food right here. It might still be warm." She pushed Fanny aside and got the plate from the larder.

Fanny cast Daniel a murderous glance and then stomped off.

Only then did Ellie seem to notice the atmosphere simmering between the two. With a sigh, she put the plate on the table. "Oh, that silly girl," she said and patted Daniel on the back.

He sat down, said a silent prayer and then ate with relish.

Opportunity

Ellie didn't stay in the kitchen. As soon as he was alone again, he felt the tension in his body unwinding together with his thoughts as the meal filled his belly. When he was done, he cleared the table, feeling pleasantly drowsy. He looked forward to a quiet evening and pulled the kitchen door open. A strong gust of wind seemed to blow the silent maid directly into his arms. She looked a bit tousled and several wayward curls had escaped her cap, framing her flushed cheeks.

Daniel grinned down at her, briefly caught up with her appearance. He didn't see the worn clothes, marking her as the lowliest of servants, nor the dirt clinging to her like a second skin. What he saw was the open, fearless expression on her face and the hint of a smile playing around her lips, showing him a small dimple both in her chin and her right cheek. His grin grew wider. She was the sweetest girl he had ever seen, and a smitten sigh escaped him. She neither giggled nor did she turn away embarrassed, like any other girl might have done. Instead, she slipped her small hand into his.

The unexpected touch caused an overwhelming urge in him to pull her close, maybe even lift her up and carry her away to some secluded spot. An image flashed through his mind of himself riding the stallion one-handed, with the girl placed before him, held close and safe with his other arm. He would free her from captivity…

The thought suddenly brought him back to reality. His fantasies were highly improper. This girl wasn't some nameless wench he could whisk away as he liked. She was the true Baronetess Brigham. She was his mistress by rights!

Daniel coughed and gave her hand a gentle squeeze before letting her go. None too soon, either, for at that moment the baronet entered the kitchen. The girl immediately darted off in the direction of the larder, but the baronet called her back. "Go up to my room to light the fire. I will be retiring early today."

The girl bowed and went through the other door instead, while the baronet addressed Daniel.

"A word in my office?"

"Certainly, sir," Daniel replied and followed his master, who closed the office door carefully behind them.

"I need you to make some travel preparations. I have been invited to Bridlington by a person of great importance. He won't be able to come here as he is bound for York, but he wants to see our stallion and two of our young geldings. He wants to participate in the new horse race at Ascot and is looking for fast runners."

"A horse race?" Daniel asked curiously.

A broad smile appeared on Brigham's face. "Yes, a horse race. There have been attempts to breed lighter, faster horses for a couple of years now. They want to race them. An exciting matter. I wish I could be there. It's supposed to take place in August."

Daniel had never heard of such a thing before. Of course, he had ridden some races against other grooms down a field, but this sounded much bigger. Would he be allowed to come along?

"I'm taking Oliver with me," Brigham continued, smashing Daniel's hopes. "I need you here. Keep a special eye on the girl and make sure to exercise Thunderboy today so he won't give me any trouble tomorrow. Prepare fodder and tack for the trip. We will start early in the

Opportunity

morning tomorrow and return late at night. I expect you to wait up for us."

"Yes, sir. Which geldings do you wish to take?"

"I'll leave that up to you. They need to be easy to handle and fit for a long ride. You know best which ones are up to it. Now get on that stallion."

Daniel left the office with a bow. He let all the geldings pass before his mind's eye, weighing up their training status and physical condition against Oliver's riding skills. Only when he placed the saddle on the stallion's back did it occur to him that the chance had come. He could exercise the stallion by riding over to Mr Ainsworth's house and inform him that the baronet would be gone all day tomorrow. Plenty of time for the solicitor to come and get the girl. Daniel wondered how he'd fare when the baronet returned and found the maid missing. Daniel didn't want to dwell on it.

He took a detour so nobody on the estate would grow suspicious. He followed the dirt track as he always did but turned right when he was out of sight of Brigham Hall. Picking his way along the tenants' fields, he soon reached the road to Flamborough. Here he could make good speed, for the road was nearly empty and thanks to the dry weather over the last few days most of the usual puddles were gone. He rode hard, pushing the stallion to its limits and hoping the horse could take it.

Thunderboy didn't disappoint him and reached the solicitor's house in good time. The stable lad looked in awe at the sweat-streaked stallion.

"Please, keep him moving until his breathing has slowed, then offer him some water. Don't loosen the saddle girth, I will be riding back shortly," Daniel told him and pushed the reins into his hands.

The butler seemed entirely unimpressed by Daniel's urgency and asked him to wait in the parlour. Daniel paced the room impatiently. He was quite relieved when the door was flung open and Mr Ainsworth stormed in, followed by a slightly startled butler who closed the door with a disapproving shake of his head.

"What news?" Ainsworth asked and grabbed Daniel's hand.

"The baronet will be absent from the estate all day tomorrow. He has business in Bridlington and will return late at night."

Mr Ainsworth beamed at him. "That's marvellous! I could be there around noon to pick Arabella up. Have you spoken to her?"

"I deemed it wiser that she knows nothing about this until you are there to collect her. Will she recognize you?"

Mr Ainsworth sighed.

"I'm not sure. She saw me many times, but you know how children are. They don't pay much heed to grownups, unless they have to. She might remember me, but it is in no way certain. It was such a long time ago, eight years! Never mind, we have to give it a try. I will tell my wife to prepare for her arrival. We are agreed that she will stay here with us, aren't we?"

"Well, yes, but for how long? And how do I explain her absence to the baronet? I have to admit, I'm a terrible liar. He will know that I have something to do with it; I have no doubt of that."

Mr Ainsworth placed his chin in his hand and thought hard. "We will have to inform the constable. And the justice of the peace. They need to arrest Riley for the murder of Baronet Brigham as soon as he gets home."

"But we don't know if he murdered him," Daniel put in.

Ainsworth gave a disgruntled sigh. "We do know that he kidnapped Arabella and practically enslaved her. That easily makes for a hanging offense."

"If it is really her," Daniel said.

"Are you in doubt?"

Daniel shook his head. He didn't know why he had said it. All he knew was that he was extremely afraid of all the things that could go wrong. "I need to ride back. Come slightly after noon, when all the servants have had their lunch. With the baronet gone, I'm sure they will take a rest. Best not to have too many people around. And don't ask for the girl. Ask to see me because you want to buy a horse. I will think of a way to hide the girl in your carriage without anyone seeing her. It's vital nobody else gets involved. I don't trust any of them with a secret like this!" Shaking hands with Mr Ainsworth once more, Daniel took his leave. He returned to the estate within a reasonable time, walking the stallion the last mile to dry him off. The baronet noted his arrival with a satisfied nod from the window of his office.

The Silent Maid

Brigham Hall, July 26, 1711

Dear Mother,

I need to write a few lines, or I will go mad with the tension. Wish me luck. It is now or never. We will attempt to bring the girl away to the safety of Mr Ainsworth's house. The baronet has left this morning and will return late. How will she react? Will we succeed in getting the baronet arrested?

And the most terrible question of all: are we right in our assumptions?

I am afraid I'm making a big mistake…

12

Rescue

DANIEL REFRAINED FROM working the horses after the baronet had left with Oliver. Instead, he turned his attention to some necessary repairs, where he couldn't do much damage with his nervousness. Every few minutes he glanced over his shoulder, although he knew it was still several hours until noon.

With the baronet gone, the atmosphere among the servants relaxed enormously. Everyone felt the relief of not being watched and there was a lot of joking and laughter to be heard while very little work got done. Before long, the maid turned up at the paddocks, greeting the white mare for the first time in weeks. The horse ran up to the fence with such speed that Daniel was afraid it might jump it. While girl and horse enjoyed some uninterrupted time together, Daniel racked his brains trying to decide what to do. Should he talk to the girl now and warn her of what was soon about to happen, or should he wait until Mr Ainsworth arrived? What if he told her and the solicitor didn't come? She would be sorely disappointed. But what if he came and she was too surprised to go with him? The chance would be lost. What if the baronet returned early and they were caught?

Daniel shuddered. The thought made him sick. He turned to his toolbox and nearly jumped out of his skin when he noticed the girl standing right next to him, watching him with a quizzical expression. He had been so wrapped up in his thoughts, he had not heard her come near. He saw amusement in her eyes, but the quizzical expression remained. He could tell she knew something was up.

"There will be a visitor today, a man named Ainsworth," Daniel said softly, after making sure no one was close. She showed no reaction at the mention of the name. Daniel's heart sank. "He will come around noon to look at some horses. Where will I find you then?"

The maid cocked her head in puzzlement.

"Listen closely. He actually comes for you. To get you out of here."

She gasped and laid a hand against her throat, slowly shaking her head.

"Arabella," Daniel said imploringly, then stopped. "You are Arabella Brigham, aren't you?"

She seemed to freeze at hearing the name.

Daniel went on, undeterred. "The baronet is gone; he cannot harm you. Mr Ainsworth was a good friend of your father's; don't you remember him? He will help you. When he comes, sneak away and head over to the turn in the road where you can see the chapel. He will pick you up there. That spot cannot be seen from the house. Be careful not to be noticed by anyone. Will you do that?"

She was still looking at him, fear glinting in her eyes.

"Everything will be all right. You will stay with Mr Ainsworth for a while until the baronet is arrested. And then you can come back and finally claim your inheritance. Do you trust me?"

She looked into his eyes, long and deep. He felt as if she was probing his heart and mind with her gaze, to judge whether he was true and reliable. A smile spread across her face, while at the same time tears collected in the corners of her eyes. Trust seemed to be a rarity in her life. When she nodded, Daniel was overwhelmed with gratitude. He spoke no more. The girl left, taking a detour past the paddock fence, where the mare was still waiting.

DANIEL IGNORED LUNCH. He was too nervous to eat, his stomach twisted into a tight knot no food could ever pass through. He tried not to look as if he was waiting for something, while he waited for Mr Ainsworth. It was a warm day and he had sent the stable lads down to the river for a swim to get them out from under his feet. Apart from that, the boys deserved a day off.

When he finally heard a carriage approach, it was almost one o'clock. Daniel stepped out of the stable yard just as Mr Ainsworth was alighting from the carriage. Russell greeted the gentleman with some surprise. Usually, visitors were announced by the baronet beforehand. Mr Ainsworth informed him of his wish to see the horses and Daniel approached, nodding to Russell that he would take over. Under the puzzled glare of the footman, he led the solicitor towards the pastures. Daniel hoped the plan he had laid out in his mind would work.

The Silent Maid

To his great surprise, Mr Ainsworth really took an interest in one of the horses, a young gelding Daniel had only ridden twice.

"This is the best thing that could have happened," he said with a breathless laugh. "I'm going to make a down payment on that horse and you will train him for me. As soon as he is ready, I will take him home. That way, everything is solid business. I have a valid reason to return and nobody will suspect a thing, you'll see!" Together they went back to Brigham Hall. Daniel had expected to find Russell waiting for them, but he was nowhere to be seen. They entered the baronet's office, where Daniel set up the contract and wrote a receipt for the payment.

"He'll know your name," he whispered, but Ainsworth waved it away. When they left the office, they ran into Fanny, of all persons.

"What are you doing in the master's office?" she asked, eyeing Daniel and his guest suspiciously.

"This is Mr Ainsworth," Daniel explained. "He wants to buy a horse and all the relevant documents are in the office."

"I'm going to tell the baronet you've been sneaking around," Fanny announced and brushed past them. Mr Ainsworth gave Daniel a questioning look.

"She wanted to marry me, and I turned her down," Daniel admitted with a shrug, eliciting an amused laugh from the solicitor.

"Let's move on to more important matters," he said and headed back outside. They stood beside the carriage, blocked from view. Nobody at the house would see them here.

Rescue

"Turn the carriage slowly and drive off," Daniel said, laying out his plan. "There is a bend in the driveway from which you can see the ruins of the chapel. Stop there and wait for the girl to come to you. You cannot be seen from the house in that spot. If she won't come, I will and let you know."

"But what about luggage? She can't possibly carry her things that far," Mr Ainsworth put in.

"She owns nothing more than what she's wearing," Daniel replied. "Besides, we do hope she will return here to claim her title. She has nothing to lose."

"Good luck," Ainsworth said and shook Daniel's hand. As soon as the driver started the team to turn the carriage, Daniel was on his way to the house.

He stuck his head into the kitchen and saw right away that Arabella wasn't there. He took it as a good sign.

"So, you have to sneak around the kitchen, too, do you?" Fanny accused him pointedly. "Or are you looking for the little witch?" Her gaze spewed venom. "Oh, of course, now everything becomes clear. The master is gone, and you want to use the opportunity. Well, I'm afraid, dear Master of Horse, you are a little late. Someone else had that idea before you." She gave a derisive laugh.

"Where is she?" Daniel asked, shocked.

"Why don't you try the washhouse?" Fanny piped with a devilish grin.

Daniel didn't wait for another of her mean comments but ran as fast as he could to the small hut situated in the shade of some trees behind the mansion. Apart from a small heap of dirty linen there was nothing to be seen. The girl wasn't here. He turned about in the small clearing in front of the low structure, searching the shadows under the trees for any trace of Arabella.

"Bella?" he called, his heart thumping in his chest. Had she gone to the meeting place already or had Russell intercepted her? Daniel couldn't imagine that Fanny had spoken of anyone else. Daniel gnawed his lip in indecision. Where should he look for her? She could be anywhere. He circled the clearing once more, this time noticing a small footpath running down into the woods. On impulse, he followed the path, praying that it led over to the chapel and that Bella had used it to evade being noticed.

The path wound around Brigham Hall in a wide arch, the terrain dropping away steeply. When Daniel emerged from the woods, the ruins of the chapel were straight ahead of him. Further up to the left, he could see the carriage waiting in the designated spot. He was just about to turn towards it, when he heard a strange mewling sound coming from the chapel. He moved closer, listening intently. There was another sound like a muffled cry. Then he distinctly heard a male voice cursing.

Without another thought, Daniel raced over to the ruins, bearing slightly to the right where the walls had crumbled. Picking his way through the debris, he suddenly came into a dark space where the ground was fairly free of rubble. Although Daniel could hardly make out a thing in the shadows, he knew immediately that he had found Bella.

"Hold still, dammit!" a man hissed in the darkest corner.

"Russell! Let her go!" Daniel yelled.

Shouting a hearty expletive, Russell jumped to his feet and faced Daniel. "What the devil are you doing here?"

"I could ask you the same," Daniel countered.

"I've been waiting for this bit of fun for ages and you're not going to spoil it for me, so get out of here," Russell said heatedly and advanced on Daniel.

An unfamiliar rage coursed through Daniel. He didn't wait for Russell to act but grabbed him by the shirt and pushed him away from the girl. Russell kept his footing and clouted Daniel's head with his fist, making his ears ring. It only made Daniel angrier. He landed quick, hard blows in Russell's belly, followed by a punch in the face.

"Bastard," the footman growled and spat on Daniel. Instead of fist fighting him further, Russell lunged at him and grabbed his hair, trying to jam his knee into Daniel's crotch. Daniel blocked him, eyes watering from the pain of having his hair pulled out in tufts. Daniel boxed Russell's stomach again and again, but he wouldn't let go. Now Russell kicked at him and landed a painful blow to his knee. At the same time, he used all his strength to pull Daniel's head down lower. Blind with rage, Daniel threw himself forward. His forehead crunched Russell's nose, but not hard enough to do damage.

"Nice try," the footman scoffed and pulled his knee up once more.

Daniel warded it off with his hands.

Suddenly Russell cried out, let go of Daniel and whirled around. Daniel threw his arm around the footman's throat and squeezed, at the same time bending his arm behind his back in a dead lock. Only then did he see the maid standing by the rubble of the broken wall, holding a large stone, ready to throw.

"Let me go! The little witch!" Russell growled and tried to squirm out of Daniel's grip – without success. He might weigh more than Daniel, but wasn't as strong. The hard work in the stables had given Daniel muscles like steel.

"Looks as if you might receive another stone. Your choice," Daniel hissed into Russell's ear. "Stop fighting and leave, or get badly hurt. Up to you."

Russell kept struggling and Daniel tightened his grip, making it hard for the footman to breathe. He hardly recognized himself. Never before had he let his anger loose like this!

"Fine," Russell croaked, clawing at Daniel's arm with his free hand.

"No tricks," Daniel said and emphasized his words with a bit more pressure.

"No." The footman's voice was no more than a whisper. He was seriously running out of air.

Finally, Daniel relented and let go of him. Russell stumbled and almost went to his knees. He bent over to catch his breath, threw one last, murderous look at Daniel and scrambled out of the ruin. He made a beeline towards the trees and disappeared.

At the sound of a dropping stone, Daniel turned back to Arabella. He went to her, putting both hands on her shoulders and bending down to look into her wide, frightened eyes.

"Are you hurt?" he asked gently.

She shook her head and sniffed.

Daniel took a deep breath. His head burned like fire and he needed a moment to get his bearings. "Arabella, Mr Ainsworth is still waiting up on the road. You have to go there now. You will be safe with him, I promise."

Tears were rolling freely down her cheeks now and she cast a frightened glance at the forest.

Rescue

"It's over, Arabella. Nobody will harm you anymore. Please, trust me. Let's go to the carriage. Come on. Come." Daniel let go of her shoulders and took her hand, leading her over the rubble of the shadowy ruin back into the warm summer sunshine. He blinked a few times to adjust to the bright light.

To his great relief, the carriage still sat in the corner of the road further up the hill. The girl followed him without resistance. He went a few paces and stopped, checking the edge of the woods for any sign of Russell. He saw none.

"Run," he encouraged her softly, letting go of her hand. "Go on!"

She didn't budge, her eyes not even looking at the carriage, but riveted to his face. Daniel sighed. What did he expect? She had been at the mercy of Riley for years now and had almost been raped a few moments ago. She was frightened out of her wits.

Daniel took her hand again and walked with her up the hill. When they finally reached the carriage, Mr Ainsworth had already opened the doors and climbed down, expecting them with breathless worry. "What happened?" he asked and then fell silent as he took in the girl's bedraggled state with her torn skirts and tear-stained cheeks, her cap lost and leaves sticking in her unkempt hair. "Good God," he whispered and reached a tentative hand out to her.

She crowded against Daniel, avoiding his touch. The solicitor looked at Daniel questioningly.

"The footman tried to force himself on her just now. She's scared," Daniel explained with a heavy heart. "But it's her, she confirmed it."

"Yes, I can see that." Ainsworth looked back at the girl and added softly, "You look just like your mother." He held out his hand again, beckoning her closer. "Will you come with me? My wife has a room prepared for you in our house. We will take good care of you until all of this is sorted out. Don't be afraid. Your father was my closest friend. Don't you remember me? I came to visit you often."

The girl blinked. Daniel thought she was wavering, but as yet she was still clinging to him.

"I'll be here to watch out for your mare. And when you come back, we will go for a ride together," he murmured and gently eased his hand out of her grasp.

"Come child, come. Let me take you to safety." Mr Ainsworth reached for her again and this time she did not pull back. She allowed herself to be handed into the carriage with Mr Ainsworth climbing in after her.

"You'll be fine," Daniel encouraged her, closing the door.

When the carriage finally rolled away, he felt oddly bereft. He ran a hand through his hair, wincing when he touched the patches where Russell had pulled it earlier. Unable to face other people at the moment, he wandered back down the hill, finding his way to Ole Pete's grave. He sat in the grass, staring at the simple wooden cross and wondering where all of this would lead.

Rescue

Brigham Hall, July 26, 1711

(…)

Here I am again. Please pray for all of us, especially Arabella. Yes, that is the silent maid's name. I can finally tell you because she is now safe with Mr Ainsworth. This part of our plan has worked out, if with some confusion. I'm now waiting for the false baronet to return, hoping the constable and the justice of the peace will be here before him.

It's no use, I'm too excited to write. More later …

13
Confession

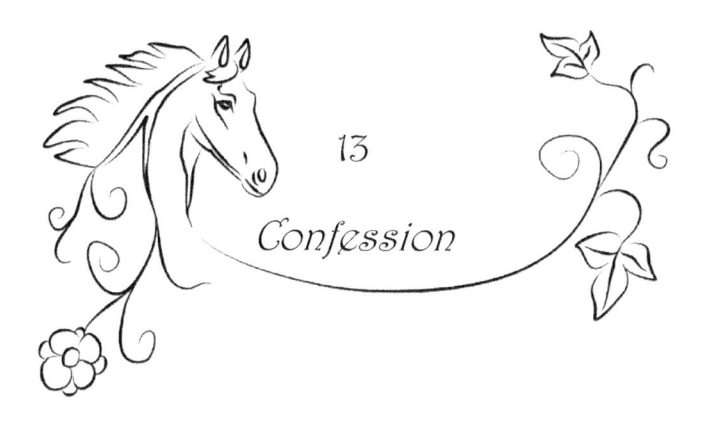

IT WAS LATE. Daniel had busied himself in the stables, avoiding the evening meal. He had overheard Russell tell some boisterous tale to explain his bruises to an audience of servants resting in the sun in front of the kitchen entrance, until Ellie had broken up the meeting and shooed everyone back to work. Daniel had not featured in that tale and he was glad of it.

Now all was quiet, the stable lads had been sent to bed and none of the other servants had ventured into the stable to seek Daniel out. He wondered if anyone had missed Bella.

It was getting dark. Daniel lit a lamp and hung it up on a nail. He was very tired after the eventful day and his head hurt so badly that he couldn't wear his usual cap. Thank God he didn't have a black eye. Russell hadn't hit him in the face. But his knee pained him. The footman had caught him at a bad angle and now every step he took was painful. Daniel sat on an overturned bucket and pulled up his trouser leg to inspect it. Warm and swollen. He looked around. When one of the horses had a warm, swollen leg, he used some of the camphor salve and bandaged the leg. Why shouldn't it help him, too? He fetched the salve and a linen bandage from the tack room and took care of his knee. To wash his hands, he limped to the stream which flowed behind the stable across the pastures. Under no circumstances did he want to get traces of the strong-smelling salve into his face. He didn't care for the sharp smell of the camphor, but its healing effects were indisputable.

On his way back to the stable, the pain was already lessening.

He loathed that he couldn't go to bed, but the baronet – Riley – had asked him to wait up for him. Daniel sat down in the pile of hay he had already thrown down from the hayloft ready for the morning. With a deep sigh, he leaned back, stretching out in a half-sitting position. His back ached as much as his knuckles and scalp. He fought to keep his eyes open, but it took only a moment before he nodded off.

A loud neigh woke him with a start. He scrambled to his feet amidst the answering snickers of the stabled horses. A moment later, the door was flung open and Riley led the stallion inside, followed by Oliver with only one horse.

"The gentleman was impressed?" Daniel asked as he took the stallion's reins. A satisfied smile flashed across Brigham's face. "Indeed, he was. He will bring three of his mares to be covered by our boy here next spring," he said and gave the stallion an affectionate pat on the neck. "Take care of him and then see me in my office," he added and turned with a nod to Oliver. Daniel noted the drooping head of the young gelding Oliver had ridden.

"Was it too much for him?" he asked and felt the horse's chest. It was warm, but not sweaty.

"Oh, give him a day of rest and he'll be as good as new," Oliver replied. He looked almost as tired as the horse, and after finishing his chores, went off to bed without another word.

Daniel stood alone for a moment, watching the horses chewing their grain, the sound soothing. He wasn't keen on meeting with the baronet. With considerable reluctance, he finally left the stable and went over to Brigham Hall.

When Daniel reached the office, Fanny was just coming out. She looked as if she wanted to stick her tongue out at Daniel as she passed him. He swallowed hard. There was nothing he could do, though, except go in and face whatever awaited him.

As he entered, he found the baronet at his desk. There was no fire in the hearth and with only one candle the room was dim.

The baronet motioned Daniel closer. "You sold a horse?" he asked, not sounding displeased at all.

"Yes," Daniel replied simply, waiting with bated breath for further questions.

"What did you do to put off that girl?"

Daniel started and bit his lip. What was he supposed to say? "Girl?" he asked hesitantly to gain time.

"She told me you've been snooping around in here. Silly cow. I don't think she will stay another year."

Daniel coughed to disguise his relief. "Refused to marry her," he explained. Brigham barked a short laugh. "Smart man," was all he said and dismissed the matter. Instead, he looked at the papers Daniel had prepared previously.

Confession

"Ainsworth. Elderly gentleman? Solicitor?" he enquired.

"Uh, yes, sir." Daniel's heart seemed to be beating right in his ears and he felt himself break out in a cold sweat.

"And he only came to buy a horse? Nothing else?"

"Yes, sir," Daniel replied, studying his boots. The less he said, the lower the chances his trembling voice would give him away.

"Do you have any idea what kind of trouble Russell got himself into?"

Daniel froze at the critical question. "He…" Lord, how was he supposed to explain that?

Brigham registered his reluctance and his suspicious glare fell heavily on Daniel. "Did he harm the silent girl?" he asked and stood up very straight.

Daniel couldn't think of a lie. "He wanted to…" he stuttered.

"He wanted *what?*" Brigham was almost screaming, an angry fire burning brightly in his eyes.

"He wanted to force himself on her, but I intervened. There was a fight and he -"

The baronet was no longer listening. Full of fury he rushed into the entrance hall and intercepted Russell on his way into the kitchen. Without warning, Brigham grabbed him by the collar and slapped him in the face with the back of his hand. Russell staggered, surprised by the sudden attack.

"Where is she?" Brigham yelled. He grasped Russell's jacket with both hands and pressed him against the closest wall. "What did you do to her?"

"Nothing!" Russell replied, his eyes wide in panic.

"I don't believe you!" Brigham growled and raised his hand for another blow.

In that instant, the door knocker sounded.

The baronet lowered his hand and looked at Daniel. "Open the door," he said quietly and let go of Russell's jacket with accentuated slowness.

Daniel ripped the door open and was immensely relieved to see Mr Ainsworth in the company of the constable. He stepped aside to let the men in.

Brigham recognized the solicitor right away.

"Mr Ainsworth," he said coolly and nodded. "I was just informed about your purchase. A splendid choice you have made. If you'd care to follow me? You too, Huntington." With that, he left Russell standing by the wall and moved back to his office at a leisurely pace. The other men followed.

Daniel's master stepped behind his desk. He didn't sit down, though, but watched the constable with a sceptical expression. The man was short and squat, swallowing hard in the light of the baronet's considerable height.

Mr Ainsworth bestowed an icy stare on the baronet. "The game's up, Riley," he said. Daniel was surprised to see a look of peaceful relief settle on the baronet's face.

"It's taken you a damn long time, old man," Riley said and pulled out a chair, making himself comfortable. "I take it you want to arrest me for murder?" he asked conversationally, looking back and forth between Ainsworth and the constable with mild curiosity.

"Right now, the charge is kidnapping," the constable informed him, making Riley laugh.

"Well, add murder. And forgery. Although, I'm not sure if it really is forgery if a baronet changes his will

Confession

because I hold a dagger to his precious daughter's throat. Would that be forgery, Constable?" The constable merely gaped at him, completely unaccustomed to people confessing their crimes so readily.

"You may certainly add arson, too. I set fire to the chapel. A merry bonfire to celebrate the baronet's death. Oh, he was dead before that. I slit his throat." Riley seemed to revel in the disgusted look on the men's faces. He crossed his arms and looked Mr Ainsworth in the eyes, smiling benignly.

"Why?" the older man asked tonelessly.

Riley suddenly jumped up and slammed both hands on the desk, thrusting his head forward to glare coldly at the man. They all flinched.

"*Why?*" he screamed. "You're asking me *why*? I'll tell you *why*. Because he made me live."

Mr Ainsworth cried out with indignation. "He saved your life!"

Riley straightened up. "Saved my life, pah! He condemned me. Condemned! I should have died, but he condemned me to this miserable existence! He forced me to be this monster, this not-man, this freak!" Riley gesticulated with his long arms and the men involuntarily took a step backwards. The fluttering light of the candle made each of his gestures dance like ghosts through the room.

"He treated you like a son," the solicitor dared to contradict him.

"Yes, but only until *she* was born. After that, Riley was history." His voice dripped with resentment. "Finally, you found out. Finally! What the devil took you so long?" He raked his hands through his thin hair, making it stand up from his narrow head. "I never expected to get away with this. Bastard! You should have challenged the will; you should have tortured the truth about Arabella out of me! But no, you just turned and shrugged it all off! Because of *you* that girl suffered at my hands for eight long, miserable years! All because of you." Riley shook his head and appeared almost dismayed. "The effort. The tension. The responsibility. To hell with it, I'm so tired of this. Arrest me, Constable. Arrest me and take me to the gallows right away." He held his hands out to be tied. The constable complied with shaking hands.

"Did you see her when you came for the horse?" Riley asked confidentially, looking at the solicitor out of the corner of his eye.

Mr Ainsworth, who had paled considerably at Riley's speech, flicked a glance at Daniel. Riley immediately caught on and slowly turned his head to look Daniel full in the eye.

"You, Mr Huntington? What do you have to do with-" He stopped short, realization dawning on him. "Pete told you." He stated it as a fact. "What irony," he said, chuckling softly as if talking to himself. "That you of all people should betray me, after all I have done for you."

Daniel swallowed hard, but finally broke his silence. "How did you make her keep it secret and stay mute?"

"Oh, nothing hard about that. Told the girl I'd kill her horse if she uttered one word. She took that quite literally. Fine by me. Told the old man I'd kill the girl. So they both kept quiet." Riley sighed deeply. "Was a damned nuisance to watch them both, though. I'm sick and tired of it. Can we go?"

Confession

Riley walked to the door, his head held high, a relaxed smile playing on his lips. Was the man truly relieved to be caught?

"He is completely insane," Mr Ainsworth whispered, and followed the constable outside, who tried in vain to look as if he was leading Riley off.

"Russell," Riley said, not in the least surprised to find the footman right beside the door, even though he stepped hastily back. "Inform the servants that they may plunder my whiskey barrel tonight. Drink my health and celebrate, because now you are rid of me. Celebrate as long as you can. I don't know what will happen to you tomorrow." He laughed loudly, sounding at the same time liberated and utterly mad. The shrill sound echoed through the dark hallways of the mansion. Nobody laughed with him.

With a stony expression, Mr Ainsworth climbed onto the carriage next to the driver, while the constable sat with the prisoner inside. When the door had closed on them and the sound of hooves had faded away, shocked silence settled on Brigham Hall.

Arabella

SHE SAT MOTIONLESS in front of the mirror, her gaze lowered, and felt her hair being brushed. The old maid was grumbling as she picked small burrs and wisps of hay out of the freshly washed curls. It hurt Arabella more than usual, and several times, while emitting a desperate sigh, the maid took the scissors and cut off a tangled curl. But she didn't scold. Nanny used to scold when she'd had to do this.

But Nanny was gone. They were all gone. Father, the maids and grooms, and even the tenants. And now Ole Pete and Riley were gone, too. Even Riley. She was all alone.

A tear rolled down her cheek.

The old maid looked at her in the mirror. "Don't cry, Dame Arabella. Everything will be all right now."

In the mirror she saw the maid smiling, but she didn't return the smile. She felt as lost as a leaf on a river. She had been torn away, away from her home, away from her beloved Kitty.

Away from the cruel Riley! a voice screamed in her head, a voice like Nanny's. Yes, she was away from Riley and his

Arabella

cruelty, and that was a relief. He had always watched her. All the time he had watched her, so she didn't say a word. All the time he had stood between her and Kitty. But he hadn't always managed. She had waited, waited patiently until his vigilance slackened. And then she had gone to see Kitty. She had even gone for a ride. And even if he'd beaten her twice as much – he hadn't been able to take that from her. She had gone for a ride and it had been wonderful. If she had remembered Mr Ainsworth then, she might have ridden to him. But she hadn't. So she had returned and learned something valuable, something very valuable. Riley didn't have absolute power over her.

Her father had told her the truth. *Those who are free in Christ, are truly free, no matter what their circumstances are.* Over the years, she had held on to that sentence with all her might. But she had only fully grasped its meaning after her midnight ride. She had understood how much Riley was bound to her; how unfree he was! She had robbed him of his sleep, had forced him to watch over her. She had worn him down until he had gone mad. Because she was free in Christ and he was not.

Hesitantly, she looked up, lifting a hand to her cheek and stroking her freckles. There were more of them since she had last looked in a mirror. The eyes looking back at her were not lost. They seemed courageous and determined. What had the maid said? Dame Arabella? Not Lady, but Dame. It meant she was baronetess. She was now the mistress of Brigham Hall. No, she wasn't lost. She could return anytime, as soon as Riley was arrested. Back home. Back to her Kitty. Daniel would take care of her. He had promised that. Then she would go riding as often as she liked, and nobody could forbid it. With Daniel, her saviour.

Thanks to him, she no longer had to clean and wash and empty the chamber pots.

She straightened.

The maid laid the brush aside. "Shall I dress you now?"

She sighed deeply and nodded. A tentative smile played on her lips. She was dressed, as in the past. With her eyes closed she let it happen, following the quiet instructions the maid gave her as in a dream. Then she was placed on the chair again and the maid pinned up her hair. When it was done, she opened her eyes.

Dame Arabella Alexandra Brigham looked at her from the mirror, a pretty, self-confident young woman with far too many freckles. Her smile deepened. Those freckles were just as wayward as her curls. As herself.

14

Uncertainty

THE FIRE BURNED brightly, and all the lamps had been lit. Pale faces crowded around the kitchen table, looking confused, shocked and scared. They had all heard the master's mad laughter when he had been led away by the constable, but nobody knew what had happened. Daniel sat silently amongst them and kept kneading his trembling hands. He felt sick. He had wanted to save the silent maid, yes. But that it conversely meant that his master would be sent to the gallows had never occurred to him. He should have thought of that. These days, people were hanged for lesser offences. And it was his fault. It was his fault that this man would be hanged. Due to his wretched curiosity. Due to his wretched kind-heartedness that always wanted to help the weak. Would there have been a way to save the girl without sealing Riley's fate?

Daniel sighed. The man had admitted a murder! Why on earth did it bother him that he would be punished for it?

"What happened, Daniel?" Ellie asked. She could no longer bear the sordid silence around the table. "Please tell us what happened!"

Grudgingly, Daniel lifted his gaze from his fingers. He cleared his throat. "Baronet Brigham is a murderer, kidnapper and swindler. His real name is Riley and he used to be the overseer here on the estate. He held a grudge against the former baronet, killed him and made himself heir to the estate. Mr Ainsworth was the former baronet's solicitor."

A murmur went through the room. Almost everyone made an exclamation of some sort.

Daniel glanced at the corner by the hearth where the girl used to sit during meals. They all followed his gaze and most of them only now noticed she was missing.

"Where is she?" Lizzie asked.

"I'm sure she took off the moment the master was gone. I haven't seen her since lunchtime," Fanny replied pertly.

Daniel made no comment. He didn't want to be the one to tell the others who they had been mistreating all these years.

"Shouldn't we look for her?" Lizzie suggested hesitatingly, which made Fanny erupt in scornful laughter.

"Look for her? Be glad the little witch is finally gone!"

"We're going to see how glad you are about that when laundry day comes around again," Ellie said under her breath.

Daniel shot a scalding look at Russell, but he sat there in silence, staring gloomily ahead.

Ellie rose. "Go to bed, all of you. There's no point in sitting around here. Tomorrow is a new day. For today, it's enough."

The servants got up as well, talking quietly among themselves. Daniel patted Ellie's arm, then hauled himself to his feet and shuffled tiredly out of the kitchen. From far off, he heard Russell babble something about whiskey. He

Uncertainty

was welcome to get drunk, Daniel didn't care. All he wanted was to go to sleep.

The next morning, Daniel woke surprisingly refreshed. As usual, he took care of the horses first. The past day would have felt like a bad dream if it hadn't been for his burning head. His knee also gave a mild protest when he carried the water buckets to the horses. He really needed to think of a way to channel water from the stream through to the stable. He chuckled. Such craziness! Nobody knew what would happen to the estate and here he was wondering how to make his work easier. When Oliver showed up with the two lads, he explained in short what had occurred the night before. The boys listened without a comment and then trudged off to breakfast, but Oliver stood there a while with his mouth hanging open. When he closed it again, there was fear in his eyes.

"What will happen to us?" he asked softly and looked at the row of horses chomping on their hay.

"Right now, nobody knows," Daniel admitted. He put a hand on the groom's shoulder. "Have trust. God will not forsake us."

Oliver didn't seem calmed by these words and hung his head. "I just started here. It's a good position." He did not continue.

"Come, let's get some breakfast. And then we'll see."

In the kitchen, the atmosphere was equally subdued. Uncertainty was written on all their faces. What would happen to them and to the estate?

Ellie alone appeared to be fairly confident. "Don't hang your heads, all of you. Get to work. It hasn't dissolved into thin air overnight, you know? Whatever happens, we need to keep things running. Animals need to be fed, cows milked, vegetables watered, and potatoes peeled; otherwise, there won't be any food. And you do want to eat, don't you?" She distributed tasks and sent them off one by one. Daniel also wanted to get started, but Ellie held him back. "You need to take the reins in your hands, Daniel," she said quietly and put a comforting hand on his arm.

"Me?" he asked, shocked.

"Yes, you," she emphasized. "You are the one who knows most about the running of the estate. The master discussed everything with you, didn't he? Nobody else has such insights. We all have our little areas of expertise, but you … you are a lot more than the Master of Horse. Even the tenants ask for you. Hadn't you noticed?"

Indecision overwhelmed Daniel. He was only a simple lad, son of a carpenter.

Ellie looked into his eyes and seemed to read his thoughts, because she smiled at him with such warmth, as if she wanted to hug him. She laid a hand against his cheek. "You are a good, humble boy, Daniel Huntington. I have thought that right from the start. And that is the reason why people would rather talk to you of late than to the baronet. They were all afraid of him, of his arbitrariness and his fits of rage. But you? You have a good heart, and you work hard. They trust you. Give them hope in their uncertainty. They are like lost sheep. They need you."

"But I…"

"We will keep things going, you and I, Daniel. With head and heart. Brigham Hall is worth our best efforts. No matter what happens, it's our home. Our chances are a lot better if we prove ourselves loyal and proficient." She held his gaze until he nodded. "You couldn't leave the horses

Uncertainty

to themselves, could you?" she added, although she knew she had long convinced him.

He smiled hesitantly. "Never," he said and felt a proud excitement gripping him. The possibilities…

It made him dizzy.

THE FLOOD OF contradictory feelings rushing through his body put him into a strangely remote mood. Despite giving his orders, working with the horses, and making necessary decisions as usual, his mind worked overtime. How should he take matters into his hands? How would the other servants react if he gave them tasks? When he made resolutions and informed them? He was one of them. They didn't have to do what he said. He was completely dependent on their good-will. And he knew at least two people he could expect nothing from in that regard. Would the others back him? Perhaps someone else was better suited.

Back and forth his thoughts jumped, but always there was this exciting tingle; this wish to prove himself. Could he do it? Could he lead such a complex organism as Brigham Hall? There was so much more to consider than in the stables, and that was hard enough. But he had managed. If he managed that, perhaps he could also manage on a bigger scale.

His thoughts were interrupted by a carriage pulling up. A hopelessly tired Mr Ainsworth got out. Deep circles smudged his eyes and his entire posture showed that he was at the end of his strength. Daniel ran to him and led him into the house, where he went into the office for lack of a better idea. It was the only room in the house, apart from the kitchen, he was absolutely familiar with. He offered the chair in front of the fireplace to Mr Ainsworth and then rushed over to find Ellie and ask her to enliven their guest with tea and pastries. After that, he sat down with him.

"Any news?" he asked and looked expectantly at the solicitor.

Ainsworth pulled a kerchief out of the inner pocket of his coat and wiped his brow. "He is insane," he said hoarsely. "The justice of the peace questioned him right after sunrise. The night in prison must have ruined his mind completely. He raved and threatened to kill the justice with his bare hands. They needed two strong men to restrain him. Until the justice sentenced him to death. He was quiet then. They haven't hanged him, yet." Mr Ainsworth sadly shook his head. "How did he get like this?" he whispered and wiped his brow again.

Daniel sat there as if hewn from stone. "It's all my fault," he said woodenly.

The solicitor's head snapped up. The next moment he leaned forward and grabbed Daniel's arm. "What are you talking about? The man was already crazy long before you ever knew him! You are the least person to have anything to do with this!" he insisted.

"But if I hadn't—"

Ainsworth interrupted him. "If you hadn't been so alert, the poor girl would still be at the mercy of this lunatic! No, Huntington, you have done the right thing. He sealed his own fate – with full intention."

Uncertainty

So why does it constrict my heart? Daniel wanted to ask but didn't. Essentially, he knew what the problem was. This thought had also revolved around his head all morning. He had developed a sort of friendship with Riley. The man had offered him chances he never even would have considered. He had schooled him. And trusted him. That was the real point bothering Daniel so very much. Riley had trusted him, and he had betrayed him.

"How is she?" he asked to change the direction of his guilt-ridden thoughts. Mr Ainsworth sighed deeply. "I believe she is in a state of shock. She still doesn't speak, only sits there and stares straight ahead." He faltered and wiped his eyes. Then he looked directly at Daniel. "As long as this is the case, I'm her guardian. Nat had given me all respective rights. I have brought the papers if you would like to see them?"

"No, I… I believe you," Daniel replied, confused.

"Mr Huntington, in my position as guardian I need to make some decisions for which I will need your help. Unless you tell me that there is someone here on the estate who knows more than you do. Who was Riley's right hand?"

"That would have been me," Daniel said tonelessly. He was glad to be sitting for his knees felt weak. At the same time, the excited tingle returned and caused a nauseous feeling in his stomach.

"I had hoped so, Mr Huntington. I would like to name you overseer of the estate until either Dame Arabella can take matters into her own hands or another solution needs to be found. Would you be prepared to do that?"

The Silent Maid

Brigham Hall, July 28, 1711

Mother,

The Lord have mercy on me! Events have unfolded rapidly. As you may derive from the letter I started the day before yesterday, which I have included, Arabella is safe. But Mr Ainsworth is deeply troubled by her behaviour. She seems calmer, but still does not speak.

Yesterday, Mr Ainsworth talked to me at length. The man I got to know as Baronet Brigham is now in jail. He immediately confessed to all his crimes as soon as the constable and Mr Ainsworth confronted him. He welcomed the death sentence and even accused Mr Ainsworth of not having found him out sooner. So many years he lived his life as unlawful owner of this estate – and within a few moments, it was all over for good. I am growing more and more conscious of the extent of his delusion, and many of his reactions that puzzled me before now make sense.

As a boy, he was unmanned by an accident and had to exist like that – a terrible thought. Time and again, I wonder how I would have felt in his shoes. Would I have been glad to have survived or would I have longed for death – like he did? I cannot say.

All of his actions, murdering his master, kidnapping the girl, the fake will – everything was planned to bring him to the gallows. But he was too smart. His plan was too intricate, so he wasn't arrested and had to play his role as Baronet Brigham. He was too ambitious to turn himself in. A curious ambivalence. As much as he wished to end his life on earth, he also strove for success. He managed Brigham Hall well.

And now, I'm supposed to succeed him. Yes, Mother, you read that correctly. Arabella is the lawful heiress and baronetess, for there are no male relatives who could inherit the estate. Although it is quite unusual, her father explicitly named her the sole heiress in his original

Uncertainty

will. Mr Ainsworth repeatedly confirmed that her father did that on purpose and was convinced she could manage the estate. However, she is unable to do so at the moment, which is why Mr Ainsworth, as her guardian, has asked me to work as overseer. I am the only one the baronet taught everything necessary for managing Brigham Hall. Mr Ainsworth will support me in all legal and commercial matters.

I know I can always be honest with you. I'm afraid, Mother. This task is too big for me. But I also see that God calls me and that I may serve him. The cook has told me something that has led my thoughts in that direction. She said the servants were like lost sheep. Confirmation is there when I look into their frightened faces. Everyone is wondering what the future will bring. They are all afraid of losing their work and having to leave this beautiful estate. With God's help, I may be their shepherd for a while.

In this sense, I will take on the task and do it to my best ability. Your loving goodbyes, so many years ago, will always reside in my heart: "You can only do your best. If you do that, nobody can reproach you."

That's exactly what I intend to do. Please pray for me, Mother, and for Arabella, too.

Love

Daniel

15
Overseer

MR AINSWORTH LOOKED at the assembled servants of Brigham Hall and cleared his throat. The parlour was spacious and would have accommodated twice as many people, but since the false Baronet Brigham had mostly kept aloof of social life and hadn't married, he had made do with fewer servants than most men of his standing.

Mr Ainsworth cleared his throat again and the excited murmur ebbed away. "As you will all be aware by now, your employer has been locked up for the crimes he has committed. He will be hanged." He stuck his finger into the collar of his shirt, trying to get a bit more air. It was a hot summer day and in addition, his arduous task made him sweat. "First and foremost, none of you need to worry. There is a rightful mistress of Brigham Hall, Dame Arabella Alexandra Brigham, the daughter of the baronet who was murdered by Riley – the man you knew as Baronet Brigham. Unfortunately, it is unclear when Dame Arabella will be able to take over Brigham Hall. Until then, you will all be employed as before and fulfil the tasks known to you. It is in all of your best interest to keep the estate in excellent shape for Dame Arabella's return."

"A woman as mistress of an estate?" Russell burst out. "Never heard of that!"

Mr Ainsworth compressed his lips into a thin line before answering, "Indeed, a woman. Since there are no male relatives who could inherit Brigham Hall and the baronet has named his daughter his sole heir in his will, there will be a baronetess."

"Where does she come from all of a sudden?" Fanny murmured.

"Do you have a question?" Mr Ainsworth addressed her.

Fanny shook her head.

The solicitor took a deep breath and continued. "In my position as guardian and solicitor of the baronetess, I hereby name Mr Huntington the overseer of Brigham Hall. I trust him completely. He is authorised to give orders, so you will do as he says."

"I've been here much longer than he has!" Russell called indignantly and stepped forward.

Daniel avoided looking at him.

"Be that as it may, Riley has involved Mr Huntington in all decisions and affairs, so he is the one with the best knowledge." Mr Ainsworth looked Russell in the eyes. "If you are dissatisfied with this arrangement, I am naturally prepared to offer you the right to terminate your employment. You will not be forced to remain here for the duration of your contract."

Daniel stopped studying the carpet pattern and looked up. Ainsworth knew what Russell had done and they had jointly decided on this course of action. Daniel hoped fervently that Russell would grab his chance and leave to find a new position.

He didn't do him this favour, though. He merely scoffed and stepped back into the line of servants.

"Can you guarantee that we will keep our positions when the baronetess comes?" Ellie wanted to know. She looked more to Daniel than to Mr Ainsworth for an answer.

"I cannot. How Dame Arabella will proceed with each of you is solely up to her."

A frightened sob escaped Lizzie's throat. Ellie put an arm around her. "Don't be afraid, it will be all right," she said, trying to quietly comfort her while casting a murderous glance at Fanny, who had opened her mouth for a tart remark. She closed it again without a sound.

"Well, as I have said," Mr Ainsworth continued, "you need not worry for the moment. Everything will go on as before. If there are any questions, please ask Mr Huntington or myself, when I am here. You may leave."

While they all filed out of the parlour, Willie came up to Daniel, who had a few things to discuss with Mr Ainsworth.

"Yes, Willie? Do you have a question?" Daniel asked the boy.

"Did I do something wrong, sir?" The boy's frightened, tearful gaze tore at his heart.

"No, Willie, you haven't done anything wrong. Everything's all right." He ran his hand through Willie's tousled hair.

"Where is the baronet now? I don't understand anything."

Daniel swallowed hard. "The baronet is in prison, Willie. He has killed someone and was taken to the justice of the peace who sentenced him to death."

"And now you are the new baronet?"

"No, boy," Mr Ainsworth chimed in. "Mr Huntington is merely an overseer. He takes care of everything until someone new comes. The baronetess I talked about."

"When will she come?"

"We don't know for certain," Daniel said, "And now go, Willie. As far as I know, the horses in the stable need to be watered. Take care of that. In this heat they drink a lot more than usual." He patted the boy on the shoulder and was glad to see him trot off.

THUNDERBOY SNORTED impatiently and pulled on the reins. The track was blocked by a farmer with his team of oxen. Daniel could have overtaken him but would have had to ride into the field to do so. He didn't want to trample the precious wheat. It had to be one of the tenants taking a cart full of hay to the barn. Should he address him and introduce himself as overseer? Daniel still wasn't sure what to do about the tenants. Riley hadn't involved him in this part of the estate. He only knew that Riley had often ridden away to check on the fields and farmsteads.

When a smaller track branched off to the left, Daniel took it and let the stallion fall into a gallop. He couldn't deal with the tenant now. His head was bursting with all the things Mr Ainsworth had explained to him. To avoid despairing completely, he had decided to exercise Thunderboy. After his long ride with Riley, the horse shouldn't stand around all day. After a short canter, the stallion slowed to a walk of his own accord. It really was terribly hot, and Daniel soon turned towards home. Nevertheless, to get away from it all and let his mind wander for a short while had done him good.

Mr Ainsworth had reassured him time and again that nobody expected him to know everything. "Do as well as you can. I don't expect more. We will all make mistakes and learn from them," he had said.

Daniel's biggest problem was not knowing how to act around the other servants. Could he still eat with them, mingle with them, laugh with them? The overseer at his previous position had never done such a thing. Now that he thought about it, he had no idea when and with whom the man had eaten.

And then there was Arabella. Dame Arabella. Daniel tried to imagine what she looked like now. He couldn't. In his mind, the image of the silent maid with her worn clothes, wind-tousled curls, and reddened fingers from the wash water kept popping up. Could she find her way back to the life of a fine lady after all of that?

The sound of horseshoes on stone pulled his attention back to the present. They had arrived at the stable. Thunderboy neighed once and seemed satisfied with the answers echoing back from various directions. Daniel laughed and patted his sweaty neck.

"Willie?" he called and saw the boy coming out of the riding arena. "What have you been doing in there?"

Willie looked guilty. "I have raked?" he replied hesitatingly.

Daniel swung down from the saddle and leaned down to the boy.

"If I go in there now, will I see that you have raked?" he asked in a whisper.

Willie swallowed and shook his head.

With a stern expression, Daniel handed him the reins. "Here, do something useful. Take off his tack and wash him down before taking him to the pasture."

"But then he will roll and get dirty again!" Willie protested.

"Yes, and then you may clean him again. That's what you get for playing in the sand instead of doing your chores."

With downcast eyes, Willie pulled the stallion after him.

I need to get at least two new grooms, Daniel thought to himself. With all the other things he had to take care of now, he would have less time to spend in the stables and Oliver couldn't do everything on his own.

As if he had conjured him up with his thoughts, Oliver suddenly stood in front of him. "Sir?" he asked in his quiet manner. "May I make a request?"

Daniel took a deep breath. "Sure, Oliver. What's up?"

"I have wondered whether I could have my own room. I'm here as a groom, not a nanny."

Daniel nodded right away. "That's right, Oliver, I understand. I … I'll think of something."

"Doesn't have to be today or tomorrow," Oliver put in. "But in the long run, I'd like to have some peace and quiet at night." With that, he went back to work. Daniel sighed and added the request to his mental list of things he had to take care of. It was getting longer and longer.

During dinner, Daniel felt the scrutinising glances of the others warming his back. The atmosphere was still solemn and hardly anyone spoke. He ate as fast as he could and excused himself. Like every evening, he went into the office, but this time there was no lamp lit and the high desk by the window was empty. For a moment, he stood helplessly in the middle of the room, overwhelmed by the sheer enormity of the task laid before him. Then he shook himself. One step after the other.

He lit the lamp, put ink and a quill on the desk, and fetched the ledger from the shelf. He had always felt uncomfortable at the high desk, so he sat down and opened the book. What was there to report today? Ellie hadn't been to the market, that much was obvious. They hadn't sold any horses or other livestock. Daniel pored over the ledger. How had the baronet gotten all the information he wrote down each day? Was it necessary at all? Daniel put the quill aside and rested his head in both hands.

He couldn't do this. Despair suddenly tightened his throat.

"What did you do to me, Lord?" he whispered. Suddenly, the name David crossed his mind. David? The David from the Bible? King, commander, ruler over the people of Israel? Daniel's hands sank into his lap and he stared blindly at the pages of the ledger. He was none of that, neither commander nor king and certainly no ruler.

Shepherd. The word sat in his head, completely out of place, but slowly it took on shape. A boy with a crook; flat, round stones in one hand and a sling at his belt. That's how David started. He hadn't been born a king; God had made him into one.

A soft knock sounded, then the door opened, and Ellie put her head round the edge of it. When she saw Daniel at the desk, she came in and closed the door behind her. "Is everything all right?" she asked.

Daniel shrugged helplessly.

Ellie sat on one of the chairs in front of the desk. "Tell me everything," she said simply.

Overseer

Daniel thought he didn't know what to tell, but then it suddenly all came rushing out of him, confused and unsorted. His doubts, his lack of knowledge, the different requests and demands and lastly even the impressions he had just had.

Ellie listened to it all without interrupting him. When he didn't continue, she nodded thoughtfully. "I think, you worry too much," she said with a chuckle. His protests were cut off with a flick of her hand. "You need to know one thing, Daniel Huntington," she went on, serious again. "You are not alone. It isn't your duty, it is *ours*. All of us who live here have to master it together. Practically, it looks like this: Everyone had to report to the baronet when he had bought or sold something, me, the gardener, the tenants, even you. And it will be the same in the future. The baronet went out over the estate a lot and talked to the tenants, so they rarely came here. Where I worked before, it was different. Everyone had to come to the master and make his report. If someone failed to show up, there was trouble."

Daniel listened attentively.

"You decide how it's done, the way you deem easiest." Ellie gave him a moment to digest this. When he slowly nodded, she took up a new aspect. "As for the servants and Oliver, I think it would be best if you move into the stablemaster's cottage now. Then Oliver can have your chamber and you would have a place to retreat to and to eat. Because you are right, the others no longer regard you as one of them. You weren't before, as a matter of fact, because the Master of Horse is as much part of the estate's management as the cook. But since I feed them, I can always be with them and they still respect me. I'm afraid it's different for you, especially because of Russell and Fanny. They yap about anything and everything, and right now, mostly about you. I would kick them out if I were you. Russell doesn't have anything to do, anyway."

"I don't have that power. Mr Ainsworth made it quite clear that he wants to leave all personnel decisions to the baronetess. I'll have to live with both of them for now."

Ellie nodded. For a moment she looked as if she wanted to ask something, but then she only said, "I was afraid of that. Fanny will be the smaller problem. She has to do the laundry now that the girl is gone. That'll keep her busy. But Russell? He lounged around half the day even when the baronet was still here. Now he doesn't do anything at all."

"Did he ever help with the harvest?" Daniel asked.

Ellie laughed loudly. "Russell and harvest? For goodness sakes, no! The thought alone!"

Daniel wasn't amused. Where could he put Russell to use where he wouldn't create much damage if he didn't do his work? "Who's responsible for the firewood?"

"Harry," Ellie replied promptly, adding, "good thought."

Harry always ignored Russell's palaver and remained unperturbed, no matter what happened around him. Daniel knew that he had cut down some trees over the last few weeks, and they now needed chopping into firewood. He nodded, pleased. Together, they would get Russell to work.

Overseer

Brigham Hall, August 2, 1711

Dear Mother,

It's so hard. Everything, everything is so hard. I catch myself fleeing into the stables, my familiar surroundings, what I know and like, just to avoid thinking about all the decisions that need to be made.

Ellie helps me a lot, and takes care of matters in the house, where I have absolutely no idea what is needed. I get glimpses of rooms being aired, windows cleaned, floors scrubbed, carpets beaten. Surely, you laugh at me now because you know all these things, but I never had to waste a thought on them apart for my personal room. But I do have the wonderful Ellie who encourages me time and again.

Mr Ainsworth is also very patient with me, even though I keep asking him the same questions over and over because I forget half of the myriad things I'm supposed to remember right after he told me.

Ellie said I should move into Ole Pete's cottage, which is rightfully mine, but I can't overcome my reservations yet. I feel way out of my depth and lonely at the same time, despite the help I get. It's not the same anymore. Where I was proud of my elevated position as Master of Horse, I now see the cleft between the servants and their masters with different eyes. I understand better what had driven the baronet into madness – apart from his unspeakable guilt. Feared by all, loved by none, he was completely alone. Fortunately, I'm not. Oliver is a great help, as well as Harry, the gardener. The latter supports me with expert advice, a lot more than I would have expected.

I hardly hear anything of Fanny's beastly tongue, thanks to Ellie, which is a relief. Mr Ainsworth wasn't able to bring any news of Dame Arabella, apart from the fact that she seems to be highly interested in the proceedings at the estate. She listens closely to all he reports. Apart from that, she only sits quietly, often lost in thought, and still doesn't utter a word.

I had thought of visiting her, but refrained from doing so without ever mentioning it to anyone. I know she is in good hands and has enough to handle herself. As Father used to say, everyone has his own cross to bear. I'll help her more if I take care of everything here as well as I can.

Thank you for your prayers!

Love,

Daniel

16

Move

SLOWLY, DANIEL PUSHED the door open and left it ajar to let fresh air stream into the cottage. He stopped in the middle of the room. The straw mattress had been removed and left the bed strangely bare. An old armchair sat by the fireplace; its upholstery worn thin with age. Next to the door on the right, there was a table with two chairs. A large cupboard covered most of the wall on the left. Daniel went over, opened it, and pulled back. The drawn-out skull of a horse was sitting on the top shelf, a few horseshoes next to it as well as a whole hoof which gave off a sickening odour. There were tufts of horsehair in various shades and the skeleton of a small mammal or two, probably mice. The shelf below that held a few simple earthen mugs and plates, one large bowl and two smaller ones, and two roughly carved wooden spoons. A dry breadcrust lay forgotten in a corner and a motheaten blanket sat on the lowest shelf. Apart from that, the cupboard was empty.

Daniel closed it again and hesitantly walked over to the table. He sat on a chair and put both hands on the table, discovering it covered with a thin layer of dust. Across from him was a window, through which he could see the pastures and a corner of Brigham Hall.

Could he live here? He got up again, stepped over to the bed and looked out of the other window. It gave a view of the back pastures with the mares and their foals. In the warm August sun, they lay flat on the grass, too exhausted to romp. Daniel put a hand on the wooden bedframe. He had expected to be overwhelmed by sadness and was surprised to find it was not so. On the contrary, the atmosphere in the cottage was peaceful and he felt himself relax. His gaze wandered over to the fireplace. He would have to invest in a new armchair. There he would sit after his work was done and read. He would move the bed into the other corner, to make room for the table under the window. Then he could look at the horses while he ate. He also needed a new mattress, but he had already prepared for that. A smile crossed his face as he remembered the confused looks the stable lads had given him on hearing his wish to collect the horses' winter fur. They had grumbled more than once, but they had obeyed. Now all he had to do was wash and dry the sacks, and then he would stuff his new mattress, not with straw but with warm, soft horsehair. With a determined nod, he started to clear out the cupboard. Next, he would find Lizzie and ask her to clean the cottage thoroughly before he moved in.

The days went by and Daniel's feeling of being out of his depth faded so slowly that he only noticed when it was next to gone. He had prepared lists for all the things he needed to do, the paper filled with many arrows and cross-connections, so that he could combine various tasks. For example, the visits with the tenants served perfectly to train the young horses. They got used to different paths, had to stand still and wait in strange places, and were separated from their herd for such a long time that they couldn't help but turn to Daniel. He often took two horses and rode one there and the other back.

Most of the tenants reacted in a good way, even though they regarded the news that there would be a baronetess in the future with some scepticism.

At first, Daniel used his rounds to get to know each tenant a bit better. He knew that he still needed support and asked many of them for advice. This showed their character fairly quickly. The farmer Miller, for example, whom Daniel had met in connection with the seed drill and who had been suspicious of the baronet, proved to be someone who knew his way around, was in touch with many other tenants and ready to take on responsibility. Proudly, he showed Daniel the fields sown with the seed drill, which now actually started to ripen due to good weather conditions. If the weather held, they would be able to bring in a late harvest.

"I would never have thought that this machine would make such a big difference, but now I am completely convinced. I have already told the other tenants about it and shown them the fields. Some of them I could talk into sowing their fields with the machine come autumn. Others are still sceptical, especially that strange Scotsman."

Daniel could imagine how the short, squat Kerr stood there in his kilt and ranted about the new-fangled devil's work without ever taking his pipe out of his mouth. He had caused trouble in the past – or rather his sons had, believing they could simply take cattle and women as they liked, in good old Scottish fashion. The baronet had cursed the union between England and Scotland more than once, stating that the Scots should have kept their parliament and borders instead of submitting to Westminster's rule.

Perhaps Kerr would have stayed in Scotland then. Rumour had it that Kerr had favoured the union and had to flee south because of that.

But instead of being welcomed with open arms by the English, he had been dubbed a foreigner and excluded. Daniel's personal impression was that Kerr was simply a person who made enemies everywhere, for whatever reason. The turmoil on the Scottish-English border had been so violent, though, that even he had heard of it.

"You've really done a splendid job, Miller," Daniel said to the tenant. "Leave the Scotsman be and concentrate on those who show interest. You've been there for the sowing. We need to coordinate everything since we have only the one machine. Someone needs to make sure that it is used properly and doesn't break."

"I know just the right person for that, sir," Miller exclaimed. "Harper's son, the one with the short leg. He can't work properly on the farm which is rough on Harper. All day long, he potters about and builds all kinds of strange inventions. Yes, I'll ask George if he will take care of the machine. He's going to keep it in order and who knows, perhaps he will build another one for you. The boy is handy with such things."

Daniel laughed, pleased. "That sounds good. Perhaps I can even pay him a small wage."

The tenant grinned broadly. "Oh sir, that would be an enormous help for the family."

"Speaking of which, do you happen to know one or two sturdy lads who'd be willing to work with the horses? We don't have enough hands in the stables."

Miller thought a while but shook his head. "The boys are all needed on the farms."

Daniel waved it aside. "I thought as much."

He was already getting back up on his horse when Miller said, "Perhaps you could ask Benson."

Daniel stopped short. "Benson? He has a son?"

"No, he doesn't, but-"

"But what?"

"Well, he has a daughter. You don't see her much. She's always hiding when someone comes. As a child, she fell into the fire and looks quite badly. She won't find a husband. Her father tried to get her a place as scullery maid somewhere, but nobody wants her because she's so disfigured."

"And that's why I should put her to work in the stables?"

"Well, that's just it. She's really handy with beasts, a real quiet one. She's even tamed deer! I could imagine she's good with horses. And she's certainly capable of pushing a wheelbarrow or carrying a water bucket."

Daniel sorted his reins. "Thank you, Mr Miller. I'll give it some thought."

At first, the idea was so alien that he didn't really want to think about it. But then he remembered Arabella, this tiny girl, and the hard work she had done every day. And how she could ride. If Brigham Hall was soon to have a mistress like that then why not a maid in the horse stable?

When would Arabella come? With all the work he had to do, Daniel rarely found time to think of the former silent maid. But whenever he entered the kitchen and saw the empty stool on which she had sat, it pierced his heart. He was probably the only one who missed her. No, that wasn't true. He had watched Lizzie and Ellie more than once as they stared at the stool, deep in thought. She was not forgotten. He alone knew where she was – and who she was. Although he had written to his mother, saying he had decided against it, he had repeatedly considered riding over to Mr Ainsworth and visiting her. But something kept him back, an inner timidity he could only explain with the fact that she was no longer a maid, but his mistress. Time and again he tried to imagine how she would treat him when she returned. In vain. Perhaps that was for the better.

"OLIVER?"

The groom set the horse's hoof back on the ground and straightened up. "Yes, sir?"

"I have cleared the room upstairs. It's yours now. Feel free to take some time later to move your things. Thanks for your patience."

Oliver beamed at Daniel. "No problem. There are so many things you need to take care of now."

"Yes." Daniel laughed and then sighed. "I would really like to work the young horses, but Mr Ainsworth has just arrived. I hope he keeps it short today."

Oliver nodded and lifted the hoof again. Daniel patted the horse's backside and then made off to the office where Mr Ainsworth awaited him.

They shook hands and sat in front of the fireplace, although no fire was burning there.

"You're looking dapper," the solicitor stated and looked Daniel up and down. "More secure than a few weeks ago. You're slowly gaining ground, hm?"

"Slowly, yes. There are some pleasing developments which I hope the baronetess will approve of. How is she?"

"She's still not speaking. Lately, she often spends hours alone in her room and writes."

"She writes?"

Mr Ainsworth shrugged. "Yes, she writes. My wife suspects that she is writing some sort of diary to come to terms with what she has lived through. She doesn't show it to anyone. During our meetings she tires easily and then simply gets up and leaves. She also sleeps late in the mornings. I wanted to consult a physician, but she refused. In such moments she is highly energetic and resolute. And then, especially when it gets dark, she is like a frightened child and starts at every small noise. Oh…" Helplessly, he shook his head. "Tell me your news."

Daniel informed him of his talk with Miller and his suggestions. He could see that Mr Ainsworth had as many problems with the idea of a maid for the horses as he himself had, but kept his reservations to himself. "I will put these suggestions before the baronetess and see how she reacts. Do you really deem it necessary to have a coordinator for this machine?" Scepticism was evident in his voice.

"I think it would be extremely helpful. He could not only take care of transport and the coordination with the tenants, but also make repairs should something break. The tenants will be more careful if there is someone watching over them. Or giving help, whichever is needed. I could not possibly do that."

The solicitor nodded. "Very well then, I will pass it on. Is everything all right with the servants?"

"At the moment, yes. If there's nothing urgent to discuss, I'd be happy if you'd let me get back to work. I have shamefully neglected the training of your new horse."

The Silent Maid

Mr Ainsworth shrugged it off. "Don't worry about that. I will come back next week and let you know Dame Arabella's decisions – if she makes any. If not, I'll leave it up to you to decide." He rose and went to the door but stopped in his tracks. He seemed unable to make up his mind whether to add something or not. Finally, he sighed resignedly. "There's no use in keeping it from you."

Daniel, who had already moved on to the next task in his mind, perked up at these words.

Mr Ainsworth cast a solemn glance in his direction. "Riley was hanged yesterday. It was very gratifying for me to see him dangle, but I know that you…" He stopped.

Daniel swallowed hard. "You're quite right, he was a murderer and deserved his punishment," he replied quietly and shook the solicitor's hand.

Once he was alone, he went over to the high desk. How many evenings had he spent there, nervous, curious, frightened, insecure? His relationship with Riley had been as contradictory as the man himself. Cruel murderer and kidnapper on the one hand, intelligent, innovative patron on the other. Daniel closed his eyes and sent a prayer of thanks upwards. Whichever craze had kept Riley in its grip, without him he would never have made it as far in his personal development as he had. And perhaps he had repented his deeds in the last days of his imprisonment. Daniel fervently wished for that. The thought of eternal suffering in purgatory unsettled him deeply. If Jesus could show mercy to the murderer who was crucified alongside him, he could show mercy to Riley. If he had asked for it.

Move

Brigham Hall, Residence of the Master of Horse, August 25, 1711

Dear Mother,

Yesterday, I moved into the cottage which used to be Ole Pete's. It is all very foreign to me and I miss the noise of the horses in the stable below me. On the other hand, the cottage is a bit removed from the usual hustle and bustle of the estate, so I have blessed peace and quiet. I was unaware of how much I craved it. In fact, I almost overslept this morning because the cock's crow was so far away. Maybe it was also because of my new mattress, which is unbelievably comfortable.

Unfortunately, my peace was ruined rather quickly, because right after breakfast Harry approached me and complained about Russell not showing up for work. He had wanted to go into the forest with him to cut some tree trunks Russell had freed of branches over the last few days. I accompanied Harry and together we pounded on Russell's door, but he gave no answer. Worried, we went in and then everything was clear. He had dragged the baronet's whiskey supply into his room and drunk himself into a stupor. We had to shake him and slap his face with a wet cloth to wake him up. Looking back on it now, we should have let him sleep it off. He was raving mad, screamed at us and probably would have started a brawl if I had been on my own. Thank God Harry was there with me. We grabbed his arms and lugged him outside, where we ducked his head into the horse trough a few times. He was a bit more affable after that. Ellie made him some breakfast while Harry took care of other things.

I had expected Russell to go with Harry into the forest after his breakfast, but I was wrong. He screamed at me again that I couldn't order him around since I wasn't his master. When Ellie reminded him that he had to obey me, he lost control. He jumped up, threw over the kitchen bench and attacked me. Fortunately, he wasn't sober yet and so sluggish that it was easy for me to avoid his blows. It made him furious. On top of that, Fanny came in and started screeching. Before I could bring myself to knock him out with a well-aimed blow, Ellie whacked him on the head with a heavy pan and he toppled like a felled tree. It was all I could do to catch him, or he would have knocked his teeth out on the table. Mo helped me to carry him outside and set him under a tree. When he woke up, he went into his room without a word and stayed there for the rest of the day. I'm sure he had an awful headache.

I really hope the baroness returns soon and sets matters right in this regard. I cannot imagine she would want to keep Russell after all he has done. Michaelmas is coming and the contracts will need to be renewed. If she returns before that and lets some of the servants go, we could find replacements at the next mop market in Bridlington.

If not… I don't want to think about that right now. What will happen? Even I am a little worried about my employment here, everything is up in the air.

Thank you for your prayers.

Love

Daniel

17
Thunderstorm

A MIGHTY CRASH tore Daniel out of his sleep. Thrice in short order, the cottage was doused in bright light, followed by a deafening bang so loud Daniel thought his head would burst. It portended nothing good. Hastily, he swung out of bed and pulled on his breeches, while thunder continued to roll. Due to the sweltering humidity, he hadn't bothered with a nightshirt and now ran outside, his chest bare. He found his worst fears confirmed: lightning had hit the huge chestnut tree in the stable yard.

Daniel ran as fast as he could, keeping his eyes trained on the ominous red flicker dancing on the building walls. The side door of the nearest stable stood open. With a mighty jump, Daniel cleared the fence. Just in time, he heard yells from inside, loud whinnying and the sound of hooves. He flattened himself against the open door so he would not be overrun by the panicked mares as they jostled to get outside. Behind them, Oliver appeared in the light of the flickering flashes, his eyes wide, his brow glistening with sweat.

"Where are the boys?" Daniel called, joining Oliver on his way to the yard. The horses would follow the trail leading from the stable to the pastures, where they would be safe for now. But the coach horses and Thunderboy were housed in the other stable. It was vital to save the stallion under all circumstances.

"They're fetching water," Oliver gasped. Fear was written all over his face.

The yard was bright as day with the tree in flames. Thank God they had cut its branches only a few weeks before so that they no longer reached out over the roofs of the surrounding buildings.

The fire hadn't jumped over, yet. What should they do?

Both boys stood frozen by the entry gate, each of them holding two buckets of water. Now Harry turned up behind them, followed by Ellie, Lizzie, and Fanny.

"One of you, man the pump, build a chain! Bring as many buckets as you can find!" Harry roared over the noise of the storm.

Immediately, Lizzie dashed off to fetch buckets from the kitchen, while Ellie positioned herself next to the pump at the kitchen entrance. There was another one by the horse trough in the yard, but it was too close to the burning tree.

"Save the horses!" Oliver said and grabbed a bucket. He ran to the tree, threw the water against its trunk and hastened away from the heat again. Daniel started to run, too. They didn't have much time. The tree was split in the middle and could break apart at any moment. Then the burning crown would come crashing down onto the roofs of the stables and their freshly gathered hay supply would be history. As well as all the saddles.

"God, please help us and keep us," Daniel murmured under his breath.

Thunderstorm

Only two horses stood in the stalls and pulled on their ropes in panic. Thunderboy owned a spacious enclosure at the far end of the stable, close to the exit leading to two more pastures grouped around a picturesque stream. He stood like a statue, his nostrils flared, and looked at Daniel unmovingly through the iron bars. Thunder rolled again and one of the horses in the stalls reared. Its leg got caught on the fence between the stalls and the animal fought for balance. Its hind legs slipped, and it crashed to the ground with a terrifying scream. Daniel believed he heard the sound of breaking bones. His stomach flipped. The horse's legs flailed like crazy as it tried to get up again, but in vain. One of the front legs wasn't working properly anymore.

Another reverberating clap of thunder pulled Daniel out of his shock. At this moment, there was nothing he could do for the fallen horse, so he grabbed the other one's halter and talked to it with soothing words. As soon as he had freed the lead rope, the horse shot backwards, nearly escaping.

"Whoa there, quiet!" he called and held the rope with an iron fist to keep the horse from bursting into the yard. Neighing, it pranced next to him to the other exit. The door was open there, so Daniel could simply let go of the horse. It raced away at top speed. Daniel looked up at the sky. Blinding flashes were still chasing each other across the pitch-dark clouds, but not a single drop fell.

"Rain, Lord, please! Let it rain!" Daniel begged and turned to Thunderboy.

The stallion remained still in his stall. Daniel grabbed his halter and carefully opened the door, prepared to jump aside should the stallion come running out. He didn't, though. Daniel had no trouble putting the halter on and

The Silent Maid

Thunderboy followed him outside, trotting, but under control. Daniel could lead him to his usual pasture and set him free there, so that he would not come into contact with the other horse roaming somewhere out there. Thunderboy neighed and then trotted off, his neck raised proudly. After a few yards he stopped and watched the fire glow from the yard, emitting loud snorts.

Daniel couldn't help but be impressed by this unusual stallion. He hurried back to the stable. The fallen horse lay motionless. In its desperate fight it had slid under the fence between the stalls and had become hopelessly entangled in the beams. Daniel's eyes filled with tears when he realized it was dead. The rope had held tight and broken the animal's neck.

"Those damned ropes always break," Daniel whispered hoarsely and knelt beside the dead horse; a young gelding, always a bit frightened, but otherwise nice and willing.

Yells sounded from the yard. Daniel jumped up. He would have to mourn later. Now he had to save the stables. Just as he stepped into the yard, a large branch broke off the tree and crashed onto the cobblestones, sending out a shower of sparks. Anxiously, Daniel watched the sparks dancing up between the roof beams. While the others poured several buckets of water over the branch on the ground, he turned on his heel, grabbed a heavy blanket and climbed hastily up to the hayloft. Perhaps he could prevent the worst.

It was pitch dark up here. Daniel carefully felt his way to the right, until his head collided with the sloped roof. He crawled on through the stuffy, dusty heat, pushing the hay aside as well as he could. Fortunately, the hayloft wasn't filled to capacity yet, so he was still able to move fairly freely. In front of him, he heard a tell-tale crackling. A mouse? Or a spark? He trained his eyes and ears on the space ahead. His nose was no use to him, the strong burning smell from outside would cover any fire in here. He listened intently, but heard nothing but a knock on the roof, then another. The knocks turned into a patter and shortly afterwards into a drumming tattoo. Hoorays sounded from the yard. Rain – finally!

"Thank you, Lord," Daniel whispered and crawled on. A shock went through him and tightened his throat. There was a weak glow in front of him, rapidly growing stronger. With a desperate groan, Daniel threw himself forward, the blanket gripped tight as if he wanted to swim through the hay. It seemed to take forever to fight his way over to the small fire, hardly bigger than a plate. He threw the blanket over it, then covered it with his body for good measure. A searing pain pierced his belly, making him hiss and then cough. Sweat was pouring down his body and the rush of rain right over his head was so loud that he had trouble hearing himself think. He kept still and looked around, but everything remained dark.

When he was sure no more fire would break out, he scrambled back. In the darkness, he almost toppled through the trapdoor in the floor of the hayloft. He managed to grab the ladder at the last moment and climbed down. Exhausted and dirty, he stepped outside into the rain, glad for the fresh coolness. More branches lay on the ground in the yard, but the tree was still standing, blackened and smoking, though no longer dangerous. The rain had put the flames out and the buildings were unharmed. A light moved toward him. When it got closer, he recognized Oliver with a lantern in his hand.

The Silent Maid

"There you are, thank God! Are you all right?" he called when he discovered Daniel.

Daniel felt too dizzy to answer. Oliver pushed him back into the stable. When the light fell on the dead horse, he jumped and cursed.

"The other two are safe," Daniel said roughly.

Oliver looked at him. "You're white as a sheet and hurt, too. Come into the kitchen. Ellie will have prepared something good for us."

Daniel allowed himself to be led to the main house. A loud babble of voices greeted them when they entered the kitchen. The fire in the stove was burning brightly and Ellie had warmed broth for them all.

"Found him," Oliver announced proudly and pulled Daniel into the room.

Talk ceased.

"What happened?" Ellie asked when she saw the burn mark on Daniel's belly.

Daniel looked down at himself and suddenly started to shake violently. Everything around him went black.

When he came to, he was lying on the kitchen bench, circled by worried faces. Laughter bubbled out of his mouth. They looked like a bunch of beggars; the faces smeared black, the matted wet hair standing wildly in all directions, the clothes wet and dirty and full of burns.

"He's gone mad now," Fanny noted.

WITH A BOWL OF the strong broth in his stomach, Daniel felt much better.

Thunderstorm

Lizzie wanted to treat his burn with a hot iron, which he vehemently refused. Mechanically, he touched the old scar on his shoulder where he had fallen into the fire as a five-year-old and his father had treated him with this method. *The heat of the iron will draw the heat out of the burn*, he had explained to him, and Daniel had held still with apprehension. He had no idea whether his father had meant too well or used the iron in the wrong way, in any case, Daniel had screamed his head off and fainted. The hot iron had been much worse than the original burn. His mother had needed to treat his fever for days.

"Then we should wash it with lime soap," Lizzie said, her eyes huge with worry.

Daniel looked at the burn on his skin. On the right side of his belly button one large and two smaller blisters had formed and a patch of skin the size of his hand was reddened.

"Yes, Lizzie is right. We need to take the skin off the blisters and wash them so that the heat devils can escape," Ellie agreed with an expert nod.

Daniel's eyes widened and he swallowed hard.

"You'll do no such thing," Harry said calmly. "Best thing is for you all to leave it alone and it will heal by itself."

Daniel sighed with relief. "Yes. Yes, I think so, too."

"As you wish," Ellie replied and shrugged.

"Oliver, Harry, will you help me get the dead horse out of the stable? Willie and Tom, you go and look for the mares. Take them back to the stable and give them a proper helping of hay. You can go back to sleep after that." Daniel rose.

The Silent Maid

Before any of the addressed could follow his request, Russell suddenly appeared in the door. "What kind of a meeting is this?" he asked suspiciously.

Silence settled in the room. If he had wanted to make a crude remark about the bedraggled state of his colleagues, he swallowed it down when confronted by so many hostile gazes. Each one of them realized that Russell alone had not helped to put out the fire. Nobody answered his question. Instead, they all rose as one. Daniel nodded to his helpers and they left the kitchen, while Ellie dished out instructions to Fanny, Lizzie, and Mo, ignoring Russell completely.

Outside, the first light of dawn was spreading across the sky; littered with thick grey clouds like ships blown by a fresh breeze. The thunderstorm had moved on and the air was clear and fragrant. Where the first sunbeams touched the ground, vapour rose.

Daniel, Oliver, and Harry had not even reached the stable yard when they heard the clatter of galloping hooves coming up the driveway. The men glanced curiously at each other. Was it the escaped horse?

Shortly, a rider appeared at the corner and raced toward them.

"Mr Huntington!" he called from afar.

Daniel stepped forward.

The rider had a bit of trouble stopping his horse next to Daniel. "Mr Huntington," he repeated breathlessly, and jumped to the ground. It was Mr Ainsworth. "She speaks!" he called excitedly. "The baronetess speaks!"

Thunderstorm

Brigham Hall, September 2, 1711

My beloved mother,

I'm fine! Finally, I get around to writing to you. So many things have happened over the past few days that my head is spinning, tragic things and wonderful things.

A couple of nights ago a terrible storm raged and the beautiful chestnut tree in the middle of the stable yard was struck by lightning. By sheer miracle the fire did not spread to the buildings and we were saved from disaster. Nobody was hurt, either — apart from a few burns — and only one of the horses died in the excitement. It is sad, but in comparison to what we could have lost, it is bearable.

This storm did some good, too, as you will learn in a moment, for at dawn the next day we received news that Dame Arabella was healed from her muteness. In the course of the following week, she will return to Brigham Hall.

At first, I could make no more sense of Mr Ainsworth's confused ramblings, and when he noticed our state and realized the amount of heavenly protection we had experienced during the night, his news moved to the background.

By now, he has been around again to report at leisure how everything came about. As had already happened here with us — I believe it was in April — the storm caused Dame Arabella terrible nightmares. Without really waking, she wandered through the house, crying. The butler caught her before she could run outside. Mrs Ainsworth gathered her in. They spent several hours behind closed doors with the girl wailing without pause. Thanks to Mrs Ainsworth's gentle encouragement, words mingled with her crying and by the time she had calmed down, she had spoken several sentences. This seemed to have broken the ban. Mrs Ainsworth said that she had to confirm over and over that Riley was dead and no longer able to harm her.

Come morning, she went back to sleep, though fitfully. When she woke, she spoke normally, if very quietly, as Mr Ainsworth said. His old ears sometimes had trouble understanding her. Anyway, she is determined to return to Brigham Hall soon and take up her rightful position.

You can imagine that everyone around here is running wild with excitement. Dame Arabella gave word to have the tower room prepared for her, which has been uninhabited over the past years. Now it's being scrubbed and cleaned, new curtains are hung up and the chimney, in which several generations of pigeons must have hatched, is repaired.

I still haven't mentioned to anyone who the baroness is and look forward to her return with mixed feelings.

Apart from Lizzie, nobody has ever mentioned the silent maid again, not even Ellie. Does she suspect something?

How will the baroness treat me? The fragile friendship connecting us is certainly inappropriate with her current status. I hope she will free me of my responsibilities as overseer and let me return to the stables. Even if I may be so bold as to say I have done a good job under the circumstances, I long to pass on the burden of watching over so many people. How often I have cursed my former masters and wished for more power to escape their arbitrariness. After weeks of walking in their shoes, so to speak, I view many things differently and feel much more gracious toward them. Those who are given much, have much responsibility.

Will she be able to carry it?

Your loving son

Daniel

18
Return

THE DAY HAD STARTED rainy, but now that all the servants were assembled in the parlour, whispering excitedly, a strong westerly wind was blowing the clouds apart. The pastures lay in a constant play of light and shadow, in which the grazing horses seemed to disappear time and again as if by magic.

Everyone was tensely expecting the appearance of the Baronetess Brigham.

Daniel stood a little apart and kneaded his cap in his hands. He was extremely pent-up and stared out of the floor-length windows with his jaws clamped tight, his entire concentration on the sound of approaching wheels. Mr Ainsworth had warned him that the baronetess was going to make some changes regarding the servants. The details he had kept to himself, though.

Daniel couldn't imagine being turned out after all he had done for Dame Arabella. And yet doubt gnawed at him. Apart from that, he was afraid of the servants' reaction. Would they accept the young lady as their mistress, when they had mistreated her for years? He was prepared to make a stand should there be turmoil.

Russell stood by the parlour door, sober and clean, but with a dour face. During the past industrious days, none of the servants had exchanged a word with him. Without ever agreeing on it, they were all unwilling to forgive him his selfish behaviour. He at least would not accept his dismissal without comment.

Talk in the room ceased abruptly when the clopping of hooves and the crunching of wheels on gravel was audible from outside.

With hurried steps, Russell went to the front door to open it. The servants lined up in two rows on both sides of the parlour door, women on the one side, men on the other. Only Mo was standing next to Ellie. When he noticed his mistake, it was too late to scuttle over to the other side.

They all watched Mr Ainsworth helping a petite young woman from the carriage. She was wearing a fairly simple, sand-coloured dress with a dark green kerchief and stays, stitched with gold. Her hair was hidden beneath a cap, only at her temples two curls framed her face. Dame Arabella, Baronetess of Brigham Hall, took Mr Ainsworth's arm and allowed herself to be led up to the entrance. She seemed to hesitate on the first step, her gaze lowered. Then she took a deep breath, lifted her chin, and looked straight ahead at the two rows of servants.

Daniel followed her every move with his eyes. For the moment, he had forgotten all about the others. The whole time he had been wondering what she would look like, but now that he saw her, he was speechless. All fear had disappeared from her eyes. Her posture was proud and confident and had there not been that moment of hesitation, he might have thought her arrogant. She did not look any servant in the eye while she passed them, but kept her gaze trained forward. Only when she had reached the end of the row and turned around, did she search for Daniel's eyes. He swallowed. For a split second, the rigid stare softened, then she looked away.

"Russell, please be so kind as to close the door and come in." Mr Ainsworth broke the silence, which seemed to have deepened with the baronetess's entry, as if everyone were holding their breath.

All colour had faded from Russell's face. He obeyed without a word and stepped in line with the other men.

"May I introduce to you your mistress, Baronetess Arabella Alexandra Brigham. You will address her as Dame Arabella or madam. Dame Arabella would like to speak a few words to you, so please pay close attention." Mr Ainsworth nodded at the baronetess and took half a step backwards. Now she took the time to look at each of the servants in turn. Daniel followed her gaze and read a variety of reactions on the faces. Open wonder, confusion, animosity, certainty, curiosity.

"I'm sure this situation is rather awkward for all of us," Dame Arabella said quietly but distinctly. Daniel was completely surprised at how full and feminine her voice sounded. He had expected something squeaky from such a small person. "I will keep it short. Fanny, Russell, Oliver, please follow Mr Ainsworth into the office. He will pay you your wages and hand out your references. You will immediately pack your things and leave. I will not suffer you to spend another night at Brigham Hall."

A murmur arose and Daniel started. Why Oliver? Fanny and Russell he could understand, but Oliver? Mr Ainsworth seemed to notice his indignation and put a soothing hand on his arm. He then went ahead of the others to the office.

The Silent Maid

Fanny stared at Dame Arabella open-mouthed. "But where am I supposed to go?" she cried, both outraged and confused.

"That is your problem," Dame Arabella replied coldly. Despite keeping her expression neutral, she managed to pack all her contempt for Fanny, and the many years of abuse, into those few words.

Fanny gasped. Russell stood beside her. "We have always served the baronet well! He would have continued my contract!" he argued heatedly.

Dame Arabella cocked her head and lifted an eyebrow. "He is dead," she said with a curiously satisfied mien.

"But he…"

"Go!" The order was given with such vehemence that all three of them turned on their heel and practically fled from the room.

"I wouldn't want to work for the little witch anyway," Fanny hissed on her way out.

Lacking a footman, Harry closed the door behind her. As soon as that was done, Dame Arabella relaxed visibly. Her gaze wandered again over the now reduced lines.

"Mo," she said and approached the boy who stared at her with huge eyes. "I know you steal food, even though it's unnecessary. Everyone here has enough. I would have to send you away because of that. But I also know how Fanny tormented you. She is gone now. I will give you another chance. If you work hard, I'm sure you will be cook someday. But you have to stop stealing. Do you promise?"

Mo hesitated a moment, then he broke into a beaming smile. "Yes, Dame Arabella," he said, awed.

Dame Arabella turned around and looked at Harry. "I would be happy to have you remain here, Harry. And both of you boys, too, Willie and Tom. Without Oliver you will have to take on more responsibility until a new groom is found."

"Gladly, Dame Arabella," Harry said with a hint of a bow and a perky smile.

Both of the lads nodded.

"Good. Then you may go back to work. Thank you."

The three of them shot a glance at Daniel and then shuffled outside. Dame Arabella stepped up to Ellie, who was fighting tears by now.

"I knew it," the cook said and lifted a hand as if she wanted to touch the young lady's cheek. She caught herself and hid her hand under her apron.

The baronetess smiled tentatively. "You will stay, too, won't you?" she asked almost tonelessly.

"Of course, child, of course! Lady, no, Dame Arabella." She laughed at her own confusion, wiping her eyes at the same time. "I shall be pleased to go back to work as well. I need to peel or knead something…" Upon Dame Arabella's nod she fled from the room to get a grip on her emotions, taking Mo with her on the way.

"Lizzie." Dame Arabella now addressed the young maid who stood there with burning cheeks and downcast eyes. "I have a new task for you."

Frightened, Lizzie lifted her head. "But there's nothing I can do!" she cried in desperation, covered her face in her hands and broke into tears.

Dame Arabella waited a moment until she had calmed down. "I would like you to be my lady's maid. You will take care of my clothes, keep my room tidy, help me with dressing, and keep me company. You will move into the chamber next to the tower room. I want to always have you close to me."

Lizzie was too surprised to breathe. "But why?" she squeaked tearfully.

"Because you are such a kind soul," Dame Arabella whispered, for the moment incapable of giving her voice more power. "I need someone who will care for me."

This admission of her weakness seemed to give Lizzie new courage. Both women looked at each other for a long time and Daniel had the impression that they renewed a connection that had been there before.

"Go and move into your new room," Dame Arabella ordered.

Lizzie curtseyed and left as well. Now only Daniel was left.

Slowly Dame Arabella turned around and walked up to him. She laid both hands on his, which were still holding the cap. "Daniel," she said weakly and he could feel his heart contract. She was fighting her tears as much as she fought for control of her voice.

Wordlessly he watched her struggle, incapable of uttering anything himself.

"I can't even begin to tell you how grateful I am to you," she finally whispered. "You have freed me. It is a riddle to me how you found all of that out, but you did and –" She paused and gave him the most beaming smile he had ever seen on her face. "You cared," she added with an incredulous laugh.

Daniel simply shrugged and smiled back. A deep contentment settled in his bones. He had done the right thing. With all the fears and sleepless nights his actions had caused him – it had been right. He sighed deeply. Then he straightened and pulled his hands out of her grasp. Her closeness provoked a flood of emotions he had absolutely no need of. The elegant dress and the tone of her voice dispersed the last doubts. She was no little girl. There was a young woman standing in front of him. One he found enticingly attractive. He caught himself grinning a bit broader when realizing that she had not tried to hide her freckles with bleach, as most ladies did. A wise decision, he thought.

He cleared his throat. "So, what happens now, madam?" he asked carefully.

She had well noticed his emotional withdrawal and responded to his business-like tone. "I know you will miss Oliver. I'm very sorry, but he forced himself on Lizzie. I will not have such behaviour under my roof," she said and stepped up to the window.

Daniel couldn't believe his ears. "Oliver would never do such a thing," he said, contradicting her with conviction.

She turned around and sadly looked at him. "He did. More than once. I saw it." She left the words hanging between them in all their harsh reality before she continued. "Mr Ainsworth has told me about that girl. Hire her if her parents allow it. We will hire more grooms at the mop market in Bridlington." She paused. "I will need your help, Daniel. My father showed and explained many things to me, but it was such a long time ago and I was a child. Of course, I have asked myself the whole time, how would I do it? How would I decide? But I couldn't see into things and Riley did everything to discourage me." She swallowed and looked at the ground. "For eight long years, he told me every day how worthless I am," she whispered almost inaudibly. "For eight long years I have begged God every day to keep my father's voice alive in my heart. He was confident I could lead Brigham Hall one day. I want to believe him, not Riley. But I cannot do it alone. Will you help me?" Her pleading gaze struck him right in the middle of his heart.

"Of course," he heard himself answer and inwardly said goodbye to the horses. It would be a while yet until he could shed his responsibility.

Return

Brigham Hall, Michaelmas, September 29, 1711

Dear Mother,

How things have changed in the short time since Dame Arabella has come back! It is hard to believe. Naturally, a lot has to do with Russell and Fanny being gone who so often caused fights and unrest. All remaining servants strive to read Dame Arabella's every wish from her eyes. Whether it is their remorse for having made the young woman's life so hard over the years or the disarming nature of the baronetess, I cannot judge. But they seem almost in love with their new mistress who doesn't count their sins. Instead, she goes to great lengths to lead Brigham Hall on a good track.

Today, Mr Ainsworth came and paid everyone their wages. The bag of silver I have now hidden in my cottage seems like a treasure to me. Never before have I seen so much money in one place, let alone owned it. It is more than the baronet – old habit – than Riley had promised me. A lot more. When I pointed this out to Mr Ainsworth, he simply smiled and put a hand on my shoulder.

"The baronetess wished to express her gratitude in this manner," he said, and then added, "She also told me to inform you that you will have free use of Thunderboy. She won't ride him yet knows how much you appreciate him."

Oh Mother, what a gift! This splendid horse has often been balm for my soul and since Riley's death we have become friends. He is much calmer. Perhaps he sensed the inner turmoil of the impostor and reacted to it.

For two weeks now, Ruth has been working in the stables. It took a while for the two lads to stop staring at her. Half her face and also her arm and hand are heavily scarred. She can open one eye only halfway and her ear is missing. There's no hair on that side of her head, either. I feel truly sorry for her and am glad that Mr Miller pointed her fate out to me. She is an excellent hand with the horses and doesn't shy away from stable work, either. She rarely talks, but for a few days now I heard her humming to herself which she did not do before. I take that as a sign that she is happy with her work. Only if strangers come into the stable, she hides right away. I can't blame her.

I think we will manage quite well until the mop market. Choosing the right grooms will require a good instinct, though. Dame Arabella has asked me to come to the market with her and help her find new servants. She is probably afraid to enter the humdrum after such a long time. She would never admit that, though. She is extremely strong headed which is probably the reason for her survival all these years.

She advised me to get a wig. I've been wearing my hair short for some years now and she felt that as an overseer on Brigham Hall I would have more dealings with gentlemen and should wear a wig accordingly. I declined. I really have no head for such vanities.

I hope this made you laugh!

Best wishes,

Daniel

19
Disillusionment

"SPECIAL OCCASION, HARRY?" Daniel asked the gardener, who did not look like an old, gnarled tree for a change, but like a proper driver.

Harry grumbled something and scratched below his arm. "The mistress was invited for tea by Mrs Ainsworth," he explained. "Can Tom help me harness the team?"

"Of course, he's in the stable sweeping. Tell him to go on sweeping when you're done, or he'll slip away again!" Daniel called in passing.

The house was astir with excitement. Lizzie came rushing down the stairs, her faced flushed. "Sorry!" she gasped and squeezed past Daniel into the kitchen. He hadn't reached the office yet when she was hurrying upstairs again with a bowl of water. Ellie followed her, laden with blankets. A babble of voices and giggling wafted down. Daniel smiled to himself. When the daughters of his former masters had been invited somewhere, the house had transformed into a chicken coop every time, everyone flapping and clucking. Torn between his sense of duty and curiosity, he hovered near the office door. He definitely wanted to catch a glimpse of Dame Arabella, all spruced up to go out. He couldn't lurk there forever, though. Pressing his lips together, he went into the room but left the door ajar so he would hear her come down.

He hadn't done much work when the voices in the corridors grew louder. His mistress' pealing laughter was unmistakable. How often had he wished to hear her laugh when she was still a silent maid! With a curious smile, he stepped into the entrance hall.

She was wearing a burgundy red skirt with a brighter blouse, elegant gloves that reached well above her elbows and instead of the usual cap, there was a hat resting on her reddish curls. Her eyes glinted with pleasure when she saw him.

"How do I look?" she asked prettily and turned about once to let him admire her from all sides. Before Daniel could even start to think about an appropriate answer, an admiring "absolutely adorable" had slipped from his lips. He felt himself blush.

All three women started giggling again, even Ellie.

"She will be the prettiest lady at the whole reception," Lizzie announced proudly, as if it was all her doing.

"Mrs Ainsworth invited other ladies to whom she would like to introduce me." For a moment Dame Arabella sobered. "I just hope I don't make a fool of myself," she added quietly and cast Ellie an insecure glance.

"Don't you worry about that, madam. Everyone will be enchanted," Ellie encouraged the young woman.

In that instant, the door opened, and Harry announced that the carriage was waiting. With an excited sigh, Dame Arabella turned to go. Over her shoulder, she said to Daniel, "Wish me luck!" and disappeared before he could answer.

Disillusionment

ONCE SHE HAD LEFT, Daniel worked diligently in the office and then rode out to look at some of the tenant farms further afield. Mr Miller had told him there was re-occurring trouble between the Scotsman Kerr and his neighbour Weldon. Daniel wanted to get to the bottom of it.

The Scotsman's farm was in such a pitiful state that Daniel didn't bother trying to talk to him. He wouldn't continue the tenancy for another year. Riley had often complained about Kerr and planned to get rid of him at the earliest opportunity. Daniel didn't waste another thought on the matter and rode on to Weldon's house. There was nobody at home. He knocked repeatedly but the door wasn't opened, and he couldn't find a soul close to the house or stables. Everything looked properly kept, though, even if there were only two scraggly chickens scratching in the dirt. Where were the sheep? Daniel's gaze swept over the nearby pastures and fields. Weldon must have moved them to another pasture further away.

Without having achieved anything, Daniel swung up on his horse and rode back to Brigham Hall.

When he returned to the office, he was surprised to find Dame Arabella standing by the window and staring thoughtfully into the distance.

He stopped in the doorway, then entered the office slowly. "You're back already?" he asked. He had not been out more than two hours and hadn't expected her to return before late evening.

She turned around and he saw that she had shed a few tears. She lowered her gaze and wiped her face. "Yes," she said in a clipped manner and sat in one of the chairs by the fireplace.

The Silent Maid

Daniel came closer. "What happened?"

A deep sigh escaped her, and she kneaded her finger for a while, before she answered quietly, "It was terrible. I don't know what Mrs Ainsworth told her acquaintances about me, but I felt like a two-headed monkey at a fair. At first, all they did was stare at me. I thought perhaps it was because I didn't use any bleach, but then they started to ask me the most impertinent questions." She fell silent and helplessly looked at Daniel.

He could feel her pain and disappointment. "What sort of questions?"

She lifted a hand, only to let it drop again in discouragement. "Whether I clean my own slops. Whether the servants obey me at all. Whether I think any man would ever marry me after living in such shame." A new tear rolled down her cheek. "Even though I never…" Her whisper faded and she looked down again.

Daniel did the same. He had not expected to hear that the upper class were not one iota better than the servants. No matter where he had worked, gossip had thrived everywhere. They had talked about their masters, their fellow servants, or the neighbours in the village. Nothing was more treasured than gossip and chit-chat. Why he had ever thought the upper class was exempt from this he didn't know. It pained him to have his delicate mistress received so tactlessly by her peers. He certainly had expected more of Mr and Mrs Ainsworth.

"So, you left?" he finally asked. Out of the corner of his eye he saw her nod.

Then she took a deep breath and rose. With a determined tone she said, "I have been through much harder things. The nagging of some silly geese is not going to kill

Disillusionment

me. It wasn't any worse than Fanny. Let them talk. Soon there will be another sensation and they'll lose interest in me." She squared her shoulder and looked Daniel in the eye. "How did it go with the tenants?"

Daniel couldn't help but be impressed by this change of attitude. This woman truly possessed an impressive strength and personality. He smiled at her absent-mindedly.

"The tenants?" she repeated.

Daniel cleared his throat. "The tenants, yes. We'll definitely have to send Kerr away. The farm is in a despicable state. I didn't meet Mr Weldon, but everything looked orderly there. We'll have to talk to him to find out what's going on between him and the Scotsman."

"Good. Perhaps you can leave him a message to come here if you don't meet him next time either. I will retire now and…" She paused. "…digest the nagging and make up my mind on how I will respond to it in the future. Any suggestions?"

"I'm sorry, but I really can't help you there."

She smiled tiredly. "I'll think of something," she murmured, nodded once more and left.

IN THE COURSE OF the next few weeks, various messengers arrived at Brigham Hall, carrying either an invitation for Dame Arabella or requesting a meeting with her. She declined many of them, but not all. When she went out, she gave the impression of a soldier preparing for battle. The exuberant joy of the first invitation was gone.

Daniel's admiration grew each time she faced this challenge and refused with an iron will to give in. He had no idea what occurred at these events because she never talked about them again. Nevertheless, he felt her relief when returning late at night and letting herself fall into Lizzie's gentle care.

It took a while, but finally she also accepted a visitor, which caused Ellie to panic on the one hand, yet be elated on the other. Only once did Daniel make the mistake of entering the kitchen in the midst of preparations. Afterwards, he considered himself lucky that she had not chased him out with a rolling pin. The breathless industry of the cook amused him for a long time, at least until Dame Arabella informed him that she wished to have him present at the dinner, since Mr and Mrs Ainsworth would be bringing an acquainted couple and she didn't want to be the odd one out.

"You want me… but I… for dinner?" Daniel stammered in shock and hoped fervently that some hole in the ground would swallow him.

"You will enjoy talking to Mr Ainsworth, and the other gentleman, Lord Dursley, will join you, I'm sure. And if you don't know what to say, simply put a potato in your mouth and look apologetic. That works perfectly."

This insight into her conversational skills made him smile despite everything.

"Have you finally acquired a wig?" she asked.

Daniel started to cough.

She interpreted his reaction correctly. "Well, at least let your hair grow; this mop is quite unacceptable."

His protests got stuck in his throat when she stepped up to him and ran her hand through his hair. He felt as if

Disillusionment

the skin on his head had caught fire where she touched him – in a much more pleasant manner than it had done after Russell had torn his hair out by the roots. It seemed to take forever to muster the strength to step backwards. The look from her green eyes held him in a much stronger grip than her hand in his hair.

"I'll go and change," he croaked and hurried away to his cottage. He needed to clean his shoes and brush his jacket down. Hopefully, his good shirt didn't have a smudge on it. Did he have a decent ribbon for the collar? Everything served to distract him from his boiling emotions, even if the distraction was anything but pleasant.

Dinner with Mr Ainsworth and the mistress, plus additional guests. How did he get caught up in that? How could she do this to him? He had no idea how to behave in such circles! A resigned sigh escaped his throat. He would make a complete fool of himself. Best to keep a potato in his mouth all evening.

"God help me," he murmured.

The Silent Maid

Brigham Hall, October 21, 1711

Oh Mother,

What a night lies behind me! I'm completely drained. Like a fish on dry land, that is how I felt during the dinner with Dame Arabella, Mr and Mrs Ainsworth and Lord and Lady Dursley. The latter own a grand estate further south and were acquainted with the late Baronet Brigham, Dame Arabella's father. They were very friendly and forthcoming. Nothing suggested the foul treatment Dame Arabella had told me about after her first invitation for tea with Mrs Ainsworth. Everyone treated her with utmost respect.

If my behaviour was as desperate and revolting as that of the said fish, the others politely ignored it. Mr Ainsworth talked to me about horses, especially the Brighams, which seemed to interest Lord Dursley immensely and filled me with gratitude. At least I could keep up the conversation. The food, however, with its multitude of dishes and cutlery, overwhelmed me completely. I ate almost nothing for fear of spilling something, ruining the tablecloth, or frightening the guests with my lack of manners. Dame Arabella kept giving me careful hints as to which knife or glass to use, but I was so confused I preferred to stay hungry.

I believe my helplessness gave her some hidden amusement. Now I know first-hand how she must have felt on these occasions when first reintroduced to society. I can only admire her courageous resolve to tackle these things. As fragile as she often seems, her core is strong.

With half an ear, I heard Lady Dursley talk to her about her father and sensitively encourage her to run the estate as he had. Obviously, Baronet Brigham was highly regarded by Lady Dursley. Lord Dursley was also full of praise for the former baronet and pointed out that I had taken on a significant task in overseeing the estate. As if I didn't know!

Disillusionment

After bidding our guests goodbye, Dame Arabella thanked me almost pityingly for my commitment. She must have noticed how far removed I am from people of such high standing. I believe I have made it more than clear that I would not participate in similar events in the future. She accepted it without comment but bestowed a strangely melancholic glance on me. I really do hope she will spare me from now on!

No, dear Mother, I'm simply not made for a life in the upper class of society.

Your loving son,

Daniel

20

Tenants

THE CARRIAGE ROLLED out of the yard, which looked strangely bare. The blackened trunk had been removed and only a forlorn stump remained of the past magnificence of the chestnut tree. Harry had drilled a deep hole into it, put a chestnut inside and covered it with earth. Daniel had watched doubtfully, but Harry was undeterred. "You'll see," he had mumbled and nodded knowingly.

A short while later, Dame Arabella appeared in the yard, an expectant smile on her lips.

"Daniel?" she called and brought him out of the tack room, where he had been hunting for a saddle that would fit Mr Ainsworth's young gelding.

"Madam?"

"I would like to ride out. Will you be able to accompany me?"

Daniel observed her thoughtfully. Obviously, the carriage that had just left had delivered a new riding habit which she was now wearing.

"Such a ride would be a bit too much for Mr Ainsworth's gelding," Daniel stated. "I wanted to ride him in the arena, first."

"Have you ridden him yet?"

"Several times, but it was not good. The saddle didn't fit properly. I just wanted to see if I could find a better one."

"Good. How long will it take?" the baronetess demanded.

"A good hour, madam," Daniel replied.

"Splendid. I will brush and saddle Kitty at leisure and expect you then."

"Should I ask one of the lads…"

"She doesn't let anyone else touch her, Daniel," she interrupted him and followed him into the tack room where she searched the rows of saddles. "The one up there, under the blankets," she said and pointed at the top left corner.

Daniel had to climb onto a stool to get the saddle down. He'd never used it before – because he hadn't noticed it.

"Yes, that's the right one!" Dame Arabella said, pleased.

"This one? For your mare?"

She nodded.

"But this is a man's saddle," Daniel noted and was rewarded with an angry look.

"Don't you dare suggest I sit sideways on a horse led by someone else! I want to ride! I've always ridden like this." She glared at him as if she wanted to challenge him to oppose her further. Daniel didn't do her that favour. After all, he had already seen her ride, without any saddle at that. Without further comment, he carried the saddle to the hitching post in the yard, carefully checking all the straps and cinches. It was well possible that mice had nibbled on them or that the leather had cracked after years of disuse. Everything seemed to be in working order, though, if rather dusty.

"I'll send Tom to clean it," he said and went off in search of the lad.

Dame Arabella was already on her way to the pasture. A short while later, Daniel heard a whistle.

He didn't know whether to laugh or be amazed. Dame Arabella was just as lively as her little white mare. He could hardly imagine what it meant to her to be free to ride her own horse again after such a long time. She looked as if she would burst out of sheer joy, which led to her mare nearly galloping in place. Thunderboy had only once sniffed in the direction of the horse and received a swift kick in return. After that, he seemed to have decided that the quirky mare was beneath him and ignored her. Daniel didn't mind.

The cool October day blew a fresh breeze into their faces and clouds chased each other across a blue sky. Dame Arabella watched the play for a while, and then turned to Daniel with sparkling eyes.

"Are we as fast as those clouds?" she asked and then shot off with a tinkling laugh and flowing skirts.

Daniel had no choice but to follow.

If he had thought she would stop at the first encumbrance or slow down after a short while, he was mightily mistaken. Like a whirlwind she flew over stick and stone, cleared ditches and walls in graceful leaps, and only slowed down after they had passed the furthest farmhouse and turned back to Brigham Hall. He hadn't been hard put to keep up with her, but he was still impressed by her endurance and riding skills. Quite a few of the grooms he had known would have ended up in the grass after some of the manoeuvres she had made. He bit his lip, while steering the stallion next to his mistress. She had lost her cap on the wild ride and her curls had loosened, streaming like a lion's mane around her flushed cheeks. She looked adorable.

"What's the matter, Daniel? Cat got your tongue?" she teased breathlessly.

Daniel smiled and thereby confirmed her question. Everything that came to mind was completely inappropriate and he had never been one for superficial conversation.

She did not pursue it. For a while, they rode silently next to each other, both lost in their own thoughts.

Only when Brigham Hall came into sight, did she say quietly, "I thank you, Daniel."

"What for?" he asked curiously. He hadn't done anything exceptional and felt rather guilty for being silent for so long.

"For letting me be me. Sometimes wild and exuberant, sometimes quiet and pensive. It helps a lot." When he looked at her, he discovered a tear in the corner of her eye. It gave him a start and he wanted to say something, but she lifted a hand to stop him. "It's quite all right," she calmed him. "It's just not that easy to be me at the moment." With a wistful smile, she studied her hands.

He wanted to tell her that he understood, but that would have been a lie. He couldn't even begin to imagine what went on inside her. He hardly knew what she had been through. Eight years imprisoned by Riley, four of them hidden away somewhere, the other four forced to work, day in, day out. Humiliated, beaten, isolated. And yet she sat proudly astride her small, tough mare, beamed like the sun itself and spread an infectious joy. How was that possible?

"Do you believe in God, Daniel?" she asked softly.

"I do."

"The answer lies there," she replied, as if she had read his thoughts.

THE DAY STARTED with an uncomfortable drizzle that a strong westerly wind seemed to drive right under the skin. Daniel muttered a curse for they not only rode out in this weather but had to visit four of the tenant farms on the estate. They wanted to inform some of the tenants about the end of their contracts and with one, Mr Weldon, they needed to talk. Repeatedly, Daniel had been to the farm and not met anyone. The tenant had ignored the request to come to the great house. Daniel would have preferred to send a messenger and meet the tenants at Brigham Hall, but Dame Arabella wished differently. She hadn't been to the farms and wanted to get a first-hand impression, despite Daniel having reported everything to her. For support, she had asked Daniel, Mr Ainsworth and even Harry along. It had been Daniel's suggestion, because he feared there would be trouble with Kerr.

The first two farms had been in a reasonable condition. The cottages, consisting of a living room and a bedroom, with stables attached, certainly needed some repairs but didn't look neglected. The tenants stoically received the news. They were used to moving on every few years and had already expected that a new mistress meant new tenants.

Tenants

Now they were drawing close to Kerr's hut, and it was obvious from afar that he had little sense for order. What had registered in Daniel's mind as general shabbiness when passing, proved to be a lot worse. One of the stables had collapsed. A hay cart was sitting in front of the heap, back wheels as well as the axle missing. All around the cabin, garbage was strewn: wooden planks, a broken ladder, rusted pots, roof laths and rags. Pigs and chickens were roaming free and an emaciated dog was chained to a post at the front door. The riders stopped at a safe distance.

"Stay in the saddle, madam," Mr Ainsworth said, and cast a worried glance at the young woman shaking her head at the chaos.

"Kerr! Come out!" Daniel called, putting the dog in a frenzy. Barking furiously, it charged the group as far as the chain would allow. The front door opened a crack and was slammed shut again. Pigs and chickens ran off squealing and clucking in all directions, making the horses restless.

Just as Daniel was about to call a second time, the door opened again and Kerr came out, his shirt half open and stuffed half-heartedly into his kilt, which presented an unaccustomed view to the group. "What's up?" he asked, his speech hampered by the pipe in his mouth. He looked as if somebody had just dragged him out of bed where he had either slept off his inebriation or was busy getting drunk. Grimy strands of hair fell around his face.

Indignantly, Mr Ainsworth made his horse move a few steps forward. "Mr Kerr," he started, but the man shook his head and kicked at the dog. "Shut up, bastard," he cursed and kicked again. This time he didn't miss, and the dog landed with a yelp in a puddle. Satisfied, Kerr looked up again. "What a grand company to visit. Is that wee lassie the new mistress? Not much flesh on that chick," he sneered and slapped his thigh, laughing. Behind him, a young man appeared in the doorway, his expression one of curiosity. It was probably one of his sons.

"Mr Kerr, a bit more respect, if you please," Mr Ainsworth demanded. "We have come to inform you that your tenancy is terminated." He cast a meaningful glance at the run-down building. "It shall not be renewed," he added coolly.

The laughter on Kerr's face froze and his eyes turned to slits. "Is that so," he said with menace.

The door behind him was opened fully and two young lads stepped out, positioning themselves to the right and left of their father, arms crossed.

Daniel met Harry's eye and nodded. Both of them jumped down from their horses.

"Cudgel," Daniel mouthed.

Harry understood and dived behind Mr Ainsworth's horse, out of sight from where the men in front of the house might see him clearly; and pulled a sturdy branch out of the grass.

"Protect her," Daniel whispered, and Harry moved closer to Dame Arabella, who watched the proceedings with mounting alarm.

A metallic click broke the tense silence. Mr Ainsworth had pulled a pistol out of his saddle bags and was pointing it at the tenant. "You will pack your things and be gone by the day after tomorrow," he said slowly and distinctly. "If not, we will return with the constable."

Kerr spat on the ground. "Ooh, aren't I afraid now," he said cockily. His eyes locked with Mr Ainsworth's and he walked with resolute steps up to the baronetess.

Tenants

Ainsworth hesitated. It was obvious he didn't want to shoot the man, especially not in front of the young lady.

A smug grin spread across Kerr's face. He passed the solicitor and concentrated on Harry, who came at him with the cudgel. Kerr ducked and landed a solid punch in Harry's stomach. Harry gasped. At the same time, Kerr's sons ran at Daniel, howling wildly. The horses shied. Daniel had his hands full to fight off the lads. Out of the corner of his eye he saw that Kerr used the confusion to make a grab at Dame Arabella. He didn't take the white mare into account, though. As soon as he reached out to the young woman, strong horse teeth sank into his shoulder. He cried out. Before he could do anything else, the toe of Dame Arabella's boot met his chin with such force that he toppled over backwards and lay unconscious.

Harry recovered his senses and ran to help Daniel. With two deft swings of his cudgel, he knocked out both Kerr sons in short order.

Breathlessly, Daniel looked at the others and drew the back of his hand across his split lip, wiping away the blood. "Are you all right?" he asked Dame Arabella, who was almost as white in the face as her mare.

"Better than you," she said with a healthy dose of gratification.

"Well, isn't that charming," a female voice sounded from the cottage. "If you knock them out, at least carry them inside. They'll catch their death lying about in the rain." The tetchy woman crossed her arms, eyeing the group full of scorn.

"Mrs Kerr?" Mr Ainsworth asked, tucking his pistol away.

"Who wants to know?"

Mr Ainsworth dismounted and carefully sidestepped the legs of one of the boys. With an outstretched arm, he held the letter of notice up to the woman. "You have until the day after tomorrow to leave the estate. I advise you to cooperate. There need be no more trouble."

With a curt movement, she ripped the paper from his hand and balled it up.

"Go to hell," she hissed and spat in front of the solicitor's feet. Then she turned around, went in, and closed the door behind her with a bang.

Mr Ainsworth shrugged and mounted again. Daniel and Harry caught hold of their horses and followed suit.

"Will they go?" Daniel asked doubtfully.

Mr Ainsworth shook his head with a sigh. "I'm afraid, we will have to make sure of that the day after tomorrow."

THE LAST HOUSE seemed abandoned. No smoke was rising from the chimney and nobody was around, human or animal. An ominous silence enveloped the place.

Daniel dismounted and knocked on the door. There was no answer. "Weldon?" he called. His voice sounded lost in the rising fog. "Weldon!" he repeated, still without answer. Why was that man never at home? He was just about to turn away when he heard a feeble scratch on the other side of the door. He listened intently and knocked again. "Is anybody home? The baronetess would like to speak with Mr Weldon!" Now he clearly made out the sound of steps behind the door. He tried the handle. The door wasn't locked, but when he entered, a boy of about five ran at him with a poker.

"Go away!" he screamed, trying to hit Daniel with it.

Daniel easily caught him and put a hand on the boy's shoulder. "Don't be afraid, I won't hurt you. Calm down."

The boy sobbed.

"Are you alone?" Daniel looked around the room. There was no fire in the fireplace but apart from that, everything looked very tidy.

The boy didn't answer, casting a secretive glance over his shoulder.

Daniel pushed past him and approached the door to the bedroom.

"No!" the boy screamed in panic. "You mustn't go in there!" Again, he attacked Daniel with the poker. This time Daniel took it away from him. The boy placed himself in front of the door to block it, but Daniel opened it anyway. An awful smell of full chamber pots met him. In the semi-darkness he could make out a shape on the bed. He started. It looked as if the shape had two heads. With his eyes adjusting, he realized it was only a woman and a little girl lying on the bed. The woman groaned.

"Is she sick?" he asked the boy and stepped back involuntarily.

"No," the woman on the bed answered. "It's just labour pains."

The girl stared at Daniel with eyes round as saucers, her thumb in her mouth. She was no older than three.

Daniel swallowed and retreated. "Madam, I think you should take a look in there," he suggested when stepping outside. All he knew about birthing had to do with horses.

They all dismounted, tied their horses, and went inside. Dame Arabella disappeared into the small bedroom. They could hear her quietly talking to the woman on the bed.

The Silent Maid

Suddenly a piercing scream tore the silence and the children started whining. Dame Arabella pulled them both out of the bedchamber by their hands.

"Harry, take care of the little ones. Daniel, light a fire and put water to heat. Mr Ainsworth, would you be so kind as to see if you can find some blankets in one of the chests? And if there is bread anywhere, give the children something to eat." With that she went back into the chamber, only to return a moment later with a slop bucket which she emptied outside.

"Madam!" Mr Ainsworth called out in shock, but she merely looked at him impatiently. "It's not the first time, you know." Then she closed the door and was gone for a long time. Screams kept coming from the bedroom, tearing at Daniel's heart. He got the fire going but there wasn't much wood left beside the stove. He went outside and looked around. At the back of the cabin, he found the firewood neatly stacked. Behind that, there was a small chicken coop and another shed. The chicken coop was empty, and the shed had housed sheep or goats judging by the smell. It, too, was empty. The two chickens he had seen outside a couple of weeks ago had also disappeared. Daniel packed his arms with wood and carried it inside.

Harry sat at the table with the children and pulled a large red kerchief out of his trouser pocket. He waved it in front of the children's noses and then stuffed it into his hand. With a wink he clapped both hands. The kerchief had vanished. Daniel had to smile at their astounded faces. He had already seen a fair share of Harry's tricks, although he still had no idea how he did them. Right now, the distraction was a blessing for the children.

Daniel went twice more to refill the wood supply which he did gladly. It was, in any case, better than sitting inside and listening to that woman scream. While he was stacking the last load, Dame Arabella showed up again and demanded a bowl of warm water, the blankets, and a sharp knife.

The next time she came out, she motioned both children to come to her. "Everything is all right. You have a little sister. Go in and look at her, but be quiet. Your mama is pretty tired."

The children tiptoed into the room, where a baby now cried.

Dame Arabella quietly closed the door behind them and sat at the table. She was exhausted, but her eyes shone with the miracle of birth. "We have come at precisely the right moment," she said softly and sighed. "Her husband abandoned her in the summer. She said he constantly got into fights with the Kerrs. They have stolen their chickens and sheep and even the dog. We are not going to terminate her contract, Mr Ainsworth. Her husband has left her because he accused her of adultery. He said the child was not his. We cannot possibly turn her out with a small babe." Pensively, Dame Arabella studied the spinning wheel in the corner of the room. "She shall have her sheep returned to her or have them replaced. I will send Lizzie down here to help with the children for a few days until she has recovered from the birth. Then we will sit down with her to see how we will set up the new contract. Perhaps she can live off the wool and spinning."

"Yes, madam, but if she has no husband…" Mr Ainsworth started and then petered out.

"Then what, Mr Ainsworth?" Dame Arabella asked pertly, her eyes sparkling. "Can't she sign a contract? Can't she be a valuable member of our estate? Look around you, Mr Ainsworth. And then please remember the last farm we visited, run by men."

"That is not a fair comparison," Mr Ainsworth protested half-heartedly.

Dame Arabella rose. "We should ride home. It's getting dark."

Tenants

Brigham Hall, November 11, 1711

Dear Mother,

What a day! It is late already, but I am too agitated to go to sleep. Way before dawn we started on our way to the mop market in Bridlington. Dame Arabella was all chirpy and exhilarated. Imagine, she got it into her head that all the servants should go along!

"But don't you dare let anyone else hire you!" she admonished.

Ruth was the only one to stay home; she absolutely didn't want to come.

Under a beaming sun, I drove the hay waggon with the lads in the back, while Harry drove the carriage with the women. The boys talked incessantly the entire way. I wanted to switch places with Harry on the way back to save my ears, but he told me he hadn't fared any better.

When we arrived, all we could do was to agree on a meeting place; then they all took off into the bustle. Dame Arabella took my arm and we strolled across the market together. Our list was long: we needed a new dairy maid, a butler, a parlour maid and a groom with experience in training horses. Not an easy task, for at first, Dame Arabella was overwhelmed by so many people and things to see, I was afraid she would turn on her heel and hide in the carriage. Her grip on my arm was almost painful. It didn't last long, though, and she soon tackled the task with great alacrity. We kept a look-out for milking stools and brooms and had soon found a dairy maid and a parlour maid. After a short introduction and a few questions about their experience, Dame Arabella handed them a penny to seal the employment, followed by instructions. The girls tied brightly coloured ribbons around their heads and went off laughing. Both of them made a diligent and modest impression on me, which I hope will be confirmed. Finding a groom was much harder. Dame Arabella approached all of the young men carrying a bundle of straw or a whip. We had agreed on this procedure, because she wanted to know if the men would respect her. Most of them merely looked her up and down, grinned, and turned to me expectantly. I talked to a few, but it was quickly clear that they did not have the necessary experience.

Then, there was this man in his forties who seemed unable to tear his attention away from the baroness. On the contrary, he studied her to such an extent, that I felt I should reprimand him. But then he asked unbelievingly, "Lady Brigham?"

Dame Arabella literally froze. We found out that he had served as a groom under Ole Pete and been dismissed by Riley. The last time he had seen Dame Arabella she had been a child. Now he was amazed at the overwhelming likeness to her mother. Dame Arabella didn't seem to remember him, but when he learned that we were looking for a groom, he basically begged us to hire him. He had always loved Brigham Hall; it had been his home and he wanted nothing more than to return there.

I regard this 'coincidence' as a gift from heaven. Of course, we hired him, and he asked to ride home with us that very evening. When I told him about Ruth, our stable maid, he merely smiled and said, "That's what the baronet would have done."

Now all we needed was a butler. We searched high and low, but nobody presented himself. There were two or three footmen, but Dame Arabella would have none of that.

"They only cause trouble," she said. I could not object. Most of the footmen I have ever encountered have been cut out of the same cloth as Russell.

We gave up in the end and bought something to eat. Then, Dame Arabella allowed herself the pleasure of looking at ribbons and books, sweets and jewellery, while I passed the time watching people. I noticed a strong-boned young man who approached any person who remotely looked like an employer. He wore a bobble on his jacket, indicating that he had no special training but was looking for any work whatsoever. No matter who he addressed, they all turned away from him in an instant. After watching this repeated over and over, and noting his mounting frustration, I pointed him out to Dame Arabella.

"He doesn't look like a butler," she remarked. I had to agree, and yet I had the impression that I should speak to him. Perhaps he was the kind of person one could use for all sorts of odd jobs wherever needed. Dame Arabella wasn't opposed to this idea, and we walked over to him. As soon as he opened his mouth, we knew why everyone else had turned away. His voice was loud and guttural, his pronunciation indistinct and hard to understand. The man was deaf. He stood before us, struggling to articulate some words while gesticulating wildly. He even pulled up the sleeves of his shirt to show his muscles. To my immense surprise, Dame Arabella put a soothing hand on his arm which silenced him. They looked at each other for a long time.

"Can you understand me?" she asked after a while. It brought tears to his eyes. He nodded. Obviously, he could read from her lips. "Are you a handy person?" she went on and he nodded again. Hope blossomed in his eyes and his breath came in quick gasps. Pleadingly, he looked back and forth between the baroness and me. I knew in the blink of an eye that he might be deaf, but was anything but dumb. I turned to Dame Arabella so that he could not see my mouth and said quietly, "I think we should give him a chance." She smiled and said, "Yes." Then she pulled another shilling from her reticule and handed it to the deaf man. A cry of joy erupted from his lungs, loud enough to make people turn. He dropped to his knees in front of Dame Arabella, kissed her hand and then laid his forehead on it. I pulled him to his feet again to end the embarrassing scene. Folks in the vicinity were whispering to each other. Quickly, we went on our way, and he followed us like a loyal dog, the shilling in his fist pressed to his heart.

On the way home, I learned that his name is Dob. The groom is Chauncey. Both of them immediately befriended the lads, who proudly showed their purchases. Mo had bought a year's supply of sugar canes while Willie had got a decent knife, receiving much praise from Chauncey. Tom has a new cap, which is a bit too big for him and presses his ears down, making him look like an elf. Of course, the other lads had to steal it and toss it around until Dob caught it and ended the game with a warning finger.

This has turned into a long letter and I am finally tired out.

I wish you a good night!

Daniel

21
Changes

DANIEL STOOD IN THE chamber above the stable with Chauncey. The groom was struggling with tears, while his fingers caressed the scratched surface of the table. Then he stepped up to the window. There was no need to explain to Daniel that he had lived in this chamber for a long time.

The two lads had towed Dob off to their loft in the other stable building and he had gone with them joyfully. Everything seemed to be all right with him as long as he had work. Daniel made a mental note to have the tailor come the next day. Dob desperately needed new clothes. What he was wearing was hardly better than rags. Tom also needed new things. He had grown considerably over the past weeks.

"How can it be?" Chauncey asked, interrupting Daniel's thoughts. "How can she be alive? She was gone. For days, no, for weeks, we combed the entire neighbourhood, without success…"

"Riley hid her away somewhere. I don't know where."

"Hid her away? For years?" Chauncey shook his head, appalled.

"He was a sick man, corroded by self-pity and hatred. For four years he kept her imprisoned, and the next four years she had to work for him, here on her own estate. She wasn't allowed to speak a single word, or he would have killed her horse. I have no idea how she survived that."

"Where is he now?"

"He was hanged for his crimes." Daniel sighed. He still felt the burden of his part in Riley's death.

"I never trusted him," Chauncey said quietly. "I always wondered whether he'd had anything to do with the baronet's death. And his daughter's disappearance."

"Your intuition didn't fail you," Daniel replied. "I was there when he admitted the murder of Baronet Brigham." He turned to go. "If there is anything you need, I'm at the cottage. We'll have breakfast after feeding tomorrow morning."

Later, Daniel sat in his armchair in front of the fireplace and stared into the flames. The day's events passed before his inner eye. It had been a strange feeling to stroll across the market with Dame Arabella on his arm, and outrageously good how she had treated him like an equal, a confidante. As if he had every right to walk with her like that. At the same time, it had been frightening. His role had invariably been that of a groom, a servant, and even that he'd had to work hard to achieve. Never in his life would he have dreamed of acting as an employer at a mop market like the one in Bridlington. He had to be careful that he didn't grow proud. Pride was a sin and the Bible stated clearly that servants should humbly serve their masters as if they served the Lord Jesus himself. He must not forget that.

Especially not when his feelings for Arabella did somersaults. Dame Arabella Brigham, Baronetess. Unreachable by Daniel Huntington, son of a carpenter, Master of Horse and overseer at Brigham Hall. He scoffed and shook his head. If he had not met her as a maid, his dreamy brain would never have come up with such nonsense as was haunting him now. He thought back to his discomfort during the dinner with the Ainsworths and Dursleys – he was not only a member of a different class, but a whole different world.

"Impossible," he whispered and threw some ash on the glimmering coals in the fireplace. It was high time to go to sleep.

THE WEATHER GOT drearier the further November moved along. Strong winds brought heavy clouds which turned every road and path into deep mire traps with their constant rain. Daniel was glad that the sowing with the seed drill had been completed without incident. Young George Harper had taken on his new task with great vigour and had repaired the machine several times. Daniel would never have been able to do that.

Now he worried about the pastures. In some of the hollows, lakes were forming, and the horses' hooves sank deep into the soil, ruining the turf. He would have liked to discuss the problem with the baronetess, but she was retreating more and more and hardly left her room. Her irrepressible courage to face life seemed directly connected to the weather. As soon as it rained, her mood changed. Then she was silent, distant, and seemed tense and frightened. When the sun came out again, her smile was back. Nobody had an explanation for this, not even Lizzie, who hardly left Dame Arabella's side.

Ever since Fanny and Russell were gone and Brigham Hall had a mistress, Daniel could eat in the kitchen again with the others, which he was glad of. He was still overseer, but the relationship of the servants had become much more familiar. They sat together after the day's work was done, enjoyed the warmth of the fire, and a cup of hot tea with honey. Around Easter, Harry had won a beehive in a card game at Flamborough and was trying his luck as a beekeeper. By now, he had separated his colony several times and had four hives which he had positioned by the fruit trees. Ellie was very happy about that since honey was expensive and the fruit harvest had been much better than in prior years.

"Have you heard what happened in the war?" Harry asked one evening.

"We're at war?" Mo looked around as if expecting to see a group of soldiers storm into the kitchen.

"Not here, don't worry. Over in America! There is a big land, much bigger than England and Scotland together. It's called Canada. Never heard of it?" Harry explained.

The lads looked at him with round eyes and shook their heads.

"There is a city called Quebec and Queen Anne wanted to conquer it. Or rather Robert Harley wanted to conquer it. He's a member of our government. A courageous man who wants to lead England to new heights as a naval power."

Daniel felt that Harry admired the man and wondered if, deep in his heart, he had wished to be a sailor rather than a gardener.

"Anyway, they went on an expedition with a large fleet and wanted to sail up St. Lawrence river to attack Quebec. But guess what, they didn't have an able navigator! Eight ships capsized in a single foggy night. Eight ships! More than eight hundred hands lost." Harry slowly shook his head.

"When's that supposed to have happened?" Ellie asked suspiciously. She didn't look as if she believed a single word of Harry's tale. He might as well have spoken of giants and mermaids.

"It was in August! Heard it last week in Flamborough. The smith's son married that girl from York, remember? Her cousin was in that fleet. His letter arrived a few weeks ago. They almost ran aground in the fog. All night long they heard the screams of the drowning men."

"Oh, be quiet, Harry. You're scaring the lads," Ellie scolded, ignoring the disappointment on the boys' faces, for they would have liked nothing better than to hear all the gory details.

At that moment, Lizzie came in and sat down on the bench at the table, exhaling an exhausted sigh.

Ellie poured her a cup of tea right away. "Here, child, drink," she said and stroked her bright hair. "Is everything all right with the mistress?"

Lizzie shrugged helplessly and stared into the cup.

"Tom, Willie, Mo, go off to bed. It's late."

The boys rose grumbling and shuffled off.

Harry also rose with a mighty yawn. "This weather robs me of my strength. And the winter isn't even here yet!"

With that, he left the kitchen. They could hear his heavy steps on the stairs. The ensuing silence was only interrupted by the crackling fire.

"She cries so much," Lizzie suddenly said. "In the middle of the night she wakes up and screams and cries. And then she says confused things about roaring trees trampling around on her. I believe she is mad." Lizzie swallowed hard. "But then she is quite normal again in the morning and really sweet. When I tell her I'm worried about her, she hugs and comforts me and tells me how much I help her and that I shouldn't worry, she will get better. Right now, I have the feeling it's getting worse all the time, though." A tear rolled along Lizzie's nose. She wiped it away with her apron.

Ellie put an arm around her.

"I have heard her cry in the kitchen in the past when there was a storm. Sometimes I went to her, but the baronet invariably came and chased me away. He was so cruel to her."

Daniel had trouble understanding Lizzie's last words due to her sobbing. He clamped his jaws tight and rose. He remembered the stormy night clearly when Arabella had run into his arms and he had comforted her.

"She is stronger than you think," he said roughly and turned to leave. Right now, he longed for the quiet solitude of his cottage.

THE NEW MAIDS, Bess and Molly, moved into Brigham Hall the following week. It took a while until the chores had been adapted to the new situation and everyone had found their place again in the overall order of things. By Christmas, everything was sorted and each of them was relieved to have the burden carried by more shoulders.

Dame Arabella had asked the priest from Flamborough to come to Brigham Hall and give a short Christmas message, to which she had not only invited all the house servants, but the tenants and their families as well. She had wanted it to be a service, but since the parlour was not consecrated ground, the priest had refused.

Afterwards, Dame Arabella wanted to make some announcements. Daniel was curious how the tenants and servants would react to her proposals. She had explained everything to him and had wanted his opinion. The sheer magnitude of plans and thoughts she had about the people on the estate had impressed him and he had strongly encouraged her. The fact that her father had been so much more successful than Riley made his doubts evaporate. Whether the tenants would accept the offers he could not fathom.

Only half of the tenant families had followed the invitation to attend, first of all the Millers. It was obvious that they came out of curiosity more than religious conviction. The people were tired of the church, even out here in the countryside. Dame Arabella was undeterred and greeted every individual with the utmost kindness.

There were many people present and the children were difficult to keep quiet. The priest did not speak for long, although he seemed glad to be able to pass the Christmas message on to people he rarely saw in his church.

When he had ended, Dame Arabella rose and addressed the assembly. "My dear fellows here on the Brigham estate, I am very happy that you have come.

Together we will work hard so that the land we are allowed to live on will not only feed us, but be taken well care of. It is entrusted to us by God, not to exploit it, but to preserve it and take God's blessing from it. That's how my father handled things and it is the way I want to handle things. It is also very important to me that you know how greatly I treasure your work in farming the land. We all strive together to have a good life."

A soft murmur arose, partly approving, partly doubting.

Dame Arabella continued. "Before my father died, he had decided to start a school on the estate. He wanted your children – and you yourselves, if you so wish – to learn to read, write and do sums to offer everyone better chances in life. This is my wish also. For this reason, I offer anyone who is interested to come here on Wednesday mornings to participate in lessons. No matter whether child or grown-up, boy or girl, everyone is welcome. I will teach you myself."

This time the murmur was much louder.

"I know you all have lots to do – so do I. But we can all sacrifice half a day a week if we want. And I would like to make another change: On Sundays, no work shall be done. Of course, you will have to feed the animals, but apart from that, you shall not do any of the daily chores. It is the day of the Lord when you shall rest and study his word. It is my wish to rebuild the chapel so that we will eventually have Sunday services again. This will take a while. To those who do not own a Bible, I will gladly give one. None of you shall be without the word of God. You may now help yourselves to some food and drink and celebrate. God bless us all."

Applause sounded and the tenants looked at each other in surprise. As long as they had lived on the estate, no such thing had occurred.

Ellie had been busy in the kitchen for days to prepare enough bread, pastries, and sweets for many hungry mouths. Apart from that, she had brewed a delicious punch, which Mo now served tirelessly from a huge cauldron.

Talk soon became a great noise, though nobody dared to speak with the mistress. She stood by the fireplace and watched the crowd with a wistful smile.

Daniel would have loved to join her but didn't get the opportunity. He was bombarded with questions about the things the baroness had announced. Time and again he tried to get the people to talk to her directly, but it was no use.

He was just glad they had talked it all through beforehand so that he could answer all the questions and encourage people to take up the offer of lessons. He explained over and over how happy he would have been as a child to get such a chance, and how important education was.

When dusk settled, the tenants went home to their farms in a jolly mood, though not without paying their respects to their mistress with a bow or a curtsey. It relieved Daniel a lot, and Dame Arabella had a friendly word for each and every one of them. She was well aware of her chance to define the future relationship with the tenants and wanted them to return home with a positive impression. After the last one had left, she sank down on a chair and sighed deeply.

Daniel stood beside her. "Are you satisfied, madam?" he asked. Never before had he met a master giving so much thought to his servants.

"I don't know," she said, sounding discouraged. "What did they say? How did they react?" She gazed at Daniel questioningly.

"They were surprised and also distrusting. Miller was excited and said he would send his children to the lessons no matter what. Perhaps he can convince others. But most of them…" He fell silent.

"Most of them think it takes a man as a tutor. Well, we're currently out of one." She stood up and scoffed indignantly.

"They were very happy about the Sunday off," Daniel added quickly.

"Of course they were. But none of them wanted a Bible, did they?" Her green eyes flashed at him.

"Give them time," he said soothingly. "Changes always take time. Riley was a tough master who demanded a lot. It's not sufficient to tell them once that everything is different now. None of them knows how your father managed the estate. Nobody knows what it is like to work together toward a mutual goal. Not even I know it; I only have a notion and hope that it will work. But I cannot imagine it." His honest words dispersed her anger.

"You can't?" she asked meekly.

Daniel shook his head.

"But you want to assist me anyway? Why?"

"I have seen your father's ledgers. They show what a generous man he was. It never harmed the estate, on the contrary. Riley was never that successful, despite all his innovations. His leadership was efficient, but it lacked kindness. There's a different atmosphere here now. And then there is Chauncey. He knew your father. And what he has told me so far sounds like heaven on earth. I will do anything to make it real."

She smiled and put her hand on his arm. "Thank you, Daniel. What would I do without you?"

He swallowed and took a step back. She kept making remarks like that which never failed to confuse him. What should he say to that? There was so much intimacy in her voice, sparking all the wrong hopes. For a partnership by far exceeding a work relationship, at least in his heart. Every time this happened, he felt helpless and overwhelmed. He couldn't think of anything but to bow and leave.

The Silent Maid

Brigham Hall, January 10, 1712

Dearest Mother,

The fundamental change accompanying Dame Arabella's return becomes more obvious all the time. The more she interacts with the people on the estate, the clearer her intentions. At the same time, her depressive moods lessen, although the weather is anything but nice. It has been raining for days on end, and humans and animals slog through knee-deep mud. An icy wind makes everything worse.

In spite of that, quite a few tenants show up for lessons on Wednesdays, not just children. Dob has also asked to be allowed to participate. Dame Arabella has started to give him speaking lessons as well to improve his pronunciation. He is learning with ardent zeal. Overall, he does everything with great joy, works hard, but always with a smile on his face. He has enriched our lives and truly is handy with most things.

The tenants' wives have begun to trust their new mistress after they learned of the things she did for Mrs Weldon. The woman now has a contract drawn up in her name to give her security. Should her husband return, she will not have to take him in or leave with him.

There was quite some trouble with the Kerr family when the time came for them to leave the estate. We had to give them a cart or we wouldn't have got rid of them at all. All of the men, including Mr Ainsworth and the constable, went out to make sure they left. They were allowed to take two pigs and a few chickens, but the dog, the rest of the chickens and all the sheep were taken to Mrs Weldon. She was extremely glad, while the dog nearly killed himself with joy at being back with his family.

Of course, the Kerrs had packed nothing, so we did it for them while they stood mutely by, their arms crossed. When everything was stowed on the cart, Dob and Chauncey rode ahead, and

Changes

Mr Ainsworth and the constable followed. They accompanied them to Flamborough, and the constable made it unmistakeably clear that they had to keep well away from the estate. They should have been punished for their theft. Mr Ainsworth thought it wiser not to pursue that, though. Scotsmen have long memories, he said, and were known to lead endless feuds. A good point he made there.

What worries him is the wish of the baronetess to rebuild the chapel. He said it was too expensive. When I put in that many of the stones still lying about could probably be reused, he got angry. On the way out, he said in my ear I shouldn't support her capricious idea. Well, whatever his reasons, I'm the wrong person to address.

The baronetess and I have gone over the books together and wondered how to finance the rebuilding. For the first time, we noticed that there is money missing. We did find a large number of coins in Riley's room but by far not the whole amount that should be there according to the books. Dame Arabella was furious and started to search the room systematically. I was sent to search the office, without result.

We are facing a riddle. Where did Riley hide the money?

All the servants have suddenly caught the treasure hunt fever and turn the entire house upside down. Every stick and stone is lifted, and every corner searched, even in the stables they knock on the floor to find hidey-holes and check every loose brick. I'll let you know if we discover something. Should that not be the case, we'll have to abandon the chapel for now.

Perhaps God will work a miracle?

Love

Daniel

22

Suitors

"LOOG WHA I FOUN!" Dob's loud voice sounded through the entrance hall into the office, where Daniel and Dame Arabella were brooding over the books.

They had counted the money stored in Riley's old room and tried to calculate how much was missing. It was hard; he had diverted only small amounts at a time, often making them look like miscalculations. In other instances, the numbers were illegible because they had been corrected or covered by ink blots. It irked Daniel when he realized that Riley had even done it in his presence, and he hadn't noticed.

Both were more than happy to flee the annoying calculations to see what Dob had found.

He was standing in the entrance hall on the second step of the stairs and proudly held up a painting. A cluster of servants had formed in front of him, admiring the portrait. When they noticed Dame Arabella, they stepped aside respectfully. Dob peeked over the frame and grinned at the sight of the baronetess. "Tha's you!" he called.

Dame Arabella approached him slowly. "No, Dob," she said softly. "It's not. It's my mother." Carefully her fingertips brushed over the picture which was covered with a thick layer of dust. She looked up at Dob and broke into a peal of laughter. His hair was full of cobwebs and dirt smeared his cheeks.

"Try to clean it with a soft rag. It used to hang over the fireplace in the parlour… where the hunting scene is now." She paused. "Are there any more paintings, Dob?"

He nodded. "Painings an chess."

"Chess?" Dame Arabella looked confused.

He cocked his head and put the painting down. Daniel came up to him and took it out of his hands.

"I fesh!" Dob cried and ran up the stairs.

While the others followed him full of curiosity, Daniel studied the painting. The woman in the picture looked almost exactly like the baronetess, the same reddish curls, the freckles and green eyes. But her gaze was softer and her figure much more voluptuous.

He carried the painting into the parlour and hurried after the others. The babble soon led him to the linen storeroom, through which one could enter the attic up a ladder. They could hear Dob rummaging about up there until he appeared at the trapdoor with a new treasure. Beaming with joy, he handed it down to the eagerly waiting servants. It was another painting, this one of a stern looking man with dark hair sitting on a chair and holding a little girl who looked just as stern.

"Papa," Dame Arabella whispered with a soft gasp. "Take it downstairs, please. Be careful!"

Daniel took it and carried it into the parlour, where he placed it next to the other one. He smiled to himself. Yes, Dame Arabella looked a lot like her mother but the determined look and the willpower evident in her eyes quite clearly came from her father. The effect the perhaps six-year-old Arabella had on him was similar to the one she had on him now: he wanted to take her in his arms and pull her on his lap, press her close and bury his fingers in her hair. The memory of her tender frame in his arms as he had come to know it on that one thunderous night rushed into his thoughts.

Time and again he had to fight this impulse. Time and again she came so close to him as to make it nearly impossible to resist her. He didn't know whether she did this in guileless innocence or with alluring intent. How often had he fled her presence because he couldn't think of anything else to do? She had never made a comment on it, but he always had the feeling that it sat between them like an unasked question.

He sighed and shook his head. No, it could never be. She was part of the landed gentry and he belonged to the lower class. As free and unconventional her thinking was in many ways, this border could not be transgressed.

Ellie, Molly, and Lizzie came down the stairs, chatting excitedly.

"Not chess, a chest!" Ellie called out to him.

"With her mother's jewellery," Lizzie added, her eyes shining. "She went to her room to look through it. She'll be down again later."

"There was also a beautiful wedding dress, completely ruined by mice. Such a shame," Molly said. "Madam wishes to have the paintings hung up in the parlour once we've cleaned them."

"Dob can help you with that. You haven't found anything else up there?"

"Only old furniture and junk. No gold," Ellie sighed and shrugged.

"I'M AFRAID WE'LL have to wait to rebuild the chapel, madam," Daniel said a few days later.

No matter how they looked at it, the money they had would only cover the costs of everyday living, no extra investments.

"If only I knew where he hid it," Dame Arabella said through clenched teeth. "What could he have wanted with it?" She was so angry he could almost see a dark cloud hovering above her head.

There was a knock on the door.

"Yes?" she called.

The door of the office opened, and Lizzie entered. "Madam, there's a gentleman who would like to see you, a Mr Winslow. He's waiting in the parlour."

"Did he say what he wants?"

"No, madam."

The baronetess sighed deeply. "I'm coming. Daniel, would you accompany me, please?"

She walked briskly into the parlour and Daniel followed.

"Good day, Mr Winslow. What can I do for you?" she greeted the visitor who proved to be a slightly overweight man in his thirties. With his black wig, the artfully embroidered green silk jacket and the flouncy shirt, he looked like an exotic bird compared to Dame Arabella in her unadorned sand-coloured dress. For a moment, her unbleached face with the large number of freckles seemed to unhinge him, but he caught himself quickly and put on a beaming smile. "My dear Dame Arabella," he said and bowed low over her hand.

Daniel kept back. He felt completely out of place, although he knew that his mistress wished to be chaperoned.

The man's stilted manner made Daniel suspicious, making him understand her wish.

"It is such an honour and – if I may be so bold to add – an immense pleasure to meet you," Mr Winslow proceeded.

Dame Arabella motioned him to a chair and sat down herself. He glanced questioningly at Daniel who stood by a little awkwardly. Not in his life would he sit in the presence of his mistress.

"May I introduce my overseer, Mr Huntington?" she said.

Mr Winslow nodded curtly.

Daniel positioned himself behind Dame Arabella's chair, his legs slightly apart, his hands clasped behind his back, and stared intently at the visitor. It gratified him to see that Mr Winslow did not seem to appreciate this behaviour in the least.

"Madam, I am sure it is unnecessary for your, um…" He hesitated. "…your overseer to be present at this conversation."

"It is," Dame Arabella retorted. "So, Mr Winslow, what can I do for you?" Her tone still carried her anger at Riley's embezzlement, which Mr Winslow interpreted as alluding to him.

"Well, it is like this…" He paused again.

"Mr Winslow, I am a very busy woman," Dame Arabella said impatiently. "You haven't come all this way to Brigham Hall for the pure pleasure of the ride, have you? What do you want?"

"This is a truly beautiful estate you have here." Mr Winslow tried a different approach. He got up and went to the window. There was a small terrace in front of it which was accessible from the parlour and surrounded by low stone wall. "However, I could not make out a formal garden, or I would have invited you for a stroll." He cast another crooked glance at Daniel.

Dame Arabella took a deep breath. "You are quite right, Mr Winslow. This is the estate of a renowned horse breeder. We rarely stroll. We prefer to ride. Apart from that, the weather is hardly fit to do the one or the other."

The snappish tone of this reply should have made it perfectly clear to him that his tactic was miserably failing him. He plodded on relentlessly. "Well, madam, wouldn't it be lovely if we could get to know each other a little? I am sure that it is an unbearable burden for a tender female like yourself to manage such an estate on her own and…"

Daniel straightened and crossed his arms in front of his chest.

At the same time, Dame Arabella had obviously had enough and jumped up. "Mr Winslow, I am far less tender than it may seem and quite happy, no, even proud to manage this estate. I have no idea who you are, where you come from, or who put the silly notion into your head that I might be open to your misplaced advances." Her eyes spewed angry fire.

Despite his superior height he appeared strangely lost, clearly not having anticipated such a reaction. "So, you're not interested in giving me…"

"No!" she interrupted him energetically. "Leave my house immediately!"

Daniel had expected him to retreat in the face of such a rebuttal. To his amazement, he did not.

"My dear madam, there is no reason to get so upset. Please, do sit back down and have some tea. Such excitement is not good for a lady." He gently took her elbow and tried to lead her back to the chair. She ripped her arm out of his grasp and looked to Daniel for help while seething with indignation.

"Mr Winslow, the mistress of this house has asked you to leave," Daniel said, much more calmly than he felt. He pumped his lungs full of air and tensed every muscle in his upper body like he did when trying to impress an unruly young horse. Even if he was only slightly taller than Mr Winslow, he was certainly much stronger than the older man, who didn't look as if he had ever had to work a single day in his life.

The subtle threat registered with Mr Winslow who acknowledged it with an unbelieving start.

Slowly, Daniel raised his hand and pointed at the door. When the man still didn't move, Daniel took a step towards him. Mr Winslow looked around once more and fled. In the entrance hall they heard him call for his footman and shortly after that, receding hoofbeats told them that their unwanted visitor had gone for good.

Dame Arabella sighed deeply. "Thank you, Daniel," she said quietly and dropped on the chair. "Do you know now why I wanted you with me?"

He remained where he was and nodded.

"Who do these men think they are? They know nothing about me. They breeze in here and believe they can sweet-talk me into handing them my inheritance. And if that doesn't work, a hint of intimidation will certainly make the little missy docile!" Her fury brought her to her feet again. "A few weeks ago, there was another one who dared come here, just like this Mr Winslow. Do you have any idea how many proposals I have received by letter since Christmas? From complete strangers?"

Daniel shook his head in surprise. He wasn't comfortable with this conversation at all.

"Three! Three letters from strangers who want to marry me without ever having seen me. They don't want me, Daniel. They want Brigham Hall." Jaundiced, she crossed her arms and stood by the window in exactly the same spot Mr Winslow had stood before. "Over my dead body," she added softly.

Daniel was silent. What could he say? Of course, he couldn't condone Mr Winslow's behaviour, and inwardly grinned at the hot-headed response of his mistress. Grinned, yes, but full of respect. She was a fighter and extremely intelligent. And she had a heart for everyone in her care, man, woman, child, or beast, unlike most others of her class. Those who belonged to Brigham Hall should have a good life.

"Do you think I should marry, Daniel? Do you think I'm too tender to manage the estate?" she asked right into his thoughts.

Daniel cleared his throat. "Well, I don't regard it as wrong to marry," he said and felt himself blush. "But certainly not for the reasons these gentlemen seem to focus on."

She gave a short, bitter laugh, and then slowly walked up to him. "I will talk to Mr Ainsworth. I want him to draw up a marriage contract securing all my rights. And if another opportunist shows up, I'll tell him he can gladly marry me, but I will remain mistress of Brigham Hall." She laughed again, amused this time. "That will probably get rid of them more effectively than a rifle."

Daniel had to laugh as well when he imagined Mr Winslow's face upon sight of such a contract.

Dame Arabella stopped two steps away from him and looked into his eyes, while the amused smile still played on her lips. "There is only one man I would marry," she said nearly inaudibly, but her gaze spoke volumes.

Daniel almost choked. He hardly dared breathe. She could not possibly mean him! He stepped back, stiffened, and studied the tips of his shoes.

"Daniel?" she asked softly.

His gaze touched her briefly before returning to the carpet. "Madam," he mumbled, embarrassed.

She came another step closer. "I distinctly remember what it was like to sit in your lap and cry my heart out while you held me," she whispered.

His eyes widened at the memory and now he looked at her, incapable of looking anywhere else. What did he think? That she had been too frightened that night to remember anything? The realization that she might think of this tender moment as often as he did hit him like a bolt of lightning. There was more. "Where is that man, Daniel? Where is that man who comforted me in that terrible stormy night? Where is that man who gave me apples and breadcrusts for my horse – against his master's will? Where is that man – the only one ever to care about my fate? Your open-hearted kindness was balm to my tortured soul. Why are you so distant now? So formal?"

She almost did it. Her pleading words crawled under his skin and made his heart pound. Just one step and he could enfold her in his arms. But what would follow? As overwhelmingly beautiful this idea was, it could not, it must not be! After years of ignominy, she was finally back where she belonged. Should he be the reason she was vilified again? This wasn't about him and his feelings, perhaps not even hers. There was much more at stake. Of course, she was attracted to him because of his kindness but it couldn't be more than an infatuation. He mustn't encourage her in the least, so he pulled himself together and stared ahead again. "You are now the mistress of Brigham Hall. Such behaviour would be highly improper," he replied roughly.

She started as if he had slapped her and involuntarily stepped back. "Is that the only thing standing between us?" she asked tonelessly.

He took a deep breath and briefly looked into her eyes once more. "It is everything standing between us," he said, turned with a slight bow and swiftly left the room. When the door closed behind him, it had something final about it.

The Silent Maid

Brigham Hall, January 18, 1712

My dearest Mother,

I could do with your calming hand on my head. How I loved to sit by your chair when you knitted. Ever so often, your hand would come down to me and stroke my hair. It was my peace. When that happened, I knew everything was all right. For too long, I've had to miss your touch.

It's a blessing that we can at least write letters and be close to each other in our thoughts.

Yes, you will guess that something unusual has happened, confusing me. I cannot write of it to you, Mother. As if fearing to release an evil, irresistible bane, I do not dare to place the words on paper.

I pray that the Holy Ghost of our Lord will give me perseverance and strength to remain irreproachable. More than ever, I dive into the word of God, although it gives me little comfort at the moment. The daily challenges are overwhelming, and I hold on to the thought that without the word of God, long ago I would have spiralled downwards. So, I stay firm, barely, but I stay firm.

With great longing,

Your loving son,

Daniel

23 Riding

DANIEL WAS AMAZED. The weak rays of the late morning sun slanted through the windows of the riding arena. Fine dust stirred up by the horse's hooves danced in the light and turned what he saw into something derived from a fairy tale.

Chauncey had asked his permission to ride Thunderboy. Somehow, Daniel had suppressed the fact that the stallion was already eighteen years old and had been trained by Sir Nathaniel, who had been a lover of the classical art of riding. It was due to a trip to Europe in his younger years that the baronet had built the arena at Brigham Hall. He had gone as far as Vienna, where he had visited the famous Spanish Riding School, sadly damaged by the war with the Turks. Nevertheless, the thought of an indoor arena to train horses and riders had impressed him to such an extent that he had decided to build one upon his return to the estate. As long as he had lived, he had stayed in touch with one of the cavalry captains in Vienna and invested much energy into the training of the stallion. He couldn't compare with the Lippizaner horses in the Riding School, but showed some talent for advanced dressage.

Daniel had never seen anything like it. Chauncey made the stallion trot in one spot, step sideways in all paces, pirouette at a gallop and even rear up on command. It looked like a graceful dance and the longer Daniel watched, the more the wish blossomed in his heart to learn this as well.

When Chauncey finally let the reins slip from his hands so that the stallion could stretch his neck, Daniel was disappointed.

Chauncey patted the animal's sturdy neck and smiled at Daniel. "He's a bit stiff but he didn't forget a thing."

"Can you teach me?" Daniel asked, feeling like a little boy.

The older man laughed. "I have to. It's unheard of that the groom at Brigham Hall rides better than the Master of Horse!"

Daniel disregarded the words with a quick gesture. Such things weren't important to him. He had learned to appreciate Chauncey in the time he had been here. A quiet, conscientious man with a lot of horse sense and much more experience at Ole Pete's side than Daniel had enjoyed. Many years he had served under the old Master of Horse.

"The baronetess would like to make use of the good weather for a ride. Will you accompany her?" Daniel asked. He hoped for Chauncey's agreement so that he wouldn't have to be alone with her again.

"No, I wanted to work with Mr Ainsworth's gelding. He's doing very well, and we should be able to hand him over shortly."

Daniel nodded and hurried back to the stable. Inwardly, he steeled himself against Dame Arabella's disastrous effect on his emotions. She might not have bewitched him,

Riding

as Fanny and Riley had claimed, but even without curses or magic she had managed to steal his heart. He met Ruth on the way, leading the gelding to exchange horses with Chauncey. Out of the corner of his eye, Daniel registered an expectant smile he had never seen on her disfigured face before.

Willie had already saddled his horse and Dame Arabella was ready as well. Together they lead the horses into the yard, tightened the girths and mounted.

"A calm ride today, madam?" Daniel asked. He wasn't up to a wild chase.

"Why? Is something hurting you?" she replied boldly and laughed. She had never wasted another word on their conversation in the parlour, but ever since she had called him by his last name. Despite her clever words there was a certain sadness in her gaze.

Daniel shortened his reins because he expected her to gallop off again. She didn't, though, and kept her prancing mare at a walk.

"I think we should give them some time to warm up," she said, and Daniel relaxed again.

The cold winter air made their breath stand out in plumes and the frost on the pastures glittered like so many diamonds in the sun. It was beautiful.

For a while, they rode in silence, following the path down into the valley to the chapel. When they reached it, they stopped for a moment to contemplate the dreary ruin. It had been built of natural stone, not big, but elegant, with high, slender windows which had been destroyed in the fire. They would need sturdy, older trees for roofbeams. Even if the rebuilding had to wait, it couldn't hurt to be prepared. Daniel made a mental note to ask Harry to mark some trees they could use. Perhaps they should ride back through the forest so he could pick some out.

With a deep sigh, Dame Arabella rode on. After a short while, she said, "Let's ride a bit faster, I'm getting cold." Without waiting for a reply from Daniel, she galloped down the path.

They had been out for about half an hour when the weather suddenly turned. Mist began to spread and where the fickle January sun had provided a little warmth, it grew uncomfortably cold. Dame Arabella agreed to ride back. She wanted to double back, but Daniel still had the trees on his mind and suggested to follow a path through the woods on their right. They had to go slowly here because there were roots and stones making the footing tricky. In addition, branches blocked the path, so they had to frequently duck.

"I hope you know this path well, Mr Huntington," the baronetess said with a sceptical glance at the thickening fog.

"Don't worry, madam, I use it quite often. The horses will learn to watch their feet." Dame Arabella didn't reply. When Daniel looked over his shoulder, he saw that she was very tense and eyed the trees almost fearfully. Her mare's ears were playing incessantly as if she, too, didn't feel comfortable.

"Is everything all right, madam?" Daniel asked.

"Yes, yes," she responded quietly, although she didn't sound very convincing.

Daniel leaned forward, for the path now climbed a small rocky outcrop. Behind it, it crossed a hollow before reaching the same level as Brigham Hall. Several large boulders lay between the trees, presenting a challenge to some horses, which was another reason why Daniel used this path.

When they had reached the hollow, Daniel heard a strange noise behind him. It sounded almost like a whimper. He stopped and turned just in time to see Dame Arabella slip off her horse, her face pale as death. She seemed to sway on her feet and held on to her mare for a moment, before frantically looking all around and then sinking to the ground. She had left the mare standing there with the reins dangling down.

"Madam?" Daniel asked cautiously and dismounted as well. His mistress was crawling along the forest floor as if she was looking for something. He took the mare's reins, who suffered him to do so without trying to bite him. "Madam, what are you doing?"

Dame Arabella did not respond.

Daniel stepped closer, but right away she whipped around.

"Don't take the horses here!" she cried, eyes panicky.

Daniel could almost feel her heart racing, despite being a few feet away from her.

A sob tore out of her throat. With dirty hands and a deeply disturbed expression she simply sat where she was.

Daniel let go of the horses and was at her side in a few strides. "Madam," he whispered and put his arm around her. Carefully he pulled her to her feet.

She grabbed him and buried her face in his jacket, while another sob shook her. Only one word formed on her lips. "Riley."

The Silent Maid

DANIEL LIFTED HIS crying mistress back onto her horse and rode home with her as swiftly as possible. It wasn't very far now. As soon as they had left the hollow behind them, Brigham Hall could be seen shimmering through the trees.

Daniel's thoughts were racing. He hadn't seen anything he could have connected to her tormentor and shook his head involuntarily. Why should she react in such a strange way? Something had to be there.

He stopped at the front door and helped her dismount. She was still crying and let herself fall from the horse into his arms. Not having much choice, he carried her to the door and kicked it a few times.

Lizzie opened and screamed immediately. "What happened?" she asked and slapped her hands to her mouth.

"She's unhurt," Daniel said, trying to calm her. "We passed a place that seems to have brought up bad memories. At least I think so. Shall I carry her up to her room?"

Lizzie nodded and raced up the stairs ahead of him to open the door.

For a moment, Daniel stood helplessly in the middle of the large, almost round room. The windows offered a breath-taking view across the valley with the chapel in the background, hardly discernible in the mist now.

"Best put her on the bed," Lizzie said and led him to an alcove on the left, into which the bed was built.

Dame Arabella was still sobbing quietly and allowed herself to be laid on the mattress. She grabbed a pillow, hugged it, and rolled into a ball. Lizzie sat down with her and started caressing her cheek.

"Madam," she whispered, "what's wrong? Please, madam…"

Riding

Daniel felt his throat constrict. There was nothing he could do here, and he suddenly remembered the horses he had left standing outside. Turning on his heel, he fled downstairs.

Chauncey and Ruth were already taking care of the horses. To his amazement, Daniel saw that Ruth could handle the white mare without problems.

"What happened?" Chauncey asked. "She didn't fall, did she?"

"No." Daniel ground his teeth. He was terribly worried about his mistress. He had never imagined she could collapse like that from one second to the next. She had been quite normal at the beginning of the ride, a bit reckless even. If only he had listened to her and returned the same way they had come and not gone through the gloomy woods. Lizzie's descriptions of her nightmares suddenly came back to him. There had been trees involved, hadn't there? He growled.

"What is it?" Chauncey asked.

"Oh, I'm just mad at myself. I shouldn't have taken that path when the mist rose. It was a stupid idea."

"Daniel, how were you supposed to know that?" Chauncey tried to ease his mind, but it was no use. Daniel felt guilty.

Brigham Hall, January 29, 1712

Dearest Mother,

It's a tragedy. Dame Arabella has relapsed after the fog surprised us while riding in the forest. She doesn't speak anymore, nor leave her room, and merely stares straight ahead. Lizzie, her maid, is beside herself with worry. She keeps asking me to talk to the baroness, but what am I supposed to do? There's nothing she reacts to.

Oh Mother, it breaks my heart over and over when I see her like this. What has she had to live through? What's going on inside her head? How can we reach her? She seems so far away as if she had left this world.

Mother, please pray for her! Who, other than God, can help her live with her experiences?

If only I knew what to do for her…

Your desperate son,

Daniel

24
Relapse

"I HAVE FOUND IT!" Chauncey yelled in the hallway.

The kitchen door burst open. Everyone lowered their spoons and looked at him in confusion.

"The gold! I have found the gold!"

They were all on their feet in an instant, talking simultaneously, until Daniel shouted, "QUIET! Where?" he added in the ensuing silence.

"In the chapel."

The others immediately perked up, yet warily – the ruin was still not an easy topic.

"What are you doing in the chapel on a Sunday?" Ellie wanted to know.

Chauncey hesitated a moment. "I sort the stones," he admitted and waved at Daniel. "Come on! There are two heavy chests. We'll need a wagon."

On his way out, Daniel heard Ellie's confused question. "He's sorting stones? Why on earth is he sorting stones?"

In no time at all, the two men had hitched up and driven down the muddy track as fast as possible. Even though the rain had eased over the past few days, the ground hadn't dried much.

"Are you looking for stones we can use for rebuilding?" Daniel asked.

Chauncey nodded. "I can't find peace of mind. Ever since the baronetess has lapsed into this condition, I go down there every Sunday to clear out as much as possible. Today, I went a bit further. I remembered a crypt below the chapel. And I found the entrance."

"And that's where he hid the gold?"

"Yes." Chauncey fell silent, as he usually did when talk turned to Riley.

"How did you get along with him back then?" Daniel probed.

Chauncey clenched his jaws. Daniel thought he wouldn't answer, but he did after all. "I never trusted him. I often warned the baronet that Riley was cheating him. But I had no proof, except the way he looked at Sir Nathaniel when he didn't notice. The hatred in that look. The contempt. I always wondered why he hated him so much when he hadn't only saved his life but opened up opportunities for him he never would have had otherwise. One day, he dropped a remark that made me see it. We had gelded a young stallion. He patted its neck and said, 'Now you're nothing, too.' I knew at once what he meant. And how deep his self-hatred went. A man who considers himself nothing cannot love the man who secured this existence." Chauncey was silent for a while. "I was the first one who had to leave. Riley knew I didn't believe a word he said. He kicked me out even before we stopped searching for Arabella. I came back a few times in secret. Looked for her. But I couldn't find her. At some point, I gave up."

They had reached the chapel and climbed down from the wagon.

Relapse

"Don't we need lights?" Daniel asked.

"There's a lamp still down there," Chauncey replied and led Daniel over mountains of rubble to the back of the chapel, where a large part of the walls remained intact. They went down narrow stairs into the crypt where the lamp was still burning. With a dramatic gesture, Chauncey threw back the lid of the first chest. It was filled to the brim with all sorts of coins, gold, silver and copper.

"Unbelievable," Daniel murmured, awe-struck. "Can we manage, just the two of us?"

Chauncey laughed. "Now we'll see how strong you are!"

"We should have brought Dob along," Daniel groaned halfway up the stairs. They couldn't walk abreast, so much of the weight rested on Daniel's bent back, who was in front.

"Let's rest at the top of the stairs," Chauncey grunted, obviously not much better off.

They sat the chest down with a metallic clank and rested for a moment.

"Do you have ropes in the wagon?" Daniel asked. "We could attach them to the handles and put them over our shoulders to distribute the weight better."

"Good idea." Chauncey disappeared and returned moments later with the ropes. In this way they managed to lug the chests across the debris and load them onto the waggon one after the other.

"I'll get the lamp, then we can go. I just hope we don't get stuck in the mud."

Twice they had to get off on the way back to help the horse pull the cart out of a hole. When they reached the yard, dirty and exhausted, they were met by everyone staring curiously at them.

"You took a long time," Willie said and tried to climb onto the wagon, but Dob plucked him down again.

"Harry, Dob, would you carry one of the chests into the office?"

"Can we look inside?" Tom asked and reached for the lid of the closest chest. Mo was also stretching his neck to get a good look.

"No!" Daniel chided the boys. "Don't touch!"

The four of them carried the chests into the house and placed them next to the other cash supplies.

Daniel felt sick as he looked at the treasure at his feet. Short-tempered, he drove all the others out of the office and locked the door. Essentially, he trusted everyone working on the estate at the moment, but the words 'do not lead me into temptation' suddenly appeared to him to be a more valuable treasure than the one behind the door.

Everyone met in the kitchen, and Daniel and Chauncey received ale and bread to renew their strength.

"Did you inform Dame Arabella?" Daniel asked Lizzie.

"Yes, I told her. But she didn't respond," the maid answered sadly.

"What are we going to do with it?" Molly wanted to know.

"We will inform Mr Ainsworth tomorrow and then I'm afraid it will have to be counted," Daniel said, not sounding overly enthusiastic.

He hoped Mr Ainsworth would have time for a meeting at short notice. He was missing the baroness' help. When she had been all right, she had taken over more and more responsibility, and Daniel had been glad about it. It was a lot easier for him to make decisions if someone else took the lead. Now that he thought about it, they had worked together very well, and he hadn't minded in the least that she had the last say in all things. Only his emotions had been in a catastrophic state, especially after Mr Winslow's visit. At least that had eased since he wasn't close to her all the time anymore. On the other hand, he now missed her terribly, although he didn't dare visit her in her tower room. It wasn't proper.

"Daniel?"

He jerked.

"Are you still with us?" Ellie asked, amused.

"Sorry, I was lost in thought."

"So I've noticed." She laughed and put a hand on his shoulder. "Go and rest, Daniel Huntington. You have done enough for today."

He gave her a grateful smile and took refuge in his cottage. Lying down on his bed, his hand reached for the Bible, but he didn't get around to reading. He had fallen asleep before he could ever open it.

MR AINSWORTH ARRIVED up the next day after Daniel had sent Willie over with a message. It was in many ways a test for the boy: for the first time out on his own on a horse, finding the right way to Flamborough and then to the solicitor's house, not lose the message and not get lost on the way home. He didn't arrive back at Brigham Hall much before Mr Ainsworth himself, but he had mastered the challenge and went everywhere to receive praise for his achievement, until Chauncey pulled him out of the herb garden by his ear where he had been telling Ellie and Harry about his ride. Daniel watched in amusement as the boy was sent back to work.

Daniel received the solicitor with great relief and led him into the office.

Mr Ainsworth was speechless when he saw the two chests, reaching inside and letting the coins tinkle back down.

"Inconceivable," he murmured.

"How much do you think it is?" Daniel asked, but the solicitor shook his head.

"It's impossible to tell. I'll have to count it…" He fell silent once more.

"Would you do that?" Daniel cast him a hopeful glance.

"One could sort and weigh it, which is likely to take as long as counting it, though. It's all higgledy-piggledy." He contemplated the coins thoughtfully, until his head snapped up and he looked at Daniel. "Did you ask me something?"

"I really don't have the time to count it and have no idea how to go about it. Would you take care of it?"

"Yes, I can do that. How is Dame Arabella? Any change? Does she know about the find?"

"Lizzie has told her, but she didn't react. For weeks she has only been sitting there. We have to cancel all her appointments and hope there won't be any rumours. Lady Dursley has asked to see her several times."

A sombre silence ensued.

"Well," Mr Ainsworth finally said with determination, "it is as it is. We have work to do. If you would provide me with ink, paper, and a few baskets, I'll get to it."

"Of course, sir. I'm afraid I have to leave now. The tenants will be meeting at Mr Miller's to talk about the use of the fields." Daniel set out paper and ink on the desk. "I'll let Ellie know to bring you the baskets." He gave the solicitor a nod and went to the door. "One more thing. You can take your gelding with you if you like. He's ready. Visit Chauncey in the stable if you need a break from counting. He will show you everything."

"Thank you, Mr Huntington. I'm glad to hear it."

Daniel wound the long scarf his mother had knitted for him around his neck. The wind was bitingly cold and the ground frozen solid, despite it being mid-February.

It had been difficult to convince the tenants to join the meeting. Everyone was used to doing things his own way in his own time. In their opinion, Riley had meddled way too much, and Daniel gave the impression of wanting to do the same. His goals were quite different, though. Daniel wanted the farmers of the Brigham estate to regard themselves as a group, a union, where each helped the other. They should share their experience and thereby profit from each other. Whether he would be able to convey this idea to them remained to be seen.

He was grateful when he reached Miller's hut and could enter the warmth. There was little room with four tenants present, one of which was Mrs Weldon with her children. Harper had brought his son George.

Mr Miller greeted Daniel with a handshake and then handed him a cup of herb tea, which he gladly accepted.

"Do you know if anyone else is coming?" he asked after nodding at everyone.

"That's all there is," Miller said. "The other farms are currently vacant."

"Not that the Scotsman's hut is any good," someone else stated and everyone hummed their agreement.

Daniel thought for a moment. "You're right, I forgot." He would have loved to run out again. How could he possibly *forget* giving notice to three tenants?

"Is it true that the mistress is sick?" Mrs Weldon asked.

Daniel rubbed his hand over his face and nodded. "Yes, she is – she is sick." How should he explain that? He didn't want the tenants to think their mistress was crazy.

"You're very worried about her, I can see that," Mrs Weldon said softly. "What can we do?"

"Pray," Daniel replied spontaneously and closed his eyes for a moment. He felt that Mrs Weldon's remark had offered both an explanation and an excuse for his failure. When he opened his eyes again, he looked at them all with determination. "Pray and take care that the estate is not run down. An attitude such as Kerr showed is a shame on Brigham Hall. We can all live here very well if we cooperate and support each other. Each of you knows the land he is working on. In addition, we now have use of the fields on the farms currently not tenanted. Perhaps you have fields that produce poor crops and would be better suited as hayfields or pastures. Perhaps you have rich ground somewhere currently not used. I want us to look at everything together, see what we have and how we can make the best of it in the future."

His words were met with approving nods. Then they put their heads together and made plans.

Relapse

When Daniel rode home that night, he felt totally exhausted on the one hand and elated on the other. There had been a lot of heated discussions and at the start, everyone had tried to get an advantage for himself. Daniel had no idea how he had done it, but after stoically repeating the same things over and over, the hard heads had softened and one by one the tenants had realized how much they would gain if they helped their neighbours.

Daniel's harshest enemy in the discussion had been Riley. While he trotted home as fast as the frozen ground allowed, he tried to count how often he had heard the words "But the baronet had…". Riley had driven a wedge between the people. He had sown mistrust and fear. He had put an immense amount of pressure on the tenants and constantly threatened to kick them out. When Daniel had explained to them that he wanted to keep them as long as possible, both Mrs Weldon and Mrs Miller had burst into tears. Gratitude was a much better motivation than fear, Daniel thought to himself.

It was way past dark when he reached Brigham Hall. His fingers rigid with cold, he unsaddled the horse and fed it. He noticed that Mr Ainsworth hadn't taken his gelding with him, yet.

Exhausted, he dragged himself into the kitchen. Nobody was around. A touched smile crossed his features when he found a covered dish in the larder, though. Ellie had thought of him. He sat down at the table and ate slowly. A strange melancholia gripped him. He should be proud of what he had achieved this afternoon. The problem was that he wasn't sure if he had achieved it. Some of the things he had said had sounded alien to him, as if someone else was using his mouth to speak. Had that been

God's guidance? He didn't know. At the moment, he felt as if he didn't know anything anymore. What was he doing here? He was a simple groom. Looking at Chauncey, he wasn't even Master of Horse. Chauncey knew much more than Daniel ever would.

"A romantic dreamer, that's what you are," his father used to say to him. As a child, Daniel had dreamed of one day owning a large estate with lots of servants. He had stood inside the chicken coop and pretended that the chickens were his servants, while he was the gracious lord feeding them. He had received a lot of slaps for wasting the feed in his eagerness. How old had he been? Four? Five? He shook his head and got up, cleared his plate away and went to the office. The door was locked. Mr Ainsworth had probably taken the key with him because Daniel had returned so late.

Lizzie came down the stairs with a tray in her hands. When she saw Daniel, she stopped, appearing very pale and tired.

"How are you?" Daniel asked.

"She is…" Lizzie paused, suddenly realizing that Daniel hadn't asked after Dame Arabella. "Oh, I'm all right I guess," she said uncertainly. Then she sighed. "It hurts so much to see her like that. It's much worse than before, when she was only a silent maid. She didn't talk then and was constantly in fear of the baronet, but at least she was alive. Now she seems like a doll to me. I miss her laughter and her brisk manner." A tear rolled down her cheek which she clumsily wiped off on her shoulder without dropping anything from her tray. "I'll take this away," she added softly.

Daniel preceded to open the kitchen door for her. Lizzie smiled gratefully at him.

He should have gone to his cottage then. To his surprise, his feet carried him up the stairs and down the long hallway to Dame Arabella's room. He knocked and entered, despite not receiving an answer. Apart from the fire, the room was in shadows. The young woman was sitting in her armchair, gazing into the flames. She was wrapped in a thick blanket and her hair hung in a simple braid down her back. Quietly, Daniel closed the door and slowly approached her. She did not react. For a while he stood there watching the light dance on her face. She seemed so sad it felt as if he was pulled into a bottomless chasm. All at once, the burden was too great to bear and he sank down on his knees next to her, leaned his hands and his forehead on the armrest of her chair and let his tears flow.

There was enough to cry for. Her lost childhood. The pain she'd had to endure. The silence holding her captive. He cried for his mother whom he hadn't seen in such a long time, for the horses he hardly had time for anymore, and for the responsibility all but crushing him. He even cried for Riley whose heart had chosen the path of hatred instead of gratefulness.

Daniel didn't know how long he had cried. At some point, the flood of tears ebbed away, and a fragile peace entered his heart. Only when he straightened up, did he notice her hand lying on his head. With a slow movement she returned it to her lap. Otherwise, she didn't stir, didn't look at him. But her cheeks were just as wet with tears as his.

Brigham Hall, February 18, 1712

Dear Mother,

There is a slight improvement in Dame Arabella's condition. She is eating unassisted again and allows herself to be dressed. Once in a while, she will make eye contact with the people in the room, but she still doesn't speak. Lizzie is happy, anyway. Since it's finally getting warmer, she is taking her mistress for little walks to the horses, hoping this will revive her further.

It took Mr Ainsworth three days to count all the money in the chests. More than three thousand pounds, a truly grand treasure. What did Riley want with it? It is beyond me.

With this fortune at our disposal, Chauncey and I have now decided to pursue rebuilding the chapel. Mr Ainsworth is strictly opposed to it, unable to name any logical arguments, however, except that it is too expensive. I assume that his own lack of faith has much to do with his conviction. Since Dame Arabella had been quite clear on the matter and in view of her family history, I don't see any reason why we shouldn't respect her wishes. We have now hired two men to clear the ruin of rubble. They are working hard and making good progress.

By now, Mr Ainsworth has taken his new horse with him and is very happy with it.

If only the baronetess would return to her former self, everything would be perfect.

Thanking you for your loyal prayers I remain,

Your loving son,
Daniel

25
Bones

DANIEL CAME BACK from another meeting with Miller and Harper Snr and saw Molly waiting for him by the garden gate. He stopped his horse next to her.

"Good thing you're back, sir," she said.

He twitched. While all the other servants called him by his first name, Molly kept calling him sir as if he was the master.

"What is it, Molly?" he asked.

"The workmen are waiting in the kitchen, sir. They want to talk to you. Wouldn't say what about."

That didn't portend well.

"Tell them I'll be with them directly." He dismounted, led the horse into the stable yard and handed the reins to Tom. Then he rushed off to the kitchen.

The workmen jumped up as soon as he entered.

"A good day to you. Is there a problem?" Daniel asked.

Mo and Molly stopped their work with undisguised curiosity.

"Well sir, perhaps we could speak in private?" one of the workmen suggested guardedly.

"Follow me." Daniel led the men into the office.

Following Mr Ainsworth's advice, they had stored the money in the cellar in a secret chamber which could be secured with an iron grid. The chamber was covered by a cupboard. Daniel wasn't sure if anyone apart from Mr Ainsworth knew about this hiding place. Perhaps not even Dame Arabella. In any case, Daniel was relieved to have the money out of the office.

He closed the door behind the men and went over to the desk, looking questioningly at them both.

"We have found bones, sir," one of them said and shuddered. "It is… that is to say… it looks like a human skeleton. Or parts thereof. Pretty charred and…" He fell silent. The other workman said nothing.

Daniel needed a moment to grasp what the man was saying. Bones in the chapel. Those could be nothing else but the earthly remains of the former Baronet, Dame Arabella's father. Hadn't they buried him? There was a large mausoleum in the graveyard by the chapel for the baronets. He had naturally assumed that the body had been retrieved and laid to rest there.

"What are we supposed to do?" the first workman asked, confused by Daniel's silence.

"I'm sorry, I… this is irritating. How far did you get?"

"We have stacked all the usable stones by the wall, just like you ordered, sir. Most of the rubble we threw in the ditch you showed us. There's a bit left."

"Good. You may take the rest of the day off and return day the after tomorrow. I will see to it that the bones are properly buried."

Both men looked at Daniel, eyes wide. "You know who it is?"

"Yes," Daniel replied quietly, "I believe I do. It's the baronetess' father who died in the flames in the chapel. It couldn't be anyone else. I wasn't here back then, and I thought he had already been buried. But don't worry, we will do that now." He could read it on the men's faces that they were thinking about vengeful spirits and other spooky tales and preferred not to mention that the baronet had been murdered. Otherwise, they would probably never come back.

When Daniel took Chauncey aside and told him about what the workmen had found, he blanched.

"He told us he had searched the ruins shortly after the fire and had only found a few bones. Everything else had been burnt."

Daniel didn't have to ask who 'he' was.

"I have seen him crawl among the stones myself. He even burned his fingers because some spots were still hot. God, what a hypocrite."

"We have to tell the baronetess," Daniel whispered.

"Are you insane? She still hasn't recovered, and you want to dish her such a shock?"

"Perhaps it will bring her back," Daniel stammered dismally. He didn't really believe it.

"Right, or it will push her over the edge irretrievably and she will go completely mad. What kind of bones did we bury back then?" Chauncey started running in circles.

"What if Riley told her everything? She said to me that he tortured her with words day after day."

"That dog!" Chauncey called and slammed his fist against the next beam. Then he leaned his head against it and closed his eyes.

"Whatever he did or said, we need to honour the remains and bury them properly. Do we have a decent chest we can place them in? I don't suppose we will need a coffin." Daniel tried to steer the groom's thoughts onto a more practical track.

On the way to the chapel, Daniel wondered whether to tell the servants about this discovery or not. None of them knew the old baronet and the spooky tales revolving around the chapel had only just been revived by the rebuilding project.

"We shouldn't tell anyone about it. Thank God the workers kept quiet," Daniel said.

Chauncey looked sceptically at him. "It won't be a secret for long. Apart from that, they will want to know why we are going down here with a wagon again. No, I think we should put our cards on the table. The baronet was a good man. His memory should be honoured."

Daniel couldn't contradict him.

When they reached the chapel, they were surprised at the amount of work the two men had already done. Most of the chapel was passable again. Only in the front, where the altar must have been, was a larger heap of rubble left. Two shovels and a pick lay on it. Daniel searched the ground at the edge of the heap and finally found what the workers had described: a scull as well as several smaller bones, perhaps from a hand. The way the tools were lying there, the workers had dropped everything and run off in shock.

"Here," Daniel said softly and brought Chauncey to his side.

He went on his knees beside Daniel and reached for the scull but didn't dare touch it after all. Tears brimmed in his eyes. "I'll fetch the chest," he said hoarsely.

Daniel couldn't blame him. His throat felt tight as well, not because he'd had a special relationship with the dead man, but because the thought of dying, and then being left under such a heap of rubble for years, scared him somehow.

Carefully, he started to clear the dirt behind the scull away with his hands. He soon noticed that it was useless, so he took the shovel after all and carefully took away layer after layer. He absolutely wanted to avoid driving the shovel between the bones.

"There!" Chauncey suddenly said next to him.

He was right. Quite some distance from the scull they found a rib poking out of the dust.

Daniel had reverently placed the scull and the other bones in the chest. Each further bone they found joined them. A lot of them were charred or broken, though much less than Daniel had expected.

"What is that?" he asked, feeling around in the dust. Then he pulled out a knife.

The whole time they had been working, Chauncey had kept up well, but now he broke down. "He killed him with that!" he cried, and then screamed all of his anger into the air, making the nearby woods echo with it. He grabbed the knife and rubbed it clean on his jacket. "It was the baronet's. Riley killed him with his own knife." Stunned, Chauncey shook his head.

Daniel put a hand on his shoulder and took the knife from him. "Come. I think we're done here. We will put the chest in the mausoleum, and I'll tell Dame Arabella what has happened. And I'll bring her this." He held up the knife and then put it away before helping Chauncey to his feet.

DANIEL WASHED AND changed before going to Dame Arabella. He felt that dust, ashes, and death were clinging to him and didn't wish to approach his mistress like that. It was late already, but Lizzie assured him that the baroness was still up. He had carefully cleaned and polished the precious knife with its buckhorn handle.

"Madam?" he said quietly upon entering the room.

She sat with her back to the door and turned her head a little, but not enough to look at him. He came nearer and stood in front of her. For the first time for many weeks their eyes met. In that instant, he felt a recognition and longing that took his breath away. It lasted only a moment and she retreated into herself once more, turning her gaze away from him. He exhaled slowly. Then he pulled out the knife and held it out to her, handle first.

"Do you recognize this?" he asked gently, trying to prepare for all sorts of reactions.

Her gaze wandered over to his hand and remained there. It was all that happened.

He swallowed a few times before finding his voice again. "Perhaps Lizzie has told you that we have started work on the chapel," he began. "The workers found something under the debris." He hesitated. It was really hard. Was he doing the right thing? Chauncey still wasn't convinced.

She was staring at the knife, unmoving, silent.

"We… we found this. Chauncey said it belonged to your father. It was him…" *God help me,* Daniel pleaded inwardly. "We found your father, madam. His bones. We have taken them to the mausoleum in the graveyard. If you wish, madam, I will let the priest come and bless his final resting place."

Daniel didn't know what he had expected, but that she showed no reaction whatsoever even in the face of this news confounded him. He dropped the hand with the knife.

Her gaze moved back to the fire.

With a tight throat, Daniel put the knife on the table and left the room.

The Silent Maid

Brigham Hall, February 26, 1712

Dear Mother,

Thank you so much for your uplifting words. You know me too well and read between the lines. I keep telling myself that God didn't place me here without a reason and yet my heart falters over and over.

Perhaps you are right. I cannot be happy while my mistress is in this state, which unfortunately hasn't changed.

For a while, everyone in the house slept badly and the boys were haunted by nightmares. Harry's horror tales, which he told with even more enthusiasm than ever before, have surely added to the problem. Despite the eerie history, everyone had hoped that the discovery of her father's remains would pull Dame Arabella from her lethargy, but no. Despite holding a ceremony in the graveyard in honour of the late baronet, with all the servants present, she showed no reaction.

I have to admit that it made me lose my faith that she can ever be freed from her predicament. What a cruel fate!

At our last meeting, Mr Ainsworth brought forth heavy accusations against me for making the baronetess exhaust herself with my attitude. I should have spared her instead of involving her in all the dealings of the estate. As if that had been an option!

No, the management of Brigham Hall wasn't too much for her. She grew more and more into it as she went. The support she needed was of a practical nature, but all ideas and decisions were hers. The whole time I had the impression she was much more at ease with making decisions than I was.

In any case, he now wants to retreat as he regards his task as fulfilled. I must say that his words disappointed me and I feel deserted by him.

Thank God, everyone on the estate is sticking together and doing their best to keep everything running. A truly strong community, which I have never encountered before, and for which I am deeply grateful.

Yours,

Daniel

26
Forgiveness

DANIEL LAY AWAKE. There was a new moon; the day had been fairly mild, and he was full of energy. He had sat up late over a letter to his mother, but even after that he hadn't felt like sleeping. Now he was in bed, staring into the dark, while his thoughts jumped from one topic to the next.

When he was finally about to drift off, somebody beat on his door.

"Daniel!" It was Chauncey.

Daniel jerked out of bed and pulled the door open. The light of the torch in Chauncey's hand made him squeeze his eyes shut.

"She's gone!" the groom cried. "Get dressed, we have to find her!"

"Who is gone?" Daniel asked, confused. Did one of the mares break out?

"The baronetess! Lizzie and Ellie have already turned the house upside down but couldn't find her. Harry and Dob are in the forest and I have searched every corner of the stables. I'm on my way to the pastures now. Perhaps she went down to her mare."

Shock raced through Daniel's veins. What if she'd had another nightmare and run off? She could be anywhere.

Forgiveness

Worry tightened his throat. He didn't want to lose her! He forced himself to think calmly. A hunch popped into his mind and quickly grew into certainty. "I'll check the chapel," he said hoarsely and grabbed his trousers. Hastily he got dressed and slipped his boots on. The night was cold, despite the warm day, so he pulled on a coat and a scarf as well.

"I thought you might want to go down there. Here's a storm lantern. If you find her, signal me and I'll come down with horses. Good luck."

They both started in the same direction but split up after a short while.

Daniel jogged slowly down into the valley, systematically checking the area on both sides of the path. Apart from a fox, he couldn't make out anything. His heart beat loudly in his ears and halfway down he had to slow to a walk. Wheezing, he went on, occasionally glancing over his shoulder to see if Chauncey was signalling him.

The night was pitch dark; the sky hidden behind a thick layer of clouds so that not a single star was visible. In front of him, Daniel saw the crumbled walls of the chapel rise up, dancing spookily in the light of his lantern. Images of the charred skull amidst the rubble popped into his head.

"Of course, what else?" he grumbled.

An owl hooted in the nearby forest and made Daniel jump. Trembling, he lifted the lantern and illuminated the graveyard. There was nothing to be seen except the bizarre shadows of tombstones and crosses. With a hammering heart, Daniel stopped and listened. He could neither make himself step between the dark walls of the chapel nor open the squeaking gate of the graveyard – as if it would disturb the peace of the dead. Should he call out? No sound came from his throat.

Fainthearted coward, he chided himself, which didn't help in the least. He started and whipped around. Was there a noise? Something flapped past him with a shrill tweet. He lifted the lantern in vain. Probably a bat. If he didn't get a grip soon, he would wet himself in fright. Daniel gritted his teeth and peered up the hill once more. No signals in sight.

Turning around again, he stepped up to the gate of the graveyard and directed the light of the lantern straight at the mausoleum. A whimper reached his ears even before he had really noticed the shape on the ground.

"Madam?" he croaked and opened the gate, which screeched terrifyingly. He hastened through, anyway, and had reached the shape in a few strides. Relief flooded him. It was her. "Madam," he repeated and squatted down next to her.

She was kneeling on the steps of the mausoleum, her hair spilling freely down her back, her cheeks covered in tears, while her fingers dug into the ground and ripped out the grass in tufts.

Carefully he touched her shoulder. She wore nothing but her shift and a coat. Her feet were bare.

A new fear gripped him. Had she lost her mind completely?

"Arabella," he whispered full of worry.

She was crying louder now, rocking back and forth without reacting to him.

Daniel didn't know what to do. The only thing he could think of was praying.

"Our Father in heaven, hallowed be thy name. Thy kingdom come, thy will be done, on earth as it is in heaven…" he murmured, tonelessly at first, and then growing stronger. He sensed the familiar words strengthening him. "…give us this day our daily bread and forgive us our sins, as we forgive those who sin against us…"

The woman's crying lessened. She seemed to listen to his voice as if spellbound.

"And do not lead us into temptation but deliver us from evil. For thine is the kingdom and the power and the glory forever, amen." He paused. She had stopped plucking grass. Lacking a better idea, he started over. "Our Father in heaven…"

She was listening to him. By the light of the lantern, he could see the crying ease and her face relax. The rocking stopped, too. Almost devoutly she sat beside him. Then her lips began to move. Daniel started the prayer over and watched in fascination how she seemed to speak the words with him, though without a sound. Once. Once again. He closed his eyes and fervently prayed to God to save his mistress from the prison her mind was trapped in.

When he repeated the prayer the next time, the full meaning of the words hit him for the first time. "Give us this day our daily bread and forgive us our sins, as we forgive those who sin against us." He stopped.

She stopped as well and suddenly looked at him, completely conscious. "No," she sighed.

Daniel wanted to say the sentence again, but she didn't let him finish.

"No!" This time her answer was almost a roar, filled with anger and pain. She straightened, balled her fists and hammered them into the ground as hard as she could.

"You have to forgive him," Daniel said and held her outraged gaze.

"No!" she screamed at him. "He killed my father!" She struggled to her feet and Daniel jumped up with her. With another roar she started pummelling her fists against his chest. "He murdered him! He cut his throat right in front of my eyes, that bastard!"

Daniel caught her hands and held them tight. "Regardless," he insisted.

"No!" she yelled again and fought against him with all her might.

A wave of anger suddenly washed over Daniel like a foreign power simply carrying him away. "You have to!" he rounded on her. "You have to forgive him!"

"Never!" she hissed and shook her head, making her hair fly in all directions. "He wanted to starve me to death, but I didn't starve! He wanted to work me to death, but I just worked on and on! He couldn't kill me; he was bound to me! He wanted to control me, but in the end, I controlled *him*! He couldn't take one step without fearing my escape! He tortured me, he tortured us both for years! I shall forgive him that? No!" She tried to twist her arms from Daniel's grip, but he held on.

"You have to forgive him!" he repeated. He would have loved to shake her. "If you don't, he will forever torture you, even from his grave! You will never be free."

"No!" she yelled again and strove to pull away.

Daniel kept his grip locked. "Forgive him!"

"No!" she called again, sounding a bit less angry and desperate.

"Forgive us our sins as we forgive those who sin against us. Say it!"

Forgiveness

Suddenly, all fight went out of her. She dropped to her knees and started to cry again. Then such an agonized howl rose from her throat, that Daniel let go of her and stumbled backwards. She doubled over and screamed until the last iota of breath was squeezed from her lungs. She put her head on her knees and remained there, drawing a trembling breath.

Something made Daniel approach and kneel beside her.

"Forgive us our sins as we forgive those who sin against us," he whispered insistently, time and again, hoping against all hope that she would be able to forgive. It was the only way to be freed from the inexplicable agony she had suffered.

Then he heard her breathless voice say the words. All the tension left her body at once and she leaned against him. In the same instant, the anger that had gripped him disappeared. Tenderly, he pulled Arabella into his arms and held her.

A strange image appeared before his inner eye: they were standing on the shore of a lake and watched a huge, dark ship drift away from them. She had held on to the ship's rope, but now it swam away on the waves and disappeared in the hazy distance.

A final sob shook her, then the tears ebbed away, and she calmed down.

"And lead us not into temptation but deliver us from evil. For thine is the kingdom and the power and the glory forever. Amen," Daniel finished the prayer.

The Silent Maid

DANIEL HAD NO idea how long they had sat there in the graveyard. All he knew was that a fundamental change had taken place – and that his legs were falling asleep. With the young woman in his arms, he struggled to his feet and somehow managed to snatch up the lantern on his way. Dame Arabella didn't stir, but it felt different than before. He stamped his feet a few times to revive them. By the time he had passed the gate, it was much better, and he started walking back to Brigham Hall with long strides.

Halfway there, he met Chauncey riding Thunderboy with another horse beside him. When he saw the burden Daniel was carrying, he whooped with joy and jumped to the ground. "Why didn't you signal me?" he called, relieved.

"I forgot," Daniel murmured.

"Where did you find her?"

"The graveyard."

Chauncey whistled. "And you carried her the entire way back? Come, I'll take her," he said and held out his arms.

Daniel felt an almost imperceptible tightening of her fingers gripping his coat. A quiet smile crossed his face.

"Just a moment," he said to Chauncey. "Madam, I can't carry you all the way back. If you will allow it, I will pass you to the care of Chauncey for a moment, mount the horse and then you can ride with me. Would that be acceptable?"

The grip on his coat eased.

Chauncey looked at him questioningly. Daniel merely nodded and handed the baroness over. Then he took Thunderboy's reins and swung up into the saddle. From there, he pulled Dame Arabella into his arms again. Chauncey raised an eyebrow but refrained from any comments. He took the lantern, mounted the second horse and together they rode back to Brigham Hall.

The house was brightly lit and busy as a beehive. Everyone was awake and had been searching for the mistress. Now that she was found, they all cheered and whooped. Daniel wasn't sure how Dame Arabella would react, but she did not resist being received by Dob who set her on her naked feet. At once, she was surrounded by the women, Lizzie first and foremost. She wrapped caring arms around her mistress and led her inside. Daniel remained in the saddle while congratulations for his successful search washed over him like a warm wave. He smiled and nodded, but his thoughts were elsewhere. Finally, he turned the stallion and rode to the stable, where Chauncey had already taken the saddle off his horse.

"Do you want me to do this?" he asked Daniel, who refused. He needed a moment to himself before facing the storm of questions. While his hands fulfilled the familiar tasks, his mind tried to process what had happened back there. It suddenly seemed as unreal as a dream.

Where had that anger he had felt come from? How had he known that she had to forgive Riley to be free? This thought had seemed totally alien and at the same time frightfully logical to him.

Had she forgiven him from her own free will? Had he forced her? Everything swam in his head. He sat on a box and put his head in his hands. He stayed like that for a long time until he had some sort of grip on the events. Sighing deeply, he rose and went back to the kitchen, where the others were awaiting his report.

Brigham Hall, February 27, 1712, before sunrise

Dear God,

As much as I love my mother, there are things that I cannot write even to her. Yet write I must, or I will go mad. I need to express my feelings somewhere so as not to choke on them. Lay all your troubles on me, you said, and that's what I will do.

The whole time I didn't want to look the truth in the eye. The whole time I pushed it away from me and I still don't see a chance of fulfilment, but I can no longer deny it: I love her.

There's nothing I want more than to call her mine and live every day in such intimacy as we shared on the back of that horse.

Oh Lord, I long for her full of tenderness and yet I dread our next meeting. It must not be! It cannot be.

What am I supposed to do?

Please Lord, take these feelings away from me so that I can meet her normally again. I'm constantly fleeing. To her, to flee my longing. Away from her, to flee temptation. I am torn like a flag in a storm, tossed about here and there by raging winds. I won't stand it much longer.

What is your will? Why have you put me here? Was my quest fulfilled last night? Was that my task, to lead her on the path of forgiveness?

Perhaps I should leave, although that thought is as alien as chopping off my own leg.

God, please be with me!

Your obedient servant

Daniel

27
Life

DANIEL OVERSLEPT. FOR the first time in his life, he had slept so long and soundly that he had no idea what was going on when he woke. Piece by piece, the events of the previous night returned to him. He crawled out of bed, rekindled the fire and thoughtfully contemplated the letter he had written before going to bed. His fingers stroked the words, then he took the sheet and ripped it lengthwise, once, and then a second time. He threw each shred into the flames, watching the paper turn brown, explode into flame and then turn to ashes. After that he washed, dressed, and went over to the house to see why nobody had roused him.

As a matter of fact, he was one of the first ones up. Although Ellie was already in the kitchen, she was moving sluggishly and yawned repeatedly. Chauncey followed Daniel on his heel, deep circles under his eyes. When he saw Daniel and Ellie, he started to laugh. "You two look exactly like I feel. I think none of us is up to much today."

Ellie merely shook her head and put a pot of fresh tea on the table.

"Did she speak?" Daniel asked after a while of enjoying their tea in silence.

"Not that I know of," Ellie replied. "But it was all such an excitement. Let's wait and see."

"I'm so glad you found her," Chauncey added.

In that moment, the door opened, and a beaming Lizzie entered the kitchen. Three pairs of eyes turned to her expectantly.

"She is awake and she's talking!" she called and clapped her hands for joy. "It's a good thing you're here, Daniel. She wants to see you. Ellie, do you have breakfast ready? Madam said she is very hungry."

Ellie jumped up. "Oh, not yet! Soon, though. We were still…"

Lizzie raised her hands. "Don't worry, there's no hurry. She said she understands perfectly if everyone is up a bit later today after the sleepless night."

Despite this message, Ellie couldn't be stopped. In no time at all she had cracked some eggs, thrown bacon into a pan, and set a few slices of bread to toast.

Daniel was still sitting at the table as if paralyzed. He would have loved to find some excuse as to why he couldn't go to see his mistress, but that was silly.

"Go on upstairs! She'll be glad to see you," prompted Lizzie.

Daniel took two steps at a time and hastened along the hallway, only to slow down before reaching her door and then stopping indecisively. He took several deep breaths. How torn he felt! He knocked.

"Come in!"

Daniel straightened, pushed out his chest and entered.

Dame Arabella was standing by the window. She was wearing a dark green dress; her hair was pinned up properly and her shoulders were covered by a yellow kerchief. Her entire posture was different from what Daniel had been used to seeing over the past weeks and months. Proud, energetic and with a perky smile, she turned to him. "Daniel," she said softly, "did you sleep at all? You look terribly tired." She came to him.

He gritted his teeth and shrugged. At the same time, he prayed she wouldn't put her hand on his arm again as she had done more than once when they had been alone. He cast a quick glance over his shoulder. Where was Lizzie with the breakfast? When he looked back at the baronetess, she had turned her back on him and returned to the window. For a while, she gazed out in silence. Daniel remained where he was, just in case.

"I would like to thank you, Mr Huntington," she finally said, much more formally than before.

Daniel sighed with relief.

"What you have done for me last night is of unimaginable value to me. I had not expected to be alive today."

Daniel flinched at these words. "What?" he asked in shock.

She turned to him again but didn't approach him this time. A sad smile was playing on her lips. "I hadn't seen any chance of living on with all of this. Everything seemed dark and despairing."

"And that's different now?" he asked nervously. With a start he remembered her father's knife which he had left on the table with her. If he hadn't found his mistress in time, would she…? He would have lost her forever. The realization made him shudder.

"Yes, it is different now. I'm not sure if it was the easiest way out to forgive Riley, but it was certainly the healthiest." She slowly moved into the middle of the room. "I had hoped…"

A clatter announced Lizzie's arrival with the breakfast. "Would you like to eat by the window, madam?" she asked.

"By the fire, please." She gave Daniel a long look but made no attempt to finish her sentence. "Once again, thank you, Mr Huntington. Please do only the most basic chores today and get some rest," she said and dismissed him with a nod.

He bowed and went back into the kitchen.

Lost in thought, he poked his breakfast. Had she had the knife with her? Would she truly have taken her own life? If he had been too late… Daniel couldn't swallow a single bite.

THE FIRST FOAL OF the year was born on March 10th and was quite a sensation on the estate, for it was as white as snow. As a matter of fact, Daniel and Chauncey noticed it late in the day because it had snowed in the night. Only when the snow had thawed by noon, everyone wondered at the white speck wandering about on the pasture.

With a mixture of relief and irritation, Daniel found during the following days that Dame Arabella was taking estate matters into her own hands, rarely consulting him. Only for dealings with the tenants, and if there were unannounced visitors, did she request his presence. The latter were coming ever more frequently, making Daniel wonder if someone was parading through the country with fanfares, announcing Dame Arabella's insufferable unmarried condition. She turned everyone down, politely but resolutely. On some days she sent the visitors away without receiving them.

Daniel's presence at these visits was more than necessary. He almost felt like the personal guard of the baronetess, for some gentlemen obviously believed they could achieve with threats and intrusiveness what must appear to them so tantalizingly easy to have.

It shocked him. On the one hand, it shocked him how little the visitors made of his presence. They seemed to think that he had no say as a hired overseer. On the other hand, the attitude of most of them shocked him. They didn't regard Dame Arabella as mistress of Brigham Hall, but as part of the furniture, free to take. More than once, Daniel bodily threw the suitors out, often requesting Dob's help, who had developed an outstanding talent at looking utterly dangerous. As much as the whole situation angered him, it strengthened his perception that he could not give in to his love. The chasm between him and the gentlemen seemed deeper than ever. However, this did not save him from jealousy. The suitors were a thorn in his flesh, and he often felt a great desire to refuse them entry and give them a good dressing down instead. Feelings he had never had before.

Dame Arabella didn't speak to Daniel about what occurred at these visits. Overall, she seemed very much alive and determined after her recovery, though also quite melancholy and as reserved toward Daniel as never before. It should have made him happy, but the contrary was the case. He kept wondering what had brought about this change of heart and whether he had done something wrong. On top of that, each new suitor brought to mind

The Silent Maid

the one sentence she had said to him after the first such visitor had left: "There is only one man I would marry."

While his heart was adamant she had meant him, his mind cursed him as a hopeless dreamer.

And yet even his mind was irritated when Dame Arabella drove off one day with Harry without telling him where she went. From Lizzie, he learned that she wanted to go to Bridlington, which made him even more nervous. It was far. What did she want there? Was there a suitor she liked after all? Lizzie couldn't tell him. Nobody could.

When she returned late at night, Daniel couldn't stand it anymore. He knocked on the office door and entered.

The room was bright and warm, and Dame Arabella sat at the desk, a few papers spread out before her.

She looked up when he came in. "Ah, Mr Huntington. What can I do for you?" she asked with a strangely knowing smile.

"I wanted to ask if everything is all right, madam," Daniel replied carefully.

She laughed. "You mean, you wanted to know where I was and what I have done there," she noted directly.

Daniel bit his lip.

"I wasn't aware that I need to report to you, Mr Huntington. But in case it eases your mind, I was in Bridlington in search of a new solicitor."

This statement surprised Daniel. "Is there a problem with Mr Ainsworth?"

She leaned back in her chair and watched him thoughtfully. "Don't misunderstand me, I value Mr Ainsworth as a person and a friend of my father's. But he is an old man and some of his opinions are – shall we say rusty? He never approved of my taking over the estate, even in my father's days, and certainly isn't happy with my position as sole mistress of Brigham Hall. I'm afraid the influx of marriage-hungry gentlemen goes back to him. He has repeatedly tried to convince me that a quick marriage is my best bet. It makes cooperation with him quite difficult."

Daniel nodded slowly. "Were you successful in your search?"

Dame Arabella's face brightened. "I was indeed. Mr Pinkney was quite charming and took up my request with surprising enthusiasm. I'm very curious of the result, which he will present to me next week." She studied Daniel with a raised eyebrow.

He didn't dare ask what her request was.

"I have another question, Mr Huntington," she went on. "Where has the money gone? Lizzie told me you found two chests of gold."

Daniel cleared his throat. "To be exact, Chauncey found them, madam. They are in the cellar. Do you know the hiding place there?"

"A hiding place in the cellar? No, I'm not aware of it."

Daniel reached inside his shirt and pulled out a heavy key, which he wore on a leather strap around his neck. "I felt it wasn't safe to put the key somewhere," he explained. "Shall I show you the place? Mr Ainsworth knew about it and thought it the best option for such treasure."

Her fingers closed around the metal warmed by his body. For a moment, she seemed irritated and swallowed repeatedly. "No, I... no. I wouldn't like to go to the cellar," she said tonelessly.

"There is a large cupboard in the wine cellar. Behind it is a hole locked with a grid where the chests are stored. Mr Ainsworth has counted everything and noted the amount in the current ledger," Daniel explained softly. Had Riley kept her in a cellar? It would explain her discomfort. He didn't ask.

"Thank you," she whispered. "If there is nothing else, I would like to close our conversation," she added with more vigour.

"As you wish, madam." Daniel nodded at her and left her to her work.

Life

Brigham Hall, March 20, 1712

Dear Mother,

Since Dame Arabella has returned to life — I cannot think of a better description of what happened in that graveyard — she shows an amazing amount of determination and independence, much more than before. She seems to require my help only in small individual matters, and I can finally return to my original tasks.

Chauncey's riding lessons are a daily joy, and he has assured me that I am making excellent progress. I can hardly describe the feeling of union with the horse that allows me to move its legs with my thoughts. I almost feel like a centaur when everything works out perfectly with Thunderboy, which unfortunately happens only rarely. But I get to the point of not getting in his way, as Chauncey puts it, more and more often, leading him to that grandeur he possesses of his own accord and which we only call forth. Of course, we ride out as well, and I can feel how much closer our relationship has grown through the lessons in the arena.

Dame Arabella seldom asks for my company on her rides anymore. She usually takes one of the lads who regard it as a reward for their work and therefore work much harder. I have no objections to that!

Unfortunately, we have lost a mare with her foal this year. We don't know exactly what happened. Perhaps she rolled too close to the fence, got her legs stuck and couldn't free herself. By the time we found her she was too weak to get up. A tragic loss. We hope to be spared any more accidents and all the other foals will be born without complications.

The positive side effect of the many visitors to Brigham Hall is that we have sold almost all of our young horses, even the yearlings. It seems as if there is an acute lack of mounts all around us. One of the gentlemen told me that the harsh winter of the year before last had weakened many horses so that they didn't make it through the last one.

Because of our generous hay arrangement this problem hardly affected us apart from lesser earnings because we needed the hay ourselves. I'm curious how this year's harvest will turn out.

Well, it is time for me to go now. Chauncey has asked me to a meeting.

Kindest regards

Daniel

28

Selflessness

DANIEL HAD HARDLY finished the sentence when a knock sounded on the door of his cottage.

"Come in," he called while he dried the ink and sealed the letter carefully.

Chauncey stamped his feet a few times and then entered, cap in hand.

"Take a seat," Daniel invited and pointed at a chair. "What's on your mind?"

"Well, it's like this," Chauncey started, unusually hesitant. He cleared his throat and turned his cap over and over, seemingly embarrassed.

This odd behaviour made Daniel guess this conversation had nothing to do with horses. "Yes?"

"Yes, well, this will probably surprise you. Actually, I'm quite certain it will surprise you a lot, but…" He fell silent.

Daniel took a deep breath and fought for patience. "Yes?" he repeated.

Chauncey looked at him and suddenly had to laugh at himself. "I act like a schoolboy," he noted amusedly.

"I can't contradict you there," Daniel said kindly.

"Well, it's like this," Chauncey started over. "I've really started to like Ruth, despite…" He faltered. "She is such a lovely, friendly girl and – well, I feel so sorry for her that she shouldn't have a family because of her accident," he went on.

Daniel raised his brows. He surely would never have expected such a statement. Besides, what did it have to do with him?

"You know, Daniel, when I was new here on the estate, the first time, you see, I was married. I had a lovely wife, and we were expecting our first child. But just like Lady Brigham, she died while giving birth. The baby didn't survive, either. That hit me hard. I've been alone ever since. For a long time, I have told myself I don't need a woman to be happy. But since knowing Ruth, I have to admit this attitude has been shaken. I know she is much younger than I am, yet she seems to like me and – well, I should like to marry her." He looked at Daniel expectantly.

"That's wonderful news," Daniel said with a smile. "I'm just not sure why you're telling me all this. It's not my place to decide whether you may marry her or not."

Chauncey twitched uncomfortably. "No, you're right. But… how do I say this? I can hardly live with her in that small chamber above the stable. It's fine for a man on his own, but perhaps the Lord will bless us with children and…" His gaze moved through the cottage.

With a jolt, Daniel realized what exactly Chauncey's request was. "You would like to ask me if you can have the cottage?" He had to grit his teeth for a moment because the thought stabbed his heart. This cottage was his refuge. He felt almost as much at home here as he had done back with his mother.

Chauncey was obviously relieved that Daniel had put the question for him. "I know you're entitled to the cottage and I would never demand it off you. I have no right to do that. It is just a favour asked from a friend."

Daniel nodded. "I understand, Chauncey. Let me sleep on it, will you?"

"All right." Chauncey rose and pushed his shoulders back. "Then I'll go and talk to Dame Arabella. If she doesn't object, I'll ask the parents. Wish me luck."

Daniel rose, too, and shook his hand. "With all my heart, my friend," he said.

Chauncey put his cap on and went back to the main house.

CHAUNCEY'S REQUEST bothered Daniel in more ways than one. While he checked the fences, armed with hammer, nails and coloured ribbons, his thoughts revolved around the conversation. He didn't need much concentration to fix loose boards and mark rotten posts with a ribbon, so he could brood unhindered.

For a long time, Daniel had shared Chauncey's attitude that one didn't need women to be happy, until a certain silent maid had crossed his path. Of course, he had felt certain desires when looking at a pretty girl, just like any other lad, but it had been fairly easy for him to supress that. Dame Arabella caused quite different feelings, exceeding simple lust by far. With a snort, he dragged his thoughts away from that dangerous trail and focussed on Ruth. How could he have missed what was developing between the two of them? He hadn't been very attentive lately. Chauncey was right though, he did wonder at his willingness to take up with Ruth, even if she was a very nice girl.

Daniel himself could never imagine kissing such a disfigured face. If Chauncey didn't have a problem with that, it was perfectly fine with him.

Could he give up his cottage for the two of them? Perhaps Dame Arabella would agree to build another one where they could live. There was enough space. On the other hand, he had been happy with the chamber above the stable and would be again. Why hold on to earthly comforts when he could do a friend and colleague a great favour? He felt his heart lock against the thought.

"Oh Lord, the tests you put upon me," he said to himself, and drove a nail into the wood with well-placed blows. "My heart shall not stick to earthly goods but serve the Lord loyally," he told the fence post in a determined tone. Then he shook his head at himself. Even if he was serious about it, he was not one bit more grown-up than he had been when ordering the chickens around. Another thought entered his head, one that he'd had several times since Chauncey had come. It was time to conquer his pride.

A FEW DAYS LATER, Daniel knocked on the door of the parlour. Lizzie opened it and informed the baronetess of his presence.

"You make a great butler," he teased and winked at her in passing, hoping she would understand his jest. She obviously did because she winked back, despite blushing crimson.

Dame Arabella was sitting by the window with a cup of tea, contemplating the dreary world outside. She seemed to enjoy that. "I hope the weather will turn friendlier

Selflessness

soon," she said softly. "We have a wedding to celebrate." With a melancholic smile she turned to Daniel. "What causes this visit, Mr Huntington?"

Even though her tone was nice, he felt a certain gloom burdening her. "Are you all right, madam?" he asked a little worried. He couldn't bear it should she sink back into silence.

"Under the circumstances, yes, thank you." She looked at him patiently.

"Chauncey has talked to you about his wedding plans," Daniel noted.

"Yes, he has. Ruth's parents are beside themselves with joy, let alone Ruth herself. You will have noticed."

Daniel chuckled. Since Chauncey had proposed to Ruth, she practically flew through the stable, sang continuously and sometimes even forgot to hide from strangers. He had never before seen such a truly happy person.

It made what he wanted to do much easier.

"He has made a request of me that I'd like to grant him, if you are not opposed, madam."

"A request?"

"Yes. He has asked me to give him my cottage."

She looked surprised. "You wish to do that?" she asked, scrutinizing him.

"Yes, madam. As a matter of fact, I want to do more. I would like to ask you to make him Master of Horse."

Now she rose. "Mr Huntington! Whyever would I do such a thing? I'm perfectly happy with you as Master of Horse."

"Thank you, madam, that…" He swallowed. It was a lot harder than he had expected. Yet the decision was made. "…that's very kind of you. Nevertheless, I believe

Chauncey would be much better suited to the position than I am. His knowledge about horses, breeding, the whole thing, is so much deeper than my own. He has worked for years with Ole Pete, side by side. If it hadn't been for Riley, he would be Master of Horse now, not I."

Her eyes widened, while her hand wandered to her throat. "You're not going to leave us, Mr Huntington?" It was hardly more than a whisper. She shuddered, turned very pale and sat down again.

For a moment, her reaction threw him completely off track. There was something in her eyes, a fear that was oddly familiar. He was reminded of saying goodbye to his mother when he was nine. He'd had the same fear. Fear of living without her.

"No, madam," he replied roughly. "That's not my intention."

She sighed and fell silent for a while. When she spoke again, her tone was firm as usual. "So, you want to give up your position as Master of Horse and the cottage accordingly, because you think Chauncey has more right to it than you do."

"No, it's not a question of right, it's only – I think he is better suited for the work, and considered practically, I don't really need the cottage, although I like living there. The chamber in the stable is sufficient for my needs. The new couple needs a home."

"Your selflessness knows no bounds, does it?" Dame Arabella said more to herself than to him. She thought for a moment, then added, "I agree with you, Mr Huntington. You have taken on so many additional tasks that your work in the stables has suffered. Tomorrow after breakfast, we will sit down with Chauncey and work out which tasks you

Selflessness

will have in the stables in the future. Please think about how much time you need for the tenants as well as the visitors. You certainly have a knack for selling horses, I'll say that much. It amuses me greatly how you throw the men out and then not let them leave without buying a horse. How do you manage to do that?"

Daniel looked at her guilelessly. "To be honest, I have no clue, madam," he admitted.

She laughed and this time the laugh reached her eyes. Yes, the golden specks in them definitely twinkled when she laughed like that. It was so appealing that he wanted to take a step in her direction. He noticed just in time and tore himself away from her sight. "I will inform Chauncey of the meeting tomorrow," he croaked and strode swiftly out of the room.

"And there he flees again," he heard her say softly behind him.

He paused at the door but didn't turn around. He had done what he had come for.

The Silent Maid

Brigham Hall, April 12, 1712

Dearest Mother,

Despite it being late at night, I still hear music and voices sounding over from the terrace of the parlour. Song and dance and joyful celebrations because Chauncey and Ruth got married today. The priest was here and all the residents on the Brigham estate were invited to join the festivities. Dame Arabella has graciously cared for everything, and Ellie and the maids did their utmost to make it a feast. There has never been a celebration like this in all the time I have been here. Even Christmas wasn't like this.

First, I was in the thick of it, tried myself at the dance, to everyone's amusement, but after a while it became too much for me and I wanted to retreat. However, Dame Arabella stopped me in the entrance hall. She asked me to follow her and led me to a room upstairs which I had never entered before. It is right at the top of the stairs in the west wing of the house and offers a nice view of the chapel and the forest. Did I mention the rebuilding of the chapel has started? For a few weeks now, workers are busy building the walls ever higher and the tree trunks for the roof are ready as well. Work continues as the weather allows. But I'm drifting off.

Dame Arabella led me to this room, which was not used all these years, just like her tower room. She had a candle with her, and the moon shone through the window so that I could see everything. It's not very large and contains no more than a fireplace, chairs and a desk. There are a few shelves with books, spreading their own comfortable smell. I looked around for a while and Dame Arabella granted me the time.

"I am well aware of the sacrifice you made for Chauncey and Ruth, Mr Huntington," she said softly. "The cottage was more to you than a room to sleep in." She let that sit between us and I had

no idea what to answer. It was correct. I just didn't know how she knew that.

"My father chose this room as his refuge. I was not allowed to disturb him here, even if he was there for me at all other times. He came here after difficult negotiations or when he had to think about something. Or when he simply needed some quiet." She paused again and I could feel the tension from the noisy wedding falling off me. The room did have a very calming atmosphere.

Now she pulled a key from her pocket and handed it to me. "I would like to make this room available to you, Mr Huntington. I won't use it; it is too painful. But I believe it will do you good. You have taken on so much responsibility here, have invested so much into Brigham Hall without ever knowing what the future might bring. Time and again you have been of greatest service to me and now you have even sacrificed your home for the good of others. I treasure your meekness, but I also worry that you will get quite lost if no one watches out for you." She had turned her face away from me so that I couldn't see her expression, but her voice carried so much warmth and care; it made me speechless. "Will you accept?" she asked, finally turning back to me. I could only nod. She turned and left without another word.

I stayed in the room for a while and listened to the sounds from below that seemed unable to disturb the peace up here. It was a peculiar sense of acceptance and appreciation that literally flooded me.

Unfortunately, the ink I found in the desk was no longer useable, or I would have written this letter right there and then. Tomorrow, I will look at the room in daylight and adapt it to my needs. First of all, my armchair will go in there because it takes up so much space in my chamber, I hardly get through to the bed.

Yes, that's how a joyful day ends peacefully. Will you ever be able to visit me here one day? It would be lovely.

Love,

Your son Daniel

29
Contract

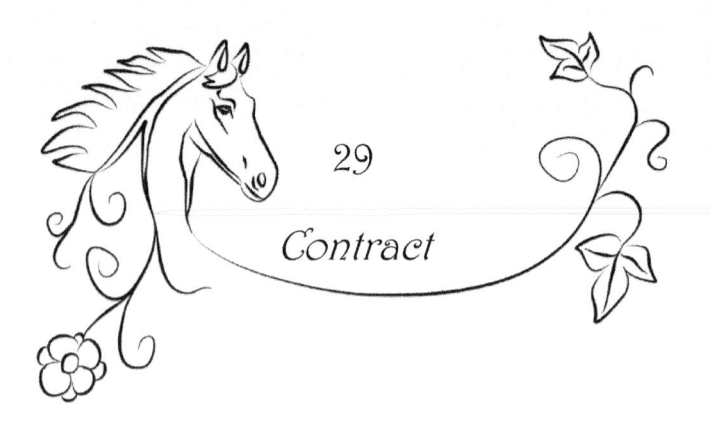

IF DANIEL HAD thought that his resignation from the position as Master of Horse would put him a step below Chauncey, he was wrong. Chauncey had always treated Daniel with respect, but now there was an awed expression in his eyes when they talked. He strictly avoided acting superior to Daniel, rather asking his opinion than giving orders. It made their work enjoyable, and Daniel felt relieved, finally being rid of his nagging conscience for not fulfilling expectations.

The room of the former baronet soon became his retreat, and he was more than grateful to Dame Arabella for her thoughtfulness.

He was sitting there, in front of the fire, on a rainy afternoon, working on a list of costs for the chapel, when a knock sounded on the door.

"Come," he called without taking his eyes from the numbers. Calculations still didn't come easy, and he had to concentrate hard to avoid mistakes. Whoever the visitor was, he waited patiently for Daniel to finish and look up. To his surprise, he was faced with a puny stranger, looking quite smug in his wig and expensive clothes. Daniel rose and put out his hand with a questioning look.

"My name is Pinkney, solicitor, at your service, Mr Huntington." The man introduced himself politely and shook the offered hand.

This did nothing to ease Daniel's surprise. "What can I do for you, Mr Pinkney?" he asked, mildly irritated. Although Dame Arabella had informed him of the new solicitor, he had no clue what the man wanted from him.

An enthusiastic as well as insecure smile appeared on Mr Pinkney's face. "I was sent to you by Dame Arabella," he explained, while turning a rather thick stack of folded papers in his hands. "This is most certainly the first time a solicitor has been intrusted with such a curious task and I am not a little proud of being a pioneer, so to speak, in the name of jurisprudence."

Daniel cocked his head in confusion. He really didn't have the slightest idea what the man was talking about.

Mr Pinkney cleared his throat, noticing Daniel's perplexity. "Be that as it may, Dame Arabella has requested me to deliver this letter with the additional papers and to await your response."

Daniel frowned. A letter from his mistress? Delivered by a solicitor? Why didn't she simply talk to him?

"Dame Arabella assumed that you might wonder why she is writing to you." The solicitor answered his unspoken question. "She has asked me to tell you that unfortunately it is impossible to talk to you about…" He paused in search for the right words. "…well, about this topic, because you…" He paused again and a meaningful smile played around his lips. "…because you invariably flee from her presence when it is brought up. Her words, not mine," he added, just in case.

Contract

Daniel's confusion was complete. At the same time, a hunch began to grow deep inside him.

Mr Pinkney held out the papers to him. "Please read these and take your time about it. I will wait in the parlour, and should any questions arise, I will be glad to help." With a bow, he left the room.

For a moment, Daniel stared helplessly at the papers in his hand, then he sat and unfolded them. The first page was covered in Dame Arabella's slim script, while the following pages were filled with a broad, energetic handwriting that had to be Mr Pinkney's.

My dear Daniel, he read and twitched in the same manner he did when she put a hand on his arm. The gesture contained – just like this address – an intimacy he couldn't accept. His eyes widened in unbelieving shock while he perused the page without letting a single line of the content enter his heart. Hastily, he flipped through the rest of the papers, shaking his head repeatedly. His throat constricted and his heart rate shot up. She couldn't mean this! In his trembling hands, the papers sank to his lap, and he stared into the flames of the fire for a while. Thoughts bounced through his head as if repelled by walls. There was only one word breaking through the melee: impossible.

He shot to his feet and stomped to the door. Shortly after that, he burst into the parlour without knocking. He was way too enraged.

Mr Pinkney rose at once and looked expectantly at Daniel. "That didn't take as long as I had expected. Did you read everything carefully?" he asked.

"No," Daniel replied. "That wasn't necessary. The idea is preposterous and I don't know how you could ever be a party to such a thing."

"Well, it was a legal challenge I couldn't resist…"

"The answer is no. It is impossible." Daniel threw the papers on the table in front of Mr Pinkney.

"Mr Huntington," the solicitor tried to soothe him, "it is the express wish of your mistress that you keep these papers in your possession." Daniel tried to object, but Mr Pinkney stopped him with a gesture. "That you keep them in your possession and think about it. Legally, it is not impossible, however you may feel about it. I will inform Dame Arabella of your preliminary answer. I may let you know that she expected this reaction from you. Nevertheless, she wanted to try. If I may be so bold as to utter this in confidence – I, in your position, wouldn't cast away this unique chance so quickly."

"That is my decision," Daniel growled and grabbed the papers off the table again. With a curt "good day" he left the parlour.

WITH JERKING MOTIONS, Daniel threw the saddle on the stallion's back and pulled the cinch tight much faster than he normally did. Thunderboy shook his head in protest. Daniel hardly noticed, trapped in his thoughts as he was. As a rule, he didn't ride the stallion during the breeding season, but right now he didn't care about anything. He had to get away from the stable and the house, away from the suddenly claustrophobic closeness of Brigham Hall.

The stallion seemed to feel his need, for Daniel had hardly swung up into the saddle when they were already thundering down the path at full speed. They shot past the pastures and caused much excitement within the herds. Daniel didn't care about that, either. The faster they were past the mares, the better. Emitting loud cries, he spurred the stallion on, who was quite willing to go even faster. Too late, Daniel noticed a group of people chatting at a crossroads.

"Get out of the way!" he roared.

They jumped aside just in time. Daniel heard some calls follow him but made no effort to slow down or make excuses. Not now. Let them think the stallion had bolted.

A pheasant suddenly fluttered up from the bushes on the left and Thunderboy jumped to the right, almost lifting Daniel out of the saddle. For several strides, he hung precariously at the horse's side before he managed to pull himself up again. Now they headed straight toward a stone wall. Neither Daniel nor Thunderboy wasted a thought on slowing down. With another cry Daniel drove the stallion on and cleared the wall with a mighty leap. Daniel hooted in triumph, following up with something like battle cries. He screamed out all of his pent-up emotion, until the path dipped into the soft green shadows of the forest.

Finally, they slowed down, for the path snaked around trees and Daniel didn't want to knock his knees against a trunk. Besides, Thunderboy was pumping quite heavily and Daniel's sense of responsibility slowly reasserted itself. He reined the stallion to a walk and let him stretch his neck. Lifting his gaze to his surroundings, Daniel wondered where he was. During the wild ride, he hadn't paid attention to anything but the turmoil in his mind. He vaguely remembered several changes of direction, unlike his previous ride of desperation after Pete's death, when he had gone straight all the way to the coast.

The Silent Maid

Sighing deeply, he patted the horse's sweaty neck. "I hope you find your way back home," he murmured and closed his eyes. He only opened them again when a branch brushed his face.

His inner turmoil had settled a bit. Now he wondered how to proceed. It was inconceivable to remain at Brigham Hall after his rejection of Dame Arabella's proposal. Michaelmas was half a year away. He would hardly find new employment in the meantime. His thoughts travelled to the sack of coins containing last year's wages. It was more than enough to live on for six months. Perhaps he should travel, look at various places in the country and finally return home to see his mother. This thought restored most of his peace of mind. It was a plan. Not a very far-reaching plan, but a plan. God would find a place for him eventually.

It was the large boulder that suddenly drew his attention to the fact that he was close to Brigham Hall again. Here was the place where Dame Arabella had suffered her relapse!

Spontaneously, Daniel jumped off and tied Thunderboy to a tree. Then he picked up a stick and poked the ground in the spot where Dame Arabella had crawled around. After a short while, he hit something hard. With powerful strokes, he wiped the dead leaves aside and uncovered a sturdy wooden board a few feet away from a majestic beech. A strong iron ring was attached to it. Daniel grabbed the ring and pulled. It proved to be a trapdoor. Below it was a walled tunnel with a ladder. Daniel knelt on the ground and peered into the dark. He would have to climb down to see more. An icy shiver raced down his back when he realized that the tunnel led below the tree. A dark suspicion dawned on him. He hesitated a moment, then went down the ladder. It groaned under his weight but didn't break. Reaching the ground, he had to bend low to move through the tunnel. The walls ended after two steps. Behind them, there was a hole in the bare earth, roughly supported by wooden beams. The beech's roots made up the roof and stretched down the walls deep into the soil.

Daniel waited until his eyes had adjusted to the dimness. On the right wall he made out some sort of bed made from leaves, straw and a few blankets, hopelessly mouldy. A chair and a table sat by the back wall. There was a wooden bowl and a spoon on it. The table was crooked because its legs had sunk into the ground. A bucket lay on its side and when Daniel tapped it with his foot, a faint smell of slops wafted up.

All of a sudden, he couldn't stand it anymore. Hastily, he turned around and climbed up the ladder.

The forest seemed incredibly friendly compared to the suffocating closeness of the earth hole. Panting and pale, Daniel dropped the trapdoor shut with a bang and sat on it. His suspicion had been confirmed and the thought was so awful that he couldn't think it. This was the prison; this was the place where Riley had kept his mistress hidden for four long years. Her fight for forgiveness by her father's grave suddenly carried much more weight.

A tear rolled down Daniel's nose and tickled its tip before he wiped it away with a swift motion. It took him two attempts to rise. His discovery had shocked him deeply. With shaking hands, he freed the reins from the tree and clambered up onto the stallion's back with little grace. He kept his hand resting on the horse's warm neck the entire way back. Inside, he felt frozen solid.

Back at the yard, Daniel slipped off the horse, emotionally and physically exhausted.

Chauncey showed up while he cared for the stallion. "Are you all right?" he asked.

Daniel considered giving an evasive answer, which wasn't fair, though. Chauncey was his friend and of those he didn't have many. "Would I go for such a ride if I was all right?" he asked with a bitter smile.

Chauncey merely shook his head.

"It did me good," Daniel said hesitatingly, "but I made a terrible discovery."

"What is it?"

"Her prison." Daniel could hardly say it. "The place where she broke down back then. There is a hole in the ground, a cave under a tree. That's where he hid her." His voice broke.

"Show me. I want to see it!" Chauncey growled. His eyes glowed with an old anger. Daniel shook his head.

"Believe me, my friend, you don't want to see that." He leaned against the horse and needed a moment to get a grip on himself again. Then he directed a down-cast look at Chauncey. "After all that has happened today, I don't think I will stay here much longer."

Chauncey swallowed audibly. "What else happened?" He seemed to sense that Daniel was at the end of his strength.

"I'm afraid I can't tell you that," Daniel replied sadly.

He did not go to dinner that evening.

Contract

Brigham Hall, April 28, 1712

Dearest Mother,

Perhaps we will meet again soon, for things have taken an unexpected turn, making it impossible for me to stay here, as much as my heart bleeds at the thought of leaving this beautiful estate.

Dame Arabella has dared to take a step I would never have expected. It is completely out of the question for me to accept her proposal. Instead of lengthy explanations, I will simply copy the letter she addressed to me so that you can form your own opinion. I'm sure you'll agree with me that such a step would be highly improper and unacceptable.

Nevertheless, I want to await your answer before I make a final decision.

Daniel

Letter by Dame Arabella Alexandra Brigham to Daniel Huntington

My dear Daniel,

Trusting what has stood between us unspoken for a long time and connects us in such a strange manner, I will make every effort of breaking down the wall which you have erected around yourself.

Unfortunately, it is impossible for me to talk to you about my feelings, for every time I try you lock up like an oyster and usually flee my presence. That is why I write to you now in hopes that you will at least read what you don't seem to want to hear.

I am lonely, Daniel. Yes, the servants have proved friendly, contrary to what I expected, and Lizzie cares lovingly for me. And yet we are separated by a chasm. It pains me to say so, but I am lonelier now than I was during Riley's imprisonment. Our relationship was terrible, but it afforded a certain closeness. Now I am free, but there is no one close to me, truly close.

You were the first one in all these years to rise up against Riley to show me some warmth. I have soaked up everything from you like parched ground soaking up the rain, every smile, every friendly glance, every kind word. Before you came, I was so desperate that I wanted to hand Riley a knife to kill me as well, just like he had killed my father in front of me.

But your presence revived me. More than that, you showed me that I could put Riley under pressure. To suppress me, he had to control me. With your help, I escaped his control more and more often. It drove him mad. He cursed and raved, yet he couldn't stop it. Not without locking me up again, and how would he have explained that? For the first time, I had hope that my fate could be turned. You kindled that hope within me and in the end, you fulfilled it. I would never have made it on my own.

You are my hero, my saviour. How often have you saved me? In the storm, when I ran into the rain in blind panic. From Russell, from Riley, and lastly even from myself.

Daniel, you are the one in whose arms I have found something I had completely forgotten: a safe haven. Whenever you have taken me in your arms, I felt absolutely secure and protected, as if nothing in this world could harm me.

Is it a childish wish to always want to have this feeling? Is it condemnable to wish for the right to lean on you any time I need it?

You have proven more than once that you possess all the traits and skills necessary to manage an estate well. The people of Brigham Hall have long since accepted you as master, only you reject it vehemently. Have you ever thought of what we could accomplish here together?

Contract

That is the reason why I have asked Mr Pinkney to set up a contract of marriage. I don't want to lose my rights as baronetess just because I marry. I don't want to place the entire burden of responsibility on your shoulders. At the same time, I don't want to carry it alone anymore, either. I want to share it with you.

If you think again that you are no more than the poor son of a carpenter, let me make one thing clear: you don't become a baronet because of a special heritage. The baronetcy is bound to wealth and property more than any other peerage. If you are rich enough, you may receive such a title from the king, no matter where you come from. That is how my grandfather, the first Baronet Brigham, received his title. Why, then, shouldn't you, who has done so much for this estate and for me personally, receive this title by marriage? If a baronetess can turn into a poor maid, then a groom can turn into a baronet.

I have already told you that there is only one man I want to marry, and that is you, Daniel. Please think about it. Please accept my proposal. That which you believe to stand between us does not exist.

Arabella

30

Accident

OVER THE NEXT FEW days, Daniel avoided everyone, especially Dame Arabella. He took refuge in his chamber to read the Bible, whenever his work allowed. Mostly, however, he simply sat and stared at the pages without taking anything in.

It was that way when Chauncey came to him.

"The foreman has a question about the chapel. He's waiting in the yard."

Daniel sighed. "Can't he ask the baronetess? She is responsible for the building site."

"He explicitly asked for you," Chauncey replied with a shrug.

It wasn't new to Daniel. The wives of the tenants preferred to approach the mistress by now, but the men? With a reluctant grumble, he followed Chauncey downstairs and crossed over to the yard with swift strides, where the foreman was leaning against the hitching post, enjoying the warming sun. The strong, cool wind didn't allow much spring feeling, despite it being May already.

"Is there a problem?" Daniel asked right away.

The man pulled his cap from his head and made a perfunctory bow. "Sir Daniel," he started, but Daniel interrupted him immediately. "I am a simple employee, no Lord. Please call me Mr Huntington."

The man started. He gaped at Daniel for a moment, before answering, "Of course, sir."

Daniel would have loved to shake him. He forced the urge down. "What is it?" he asked once more.

"Well, sir, one of the beams intended as a roof beam is cracked. We can't use it like that and need a replacement."

"That's annoying. How did that happen? All the beams were in order when I checked them the day before yesterday."

The man lowered his gaze and studied the tips of his boots. "Yes, well, there was an accident. I suppose we didn't fasten it properly when pulling it up. It slipped from the ropes."

"Did someone get hurt?" Daniel asked, shocked.

"No, sir, not seriously. One man has a wound on his hand because the rope slipped through it. But that's all."

"All right, that couldn't be helped. I will talk to Harry to see where we can find a new beam. Is everything else secured at the site? Or is there a danger of everything collapsing with the beam missing?"

"You're welcome to come down and look at it, sir. The long beam is set, nothing can happen."

Daniel spontaneously decided to go and take a look. The building works fascinated him, especially the building of the roof. There were scaffolds and ladders all over the place, as well as a long ramp that ran along the outside wall to transport material to the top. To think that much larger churches than their small chapel were built in the cities; he got dizzy simply imagining the heights the workers had to move in.

When they reached the chapel, Daniel heard someone rant. Turning the corner with the foreman, he saw a group of workers assembled. In front of them, the building master marched up and down, giving them a piece of his mind. He must have seen Daniel out of the corner of his eye, for he stopped suddenly and made dismissive gesture. "Get back to work," he growled and then approached Daniel.

"I just wanted to see how the work is proceeding and then I find this!" Indignantly, he threw up his hands and then waved at the sturdy beam cracked down its length.

"It's so difficult to get decent beams for such use! It sets us back for days. It's very annoying and I apologize for the delay." He bowed to Daniel.

"Yes, it is annoying, but thank God nobody was hurt. I will…"

"No, sir, under no circumstances. I will take care that a replacement is found as soon as possible. You don't have to do anything. Fortunately, I have talked to a man only last week who had excellent beams in stock. I just hope he hasn't sold them all, yet. I will ride over immediately. Would you inform the baronetess?"

Daniel swallowed. "What about the costs?" he asked hurriedly to avoid thinking about meeting his mistress.

The building master's enthusiasm was thoroughly dampened by this question. "Well, Dame Arabella told me more or less that money wasn't an issue…"

Daniel looked him resolutely in the eye. "That does not mean she wants to throw it out the window by the bucket full," he said drily. "Your workers have caused these additional costs. If you want to buy a new beam, you will at least pay the transportation. Deduct it from the workers' wages, that will teach them to be more careful in the future."

"We cannot use a freshly cut tree, it will warp the entire structure, sir. You are right, of course, that... well, yes. I will keep the cause in mind when listing my costs."

And add the money elsewhere, Daniel thought, but held his peace. It wasn't *his* money, even if the waste angered him. In any case, he would minutely check the bill. If he was still around.

"Get going," Daniel said.

The building master hastened to his horse, which he had tied to the graveyard gate. Daniel heard him canter away. He remained at the site until evening. Then he had no choice but to return to Brigham Hall and inform Dame Arabella of the latest occurrences. He wasn't comfortable with that.

WHEN DANIEL ENTERED the corner room where Dame Arabella was having her dinner, Lizzie wanted to leave right away.

"You can stay," Daniel murmured and fervently hoped she would listen to him.

She looked over at her mistress for confirmation and since she didn't contradict him, Lizzie stood beside the fireplace and waited.

Dame Arabella took a long look at Daniel before speaking. "Mr Huntington," she said softly. Her voice carried so much sadness, it cut straight through his heart. "What brings you to me?" There was no glimmer of hope in her eyes. She had accepted his answer as irrevocable.

Daniel had to swallow several times before being able to name his intent. "The building master is on his way to get a new roof beam. Unfortunately, there was an accident and one of the beams was damaged. He said the building process will be delayed for several days. I…" He cleared his throat because his voice had suddenly turned into a croak. "I have told him to pay the transportation out of his own pocket, at least. I hope you agree."

"Yes, of course. Thank you…" She hesitated. "…Mr Huntington," she completed the sentence almost inaudibly. Daniel bowed, turned, and fairly shot from the room. He knew exactly why she had hesitated. She would rather have said 'Daniel'.

He made his way through to the kitchen where he met Ellie.

"Daniel!" she called. "What's the hurry? Come here, lad, you haven't eaten all day."

Almost scared, he looked at her as if she was a fairy that had suddenly popped up in front of him.

"No, thanks," he replied roughly and continued his flight.

Back in his chamber, he slammed the door and put his back against it, knees shaking and pulse racing. This could not go on. He wasn't even able to be in one room with this woman and speak a few civilized words. He had to leave. He had no other choice left.

Accident

Skipwith, May 4, 1712

My dear son,

It is indeed a highly unusual message you have sent me with your last letter. However, despite your expectations, I cannot agree with you. On the contrary.

My dear Daniel, as intelligent and prudent as you usually are, right now you are acting like a twit. What has got into you?

As early as your first letters concerning the silent maid, I sensed how much your heart belongs to this girl. I have hoped with you, trembled with you, brooded with you, and was more than surprised and joyful when it came out that she is the true baroness.

How immensely proud I was of you, my son, who freed her from her terrible fate, and took on responsibility exceeding every measure anyone might have expected. You have given her every support she could have wished for.

What I have not understood the entire time, however, was your strange conviction that she was unreachable for you. I have tried repeatedly to make you see differently, but obviously my efforts were too tentative. So now I will write it in all clearness:

Daniel, love will always find a way and I see absolutely no reason why you shouldn't marry this wonderful woman. Her letter has touched me to the core, for she seems to know you very well and to accept you with all your strengths and weaknesses. I'm prone to believe that you need her more than she needs you; to show you what's inside of you.

Remember how God called Moses. A shepherd, an escaped murderer, but God wanted to use him. Or David! A small boy conquering a giant and turned into a king by God.

Daniel, I firmly believe that God is calling you to serve him on this estate. Not he is master who gives orders to others, but he who cares for what has been entrusted to him. And that, my son, has always been within you. No matter whether man or beast, those living under your care live well.

Do not flee your fate out of false modesty, Daniel! Be courageous and strong and fear not, for the Lord is with you in all that you do. Do I really have to remind you of your baptismal verse?

In the time you have been at Brigham Hall, you have matured and surpassed yourself. I know your father never saw your potential, but I always knew that you had much more inside you than anyone – including yourself – suspected. Yet even I am amazed at the things you have managed in the past year. And I know it's not the end of it. You can do more, so much more!

Now go and ask Dame Arabella Alexandra Brigham to be your wife. I have added a ring so that you will have no excuses not to ask her. It is my wedding gift to you, my beloved son.

I am so proud of you.

Love,

Your mother
Mary Anne Huntington

31
Awakening

DANIEL LOWERED THE letter and stared at the ring, thunderstruck. It was a simple gold band with a tiny stone set in it, and tears brimmed in his eyes when he realized it was his mother's only heirloom, her grandmother's ring.

Had his mother actually called him a twit? He scanned the first lines again. Yes, she had. He pursed his lips and felt like a dumb little boy, while his heart rate picked up. His mind was still struggling with the information he had received, but hope was already taking over his heart.

His mother didn't think it was completely preposterous that he should marry a baronetess? On the contrary, she even urged him to it? A surprised laugh escaped him. He had been so convinced it wasn't right! All at once, he no longer knew why he had ever believed that, why the worldly restrictions and social barriers had appeared so invincible to him.

From a whole new perspective, he pondered the events of the past months. What had Dame Arabella written? The people of Brigham Hall had long since accepted him as their master… His anger at their addressing him with 'sir' suddenly seemed silly. And then the entire momentousness of what Dame Arabella had confessed in her letter struck him. There was no need for him to repress his feelings for her. He didn't have to shrink back from her touch. They would lead this estate together. He could enfold her in his arms… A powerful wave of joy and longing rolled over him. He jumped up and tore open the door, only to close it again and sit on his cot.

How? He couldn't simply burst in on her and tell her he had changed his mind.

The sound of hooves reached his ears. Upon a quick look out of the window he saw Dame Arabella lead her mare up to the hitching post. She was wearing her riding attire. It was all he needed to know.

Putting the ring in his pocket, he hurried down into the stable. One of the horses was being saddled by Tom.

When the boy saw Daniel, he grinned happily. "The mistress has asked me to go for a ride with her."

Daniel never hesitated, although he felt bad to disappoint Tom. "I'm afraid that won't be happening," he said decisively. "I have something to discuss with the baronetess. I will ride with her."

Tom's shoulders drooped. "That's not fair. She asked me!" He pouted.

"Don't talk back," Daniel reprimanded him curtly.

"I'm quite ready," Dame Arabella called from the yard.

Daniel led the horse outside. The white mare was already prancing toward the gate with her mistress in the saddle. Daniel hurriedly tightened the saddle girth. When he had mounted, the baronetess' surprised eyes met his.

"You accompany me, Mr Huntington?"

"Yes, madam," he answered and could hardly believe what he was about to do. In the same instant he had seen her in the yard, he had known where and how to ask her.

"Have you ever gone straight in that direction?" He pointed north.

"Not that I know of," she replied with a strangely questioning look.

He chuckled. "Then follow me," he said and trotted off.

Daniel didn't recall the details of his ride with Thunderboy after Ole Pete's death. All he knew was that he had gone straight on the entire way and had at some point reached the ruined castle by the sea. Since the baronetess was always game for swift ride, he galloped ahead without worrying whether she could keep up. Once in a while, he threw a glance over his shoulder, and every time he saw the eager face of the little mare who would have liked nothing better than to overtake him. But Dame Arabella kept her back, against her usual habit. Normally, he only saw her slim figure in the dark blue riding habit from the back and could watch at leisure how the wind tore more and more strands from her pinned up hair until the unruly curls streamed behind her as if they had a mind of their own. When he looked back now, he saw her reddened cheeks and the unvarying questioning expression in her eyes.

Daniel sensed his horse growing tired and slowed to a walk. Dame Arabella closed the gap between them but said nothing. Despite avoiding looking at her, he felt her curious glances. He didn't want to give himself away before reaching the ruin.

After a while of riding in silence, she said softly, "Something is different."

It was a fact stated, so he didn't have to answer and refrained from doing so.

"I take it you follow a certain aim?" she went on to ask.

Daniel glanced at her briefly and nodded. The longer they went on, the more nervous he became. What if he didn't find the ruin? What if all courage left him and he wouldn't dare to ask her after all? Just as the doubts threatened to overwhelm him, they reached the top of a hill and saw the crumbled walls of the castle lying before them. Dame Arabella gasped.

"Have you ever been there?" Daniel asked.

"No. My father strictly prohibited it. He said it was an evil place."

"An evil place? Why is that?"

"It is rumoured that several people have jumped to their deaths from those cliffs," she replied with a shudder.

"Well, to me, this is a place of comfort. There is nothing evil there." Their eyes met. He could see her inner turmoil. "Are you afraid of heights?" Daniel asked, just in case.

She laughed. "No, heights don't bother me. It is the dark, tight spaces that pose a problem."

Daniel nodded. He understood only too well. "Then there is nothing to be afraid of," he said.

They came near the tumbled walls.

Daniel stopped and dismounted. "There are a lot of loose stones here. We should tie the horses to this tree and walk the rest of the way."

Without a comment, she followed his example. Then they carefully clambered over grass and weeds and up the stairs to the highest intact wall. A fresh sea breeze blew in their faces, the sun sparkling on the waves. As the first time, the view was both surprising and majestic. Dame Arabella put both hands on the wall and rose on tiptoe to be able to look down over the broad stone railing. Below, the surf broke on the cliffs with a strong roar. Seagulls swooped over the beach, their shrill cries rising on the wind.

Daniel felt this rough wilderness grip his heart and blow the last shreds of hesitance away. *Be courageous and strong and do not fear, for the Lord is with you in all that you do.* For the first time in his life, he made these words his.

With a hammering heart, he turned to the delicate woman next to him. "Bella," he said so quietly that it was hardly audible above the wind and the waves. He had wanted to say her full name, but only those two syllables came out.

She jerked her gaze away from the view and fixed it on his face. He took time to study each little golden speck in the glowing green of her eyes. His feelings took up so much space in his head that he wasn't sure what he would say next.

"Have you changed your mind?" she asked before he could think of something. Her voice sounded almost childish with unbelieving hope.

He laughed and took her hands in his. "Yes," he said simply.

A smile all but exploded on her face while tears shimmered in her eyes at the same time.

"I'm so sorry I was such a… twit. I thought…"

She put a finger on his lips and slightly shook her head.

With a chuckle he took her hand back in his. "Arabella Alexandra Brigham," he said determinedly and took another deep breath. "Will you be my wife?" At the last moment, he remembered the ring. Putting his hand in his pocket he took it out, didn't get around to holding it out to her, though. She had already wrapped her arms around him with a sobbed, "Yes".

Putting one hand into her tousled curls and the other on her back, he held her while she cried with relief. A shudder ran through his body and he suddenly had the impression that his entire world had shifted. Something had been straightened. He felt complete where something had always been missing. And he was happy, as he never had been before.

Tenderly, he slipped his hand under her hair at her neck and caressed the soft skin. The touch made her look up and lift a hand to his cheek. She didn't need to tell him how much she loved him. He could read it in her eyes.

Epilogue

THE TREES SCREAMED their cruel war cries. They raged with roaring branches against the storm while their roots gripped the earth. Drops and clumps rained down on her as she hid beneath the blanket. In the dark, she believed she could sense the trees growing new roots to increase their hold in the ground. Like invisible tentacles they squirmed down, touched her, enveloped her, and threatened to crush her. From somewhere, a loud crash sounded, and she jerked up. A scream rose from deep inside her, nameless fear looking for a way out.

"Bella?" The warm voice next to her broke the bane of darkness. "It was only a dream, Bella, only a dream. Don't be afraid."

Strong arms wrapped around her. The scream in her throat died.

"Come here, love." He pulled her close so that she could rest her head on his chest. The calm, regular beat of his heart drove the trees' roaring out of her head. A few tears dripped from her eyes, but soon dried up. She was safe. Loved.

Thank you for reading *The Silent Maid*. I hope you have enjoyed it and would greatly appreciate it if you would leave a review and/or recommend this book to others. As a self-published author this helps me tremendously in gaining visibility among the masses of wonderful books out there.

My special thanks go to three of these wonderful writers who have helped me tremendously in the hunt for typos, awkward wording and faulty grammar: Toni Allen, Helen Pryke and Allie Cresswell. All three of them have written wonderful books which I have greatly enjoyed and highly recommend to you. Their selfless support, however, is what makes me feel rooted in the bookish universe and gives me the confidence to publish a book written in another language than my native one.

This is my first historical novel, but others are due to follow. Meanwhile, you might want to take a look at my contemporary romance series *The Way of Life*.

According to her parents, Josie should be in college studying law. After what happened to her, it's out of the question. She needs to find out who she really is.
Leaving the glamorous life in New York behind her, she starts over in Oklahoma, where she meets Jim, an attractive, but shy horse trainer. They recognize each other as soul mates at first glance, something Josie has longed for all her life. But is she ready for it? Because in the depth of her soul the trauma is hidden which she so desperately tries to forget.

Learn more at https://annettespratte.org/books

Printed in Great Britain
by Amazon